Too Close to Home

The City of Dreams: Book 2

Tess Shepherd

Edited by Megan Powell
Cover illustration by Dorina Nemeskéri
Cover design by Tami Boyce
ISBN: 978-1-7374740-0-5
First Edition: August 2021

Visit the author:
Website: www.tess-shepherd.com
Instagram: author_tess.shepherd

BOOKS BY TESS SHEPHERD

Standalone Novels
The Fire Drill

The City of Dreams Series
Public Trust
Too Close to Home
The Kismet Equation (July 2022)

Dungeness Hollow Series
Jessie's Point
Spring Tide (January 2022)
Mainstay (October 2022)

Bar Hopping for Singles Series
*Bar Hopping ~~for Singles~~
*Bar Hopping for Singles

* Sign up for my newsletter at hello@tess-shepherd.com to stay updated on latest releases, free downloads, news, and other promotions!

For my niece, Gracelyn Rayne—

Too Close to Home

Prologue

Maggie Simmone had always had a sense for people. She had been born the mahogany-haired, blue-eyed child of a trauma nurse and an LAPD officer—then LAPD Captain, then Chief—one of five wild children who'd always seemed to be getting into trouble.

She had always wondered if being the eldest girl—the most responsible of her rowdy siblings—had imparted a sense of understanding in her. A sense of when a person was hurting and what would make them feel better. At the very least, having to corral four siblings was certainly the reason she was a terrible friend to go to in an argument. She could always see both sides of the disagreement and, by default, was never helpful in resolving it.

The simple truth was that she had always had a sense for people because she listened where other people talked, nodded when others would have hopped in with a story of their own. It was a trick of human nature that made people want to be around her, made them comfortable enough to tell her their problems.

Maggie *cared*.

To her, her penchant for listening was not unusual at all; it was something that she had inherited from some genetic cocktail that was half of her mother and half of her father.

Now, her penchant for knowing exactly when Logan Cane would show up again—and when he'd leave—well, that was pure juju. A tingle between her shoulder blades, a sick swooshing in her stomach that lasted for days, sleepless nights that somehow left her too nauseous to eat, too

1

anxious to focus, and too exhausted to care about much else.

Maggie knew when Logan was on his way home. And she hated every second she spent waiting for him to arrive.

She didn't label it herself, but she thought of it as predestination, a magnetic pull that brought them together in life…and probably had in past lives too.

Kismet.

Fate.

Destiny.

It was that pull now which made her hesitate at the door, her hand already on the handle, her eyes staring blankly forward as if she could see through it, to him.

With the cold metal under her palm, she took a moment to clear her head, to push all of her rising emotions into the smallest box in the furthest corner of her mind.

If she had thought more on it, she would have been surprised by how calm she was. Usually, she was a mess of nerves and excitement when Logan arrived.

But not anymore.

Now she would have been happier if she'd never seen him again.

When the doorbell rang a second time, she scowled, letting just two of those boxed emotions back out. But because she couldn't procrastinate any longer, and because she didn't want her mom coming out of the other room where she watched Gracie, she took one quick breath, set her shoulders, and pulled the door open.

He stood on her front step, a pretty African Violet in a bright blue pot in his large hands and a grin in his predatory gray eyes. His hair had grown out, and he'd tied it back into a little bun that highlighted his square jaw.

Her stomach gave one long pull at the sight of him, one there-he-is kick before settling. *He looks so good. Always.* The thought was resigned. Accepting.

The dark blue jeans and gray tee-shirt would have looked bargain brand on any other man, but on Logan Cane they looked like they'd been custom made just for him. Muscled shoulders and arms met a wide, strong chest, before tapering to a narrow waist, then to strong thighs and the impossibly long legs that gave him his six-five height.

She could see his bunched muscles contoured by the shirt and consciously refrained from pulling her sweater tighter around her middle. She'd put her body through a lot since the last time she had seen him. Nearly two years earlier she'd carried and birthed a child.

His child.

A thousand memories flashed through her mind at once, too quick for her to pick out specific events from the reeling montage. From children to friends to lovers, the reminders were all there, and having them swirling in her mind pulled her chest tight and blocked her breath in the back of her throat.

"Hey, Mags," he said finally, his catlike eyes cautious as he held out the plant for her. "Long time, no see."

"What do you want, Logan?" She kept her tone deliberately flippant to counter the hot thump, thump, thump of the blood pumping through her heart. She was aware of a nervous flutter that had climbed back into her stomach the moment he'd opened his mouth.

He looked stunned for a moment, as if he wasn't quite sure that he'd heard her right. He dropped his gaze as if searching for something at her feet, shook his head once before whispering, "What do I *want?*"

The words that she had practiced dozens—no, hundreds—of times didn't come to her, so she nodded instead, making sure to keep her eyes cool, detached.

He shook his head again, incredulous. "You…you had my baby. *Our* baby."

"I did," she said softly. There was no point in denying it. "Over a year ago."

"I came as soon as I found out," he said, his words barely a whisper now.

A lifetime of knowing him told her—by the way that he clenched and unclenched his jaw—that he was struggling with what to say. And, for just a moment, she felt sorry for him, felt sorry that she was about to hurt him even more.

"I had no idea until my mom tracked me down a month ago...I didn't...I swear, Maggie."

I know. She smiled sadly into gray eyes that were so familiar to her, gray eyes that she had looked into for nearly thirty years.

She wanted to laugh.

Or cry.

The only reason he was home was because of some confused sense of responsibility. And knowing that brought the same dull ache to her chest, the one that had faded from a sharp slice of pain to a more consistent pang over the years he'd been away. Still, she couldn't help but tell herself: *You knew this would happen.*

He clearly had no intention of moving from her front porch, so she pulled her sweater closer around her body and blinked back the tears burning her eyes. "I think that you should go."

"No." He countered her instantly, took a single step towards her. "We have to talk about this, Maggie. I'm back...I'm back for good this time."

The bitter laugh slipped through her lips before she could smother it, but the moment it snaked through the air between them she regretted the slip in her control. "No. You're *not.*"

The weight of her words filled the air between them. A wet blanket of truth seemed to descend from above to cover them both, making it hard for either of them to breathe. But even through that familiar claustrophobic haze of pain, Maggie felt relief.

She hadn't caved.

She hadn't flung herself into his arms as had been her habit through their twenty-year, on-again-off-again relationship. She'd held her ground, just like she'd said she would. And sure, her stomach still pulled tight at the sight of him, and her skin screamed for contact. Even her treacherous mind was telling her that if she took two steps closer, just two steps, she would be able to breathe in the scent of him.

"I understand if you need time."

She could see from where she was standing that his free hand was fisted, the knuckles bone-white. Again, and for just a moment, she felt her bubble of resolve dip. It was as if a careless child was pressing against the edges, bringing it alarmingly close to popping.

"I don't need time." Grabbing onto the anger that had fueled her through the last two years alone, she took one solid step toward him, pleased when he took one step back. She knew that the glint in her eye was murderous, but she didn't care. Not anymore. "What did you think, Logan? That you'd just show up, ride in out of the blue whenever you want, and things would just go back to normal?"

His eyes flickered to her face and she knew that he was surprised by her dead-calm tone. "I'm done with you. For good."

"Mags…"

Holding up a hand, she silenced him. "Don't come to my house. Ever." She forced her eyes back to his, barely keeping the grief from slipping over her features.

He looked shocked.

"We're done, Logan." Turning on her heel, she marched back inside, only spinning around so that she could slam the door in his face.

"I have rights, Maggie."

She laughed again, a cold, bitter sound that broke her own heart. "Yeah. Let's go talk to a judge and we'll explain where you've been for the last two years."

"I didn't know!" He shouted back at her, raising his voice for the first time since they'd started the conversation.

She flew out of the door before she knew what she was doing, before she knew what she was planning. But the sharp slap to his cheek had him raising his free hand in reflex, and he caught her wrist as she was winding up for a second offense. "Don't. You. Dare." His whispered words were cold, lethal.

Ignoring the feeling of his big hand wrapped around her, she focused on the sting in her palm—a flood of tingles spreading outwards—and the look of surprise on his face. She was not above admitting that both brought her immense pleasure.

Despite the dangerous look on his face and brittle flex of his fingers around her wrist—and the fact that he was a violent man—she knew that he would never physically hurt her.

When the silence between them stretched to paper-thin, Maggie snatched her hand back. "You *knew*, Logan." He opened his mouth to object, but she didn't give him a chance to argue. "You knew what you were doing."

"That's not fair."

"How about we count the times I've cried in a puddle on the floor with your own mother after you up and left us?" She saw his eyes darken but barreled on. "Marlene left LA because she couldn't take the waiting. Waiting for you to come home. Waiting for a call. Waiting for news of your death to come in with the mail. Jesus Christ," raising her hands, she gripped her hair on either side of her head as if she could yank it from the roots, "you literally have no idea."

"My mom left to go and live in Vegas with Bob. It had nothing to do with me."

"Do you know that I take your dad to his doctor's appointments?"

He didn't reply, but she knew by the way his eyes widened that he probably didn't even know that his dad had been sick.

"Do you know what it feels like returning your wedding dress because your fiancé left you without saying goodbye? Or, how it feels to give birth knowing that you can't track down your newborn's father because, after. *thirty. years.* of knowing him, he couldn't even leave you his contact details?"

"Maggie…"

"I don't *owe* you anything. And I certainly don't owe you half of *my* child. Do you understand me?"

He didn't move.

Spinning around, she hurried back into the house and slammed the door behind her—this time without looking back.

"This isn't over, Maggie." His words crushed the last of her resolve and she slid to the ground, her back supported by the weight of the heavy oak door.

For the hundredth time, she felt her heart break over Logan Cane. Putting her head in her hands, she gave in to her tears. She cried for the little girl who'd grown up to only ever love one man. She cried for the young woman who'd dedicated her entire life to the same man, and she cried for the woman that she was now. The woman who had nothing left to give to any man.

Anyone, really.

Except for Gracie. Her own voice in her head forced her to function past the choking heartbreak expanding in her throat. As much as he'd hurt her, and as much as she wanted to hurt him in return, he had given her the single biggest joy of her existence.

She wouldn't deny that if it weren't for Gracie, she and Logan would probably be undressing each other in a frenzy already. But now…everything had changed.

The irony was not lost on her.

7

Funny though, that one tiny, innocent human could change a life so completely. It was Gracie who'd altered her perspective. Gracie who'd made her realize that her love for Logan wasn't enough—that it would never be enough. She might have been taken for a fool, might *still* be a fool, but she'd make damn sure that her daughter wasn't.

Pushing to her feet, she wiped the last of her tears from her face. Then she straightened her spine and forced a casual smile. Her daughter was in the other room with her own mother, and neither of them needed to see her fall apart.

You've survived day one. There was no joy in the victory. She knew, as sure as she knew her own name, that Logan would be back. He was immovable when he got an idea in his head.

You've got this. You're in control. Her inner diva—the voice that had held her up through solo pregnancy, birth, and the first year of being a single mother—gave her a solid pep talk.

It didn't matter that she could still feel her body's response to him, still feel where his skin had branded hers. She'd take the victory for today because if there was one thing that she knew about Logan Cane, it was that he didn't give up without a full twelve rounds.

Chapter 1

One Month Later

Maggie pushed open the upstairs door to her soon-to-be sister-in-law's art studio. She paused just inside the room as her brother and Lola jumped apart like two kids getting caught behind the bleachers. "Dad wants your help with the barbeque."

Jake grinned down at Lola, his fiancée as of about twenty minutes ago, the look in his eyes adoring. Her own heart skipped when her baby brother leaned down and brushed his lips over Lola's before he strode from the room to go and rescue dinner.

"I can't believe that you guys planned all this." Lola twirled on the spot, her big, brown eyes glistening.

Maggie knew that she was referring to the house and the fact that the entire family had rallied over the last two weeks to help Jacob organize his surprise purchase for his proposal. Her little brother had pulled out all the stops. He had gotten down on one knee in front of their new home—something that Maggie thought incredibly romantic considering that Jacob was half Neanderthal most of the time.

"We're glad we managed it with the timeframe he gave us." Her voice was gentle and teasing, deliberately moderated for Lola, who hadn't quite adapted to the Simmone's way of communicating yet.

Lola chuckled and lifted a hand to swipe at her eyes. "I can't believe how fast this all happened...I've known Jake for such a short time, but it feels like..."

"Lifetimes?"

"Exactly." Spreading her arms wide to encompass her studio, Lola spun in another single circle. "I'm *so* happy."

"Welcome to the family. Officially."

Lola turned to face her and cocked her head, sending her pretty curls flitting forward and into her eyes. She crossed her arms over her chest, sending a bevy of bracelets on her wrists dancing. "How are you doing, Maggie?"

There was no use in pretending that she didn't know what Lola was talking about. The entire family had been switching between checking in on her and Lola for the last month.

They all thought that they were so clever, alternating which days one of them stopped by and always bringing something for Gracie so that it didn't seem pre-planned. They'd been not-so-subtly dropping in because Logan was back in town. They had been doing the same to Lola because, unlike Maggie, Lola had been in a life-threatening situation only a month earlier—one that had wound her up in the hospital for nearly a week.

"I'm going to be fine this time," she replied, seeing that Lola was quietly waiting.

If there was a forced deliberateness in her words, Lola didn't comment on it. Instead, she walked over to where Maggie stood and gave her a quick hug. "Jake and I...We're here for you. We'll support you. Whatever you decide."

"Thanks." Maggie knew that Lola wasn't one for overt displays of emotion, which is why she returned the hug before taking a solid step away.

The truth was that she'd been walking on eggshells for the last month, one eye always trained on the horizon as she waited for Logan to make his next move. "Right now I just need to pretend that everything is normal."

"Has he come around again?" Lola asked, her eyes slit in the closest thing to anger that Maggie had ever seen in her.

Shaking her head, she wrapped her arms around her body. "No, but I know he's still here. Chances are he's giving me enough space to cool off before he plays his hand."

"Plays his hand?"

"Oh, yeah. Logan Cane loves to win."

"Sounds like you do too."

Maggie looked over at Lola, unbegrudging of the fact that her brother had clearly told his fiancée everything that he knew about her and Logan. Love was supposed to be like that—a mutual agreement to be around when shit went sideways, a promise to try when things got rough. An understanding to keep no secrets from one another.

"I used to enjoy keeping him at bay for the first few days once he got back," Maggie admitted with an incredulous laugh. "I used to like making him suffer a-a little." She choked on her words. "God, I was such a *child*. So *naïve*." Pulling her sleeves over her hands to block the chill in the room, she added, "I thought he'd stay every time. I believed what he said. Every. Single. Time."

Idiot.

"I'm so sorry." Lola took a step towards her again. "I can't even begin to imagine…"

"It's my own fault." As if looking up into Lola's sympathetic gaze made the fact clearer, she barreled on, "Logan came home and left me again…countless times. And, still, *like an idiot*, I threw myself at him every time."

Lola nodded silently, her eyes misting.

"Do you know that he is the only man that I've ever slept with?"

"What?" Lola frowned, surprised by the admission. "Really?"

Maggie nodded and, feeling the tight ball of anger spreading in her stomach, she welcomed it, enjoying the searing rage that spread through her body and replaced her tears. "I was hung up on him for so long. And look where it got me! I'm forty-two! I'm a *middle-aged*, single mom!" Lowering her voice, she cast a glance at the door then whisper-shouted, "I haven't showered in *three days!*"

Lola squeaked, a hysterical bubble of laughter that made Maggie smile. "You look great?"

Maggie felt a sudden laugh gurgle up in her chest and collect in her throat, rapidly dissipating her brief need to punch something. Biting it back, she glanced at Lola.

Mistake.

The moment they made eye contact, they erupted in laughter, their belly laughs echoing through the house.

They laughed for minutes, their hysterical giggles coming in fits and starts as they alternated trying to calm down—and failing.

Several times, Maggie managed to even out her breathing by sucking in a huge gulp of air. But then she'd look up again and see Lola bent over trying to do the same, and her resolve would crumble into another burst of giggles.

When Lola slapped a hand over her lips, trying to be quiet, her muffled laughter sputtered through her fingers. Maggie wrapped her arms around her stomach, trying to contain the stitch that had started to form. "Oh, God," she wheezed eventually, "I'm going to pee."

"Ahhh," Lola wiped her eyes with her sleeve, sniffling on a last chuckle. "You're a mess."

"I know," Maggie groaned.

"But you're our mess."

Maggie smiled. "I know."

"So, what is your plan?"

The answer burned like acid in the pit of her stomach before she let it rise up her throat. "I'm going to let him be a dad. For Gracie's sake."

"And you?"

"I don't know." Panic fluttered in her chest. "I want to say that I hate him, that I can...resist him."

"But you don't think you can."

"I…" she exhaled loudly. "I've loved him for over twenty years." Tears burned her eyes again. "Right now, I'm happy being angry because it gives me space…"

A rapid-fire knock on the door had them both turning before Zac opened it, glancing in at their tear-streaked faces and serious expressions with open skepticism. "June said to check what the ruckus was about," he said, his gaze dancing between Lola and Maggie.

"We were just lamenting my un-showered, unkempt state," Maggie replied, changing the subject and making Lola giggle again.

Zac looked her up and down. "You're a smoke show, Maggie Simmone. A little scrawny these days, but nothing that June's apple pie won't fix. I'll prove it to you," he said, taking a full step into the room.

"You're full of shit." She knew the game that he was playing. They had, after all, been playing it for at least twenty years.

It had started when she had overheard Zac telling Jake that his older sister was a 'babe' and asking if she was single. *That* had been at their LAPD swearing-in ceremony. She had found it sweet at the time, that one of her little brother's friends, a hunky twenty-one-year-old who had been five years her junior, had thought to ask after her.

Not that she'd ever considered taking it further. Although Zac was a swoon-worthy six-foot package of broad shoulders, long legs, hair as black as midnight, and ice-blue eyes, he would always and forever be Jake's best friend. An honorary little brother of sorts.

"I'm serious, Maggie. One kiss and you'll be mine forever," he said, holding out his arms for her even as he sent an appalled Lola a cheeky wink.

"Har. Har. We both know that best friend or not, Jake would lose his shit."

"I'm prepared to risk it if you are."

Maggie laughed, enjoying the banter. It had always been so easy with Zac, so...natural. "I don't trust where you've been, Murph. Word on the street is not in your favor..."

"They're just filling the gaping hole in my heart." He waved his hand, brushing off her jibe nonchalantly.

Because this was also part of their routine, she rolled her eyes and stepped into his arms. When they encircled her, she smiled and let her head rest on his shoulder. It did feel nice to have the solid wall of male chest, the contact of a friend who would always be on her side.

"Lol?" Zac held out a hand for her. "You gonna join this cuddle fest?"

Maggie laughed when Lola rolled her own eyes exaggeratedly and stepped into the group hug, slotting under Zac's free arm.

"You smell really good," Lola said after a moment, her eyes squinting up at him.

"Thanks. It's sandalwood. Babes love it." When they chuckled, he turned them both and propelled them towards the door. "Enough moping. We're going to drink and barbeque and," he tapped Maggie's nose with the hand that was slung around her shoulders, "not think about unappreciative assholes who don't deserve us."

"Amen to that," Lola chimed in.

"Thank you, guys. I really love you...And you're right! Today is a day for celebrating! My baby brother is getting married."

"And I hear she's not half bad," Zac added, nudging Lola.

They came down the stairs like that, the two girls tucked on either side of Zac, his rangy arms roped over their shoulders.

"Dude?" Jake said, holding out his hands. "My sister *and* my fiancée. Come on!"

"What can I say, man. Gotta spread my bets."

Everyone chuckled and kept on with what they had been doing, ignoring the routine that was as much a part of their family gatherings as Zac was himself.

Phil Simmone stood outside in his flip flops burning hamburgers. Jacob, and Hudson—the baby of the Simmone five—stood side-by-side at the make-shift table that Hudson had set up earlier. Their big shoulders formed a wall in the sizeable front room.

"Where are Mom and Gracie?" Maggie asked, slipping out from under Zac's arm.

"She needed to be changed," Jake said first. "I think she said she'd do it on the laundry table." He shrugged. "Sorry, it's the only available surface at the moment."

Nodding, she walked through the house. She took her time so that she could appreciate the hand-crafted ceiling beams and the ornate side paneling that led through to the kitchen before disappearing to the laundry room and garage. "Mom?"

"We're in here."

Maggie walked through just as June clasped a fresh diaper on Gracie. When her daughter saw her approaching, she giggled and rolled into a sitting position. She held out her chubby arms, and scrunched her fingers together, grasping for her.

Maggie's heart bloomed.

Big gray eyes like Logan's grinned back at her and Gracie, seeing that she had the attention, gurgled, "Ma."

Gracie was trying out all her sounds, but so far her daughter had three words in her repertoire, one of which was, 'Ma' or 'Mama'. The other two were 'Gama', which naturally June claimed was 'Grandma', and 'Spuk', which was close enough to 'Spunk' for her to know that her daughter had been listening to her long, often rambling conversations with her thirteen-year-old pit bull.

Maggie leaned down to pick her up as June moved off with the sealed bomb bag that contained the diaper. "Hi, baby," she said, nuzzling Gracie's bare tummy and sending her into a fit of baby giggles.

Laying Gracie back on the table, Maggie quickly redressed her in a yellow onesie, chatting about everything in general and nothing in particular until she finished the ensemble with a cute pair of bumble-bee socks that had little yellow bows on the tops.

"There you go. All done." Maggie clapped her hands once, the loud tap sending Gracie into a fit of giggles as she clapped her own tiny hands together.

Looking at her daughter, lying there on the laundry table, Maggie wished that she could freeze the moment in time. Pause it and keep it just for herself.

Gracie was so happy, so carefree. In her daughter's world, there was no pain, no disappointment.

"It never gets easier."

Leaning down, Maggie picked up Gracie, tucked her neatly on her hip before turning to face her own mom. June was looking at her face, her green eyes clouded with concern.

Maggie smiled, trying to hide the flutter of panic whispering under her ribcage. "I don't know how you managed five. Sometimes…it all just feels like too much."

Her mom just raised her eyebrows. "I had your dad." She shrugged. "And women are more resilient than men give them credit for. Hell, we're more resilient than we give ourselves credit for."

"I couldn't have done it without you and Dad, without Jake and Hudson. God, even skype calls with Emma and Lyle have kept me sane over the last year."

"We're family." And that's all it was to June Simmone. Simple. You protected your family. You lived and died for family.

"Yes, we are." She switched Grace's significant weight to her other side. Gracie yawned before laying her head on

16

Maggie's shoulder, her light brown curls soft against Maggie's skin. "Somebody needs a nap."

"Let's go through. You can put her in her stroller while the adults drink and eat. Your brothers should have set up everything already."

Maggie followed her mom back through the kitchen, stopping only to grip the stroller with her free hand so that she could push it through to where everyone was standing in the lounge.

"Here," Jacob held out his hands for a sleepy Gracie. "I'll put her down."

"Thanks." The baby went to Jake without fuss. She was a child who was used to being passed around and doted on—something that Maggie was grateful for. They'd have to address her comfort with strangers when she was old enough to get into trouble. But for now, she loved that her little girl could fall asleep in her brother's arms as easily as she could in hers.

Moving through the lounge, she stopped to pull her sweater a little closer. It was late October in Los Angeles, which meant that the temperature danced around eighty during the day, and dropped to a cool sixty-five at night. For Maggie, that meant sweater weather.

She wouldn't mention it to her family, but she'd been having some trouble since a little before Logan had come home. Even before he'd knocked on her door, she'd been down ten pounds, and in the month since then she'd dropped another ten. If her family noticed, they didn't say anything about it.

Probably because, like her, they knew it wasn't deliberate. It was just a gnawing nausea that followed her around all day, bubbling in her stomach and making her feel like she was two coffees away from a stomach ulcer. But she knew that she needed to realign her life, find a new balance before she could focus on being hungry again.

"Dad, do you want a drink?"

Instead of answering, Phil picked up the beer that he had propped on the side of the barbeque and waved it at her. Maggie picked a can of Guinness out of the ice chest for herself before moving over to where he stood, blissfully unaware of the fact that he was killing the hamburgers.

The corporate lawyer in her—the girl who used to entertain clients at the best restaurants in town—cringed. But the daddy's girl in her won, had her taking a solid step back so that she didn't interfere.

"How you doing, Maggie Mae?"

Her father looked at her, his blue eyes sharp and assessing. She knew that he was taking her in, studying her as she imagined he'd done to suspects right before he'd started interrogating them. *He's still such a cop*, she thought fondly.

"I'm good." The lie came easy. "I called the firm yesterday. Told them I'm not coming back." Saying the words out loud released a little flurry of panic into her system and she wrapped her arms around herself to try and stifle it.

He stopped what he was doing, held the tongs loosely in his hand. "When did you decide?" he asked, his bushy, gray eyebrows raised.

"Well, you know that I've been thinking about it since Gracie, Dad…"

"I know." He put down the utensil, and Maggie had to refrain from stepping in to save the meat. "I don't care about the fact that you quit your job, baby girl. I just wish we'd been there with you."

When tears filled her eyes, he wrapped one arm around her. "It wasn't easy," she managed after a minute. "I know that it's what I want but it still feels so…irresponsible."

"You're a parent." He squeezed her. "Nothing you ever do will feel responsible. Ever again."

Laughing, Maggie hugged him back. "Well, it's officially do or die. I have enough savings for one shot at my café…"

"We'll all pitch in where we can." Phil turned to meet her eyes. "Your mom and I are so excited to have a new favorite…wine bar."

The truth was that he didn't really understand the concept, even though June and Maggie had explained it to him on separate occasions. But Maggie didn't mind. Her small business, the one that she'd been thinking about since she'd graduated from law school was a café by day, wine bar by night type establishment. But Phil didn't get it because 'Didn't most wine bars serve coffee too'?

"Once I've picked a location, and once I've set up, you'll be on my short-list for opening night." Leaning in, she kissed him on the temple. "Promise."

"Phillip Simmone, you done killing those burgers yet?"

"About!" Phil didn't hesitate to yell back.

Laughing, Maggie caved to her compulsion and moved forward to pull the hamburgers off "Here, let me carry them to the table." She used the extra barbeque spatula to stack the burgers on a paper plate, carried them to the makeshift set up.

"Dinner!" she shouted.

Three huge males suddenly surrounded her. Maggie rolled her eyes, letting her grin flash.

Zac, Hudson, and Jake piled food on their plates, each stacking two huge burgers full of tomatoes, onions, and lettuce.

Amused, she watched Jake balance his plate precariously as he walked across the lawn to where Lola sat before handing her one. The gesture, so simple, had her own eyes tearing up, and Maggie looked down at her plate, which was getting heavier in her hand. It was piled with two patties, a huge dollop of mayonnaise, and tomato and onion.

Her stomach heaved, but she watched in silence as Zac plopped three slices of cheese on top of the patties on her plate. "Zac!"

"What?" he asked, his blue eyes grinning. "I know that you don't eat carbs."

"I can't eat half of this! You're just wasting it."

"Wanna bet?" He winked at her. "Your problem isn't that you're limited by your size, Mags. Although," he nodded mock-seriously, "you're pretty scrawny."

She snorted.

Undeterred, he carried on, "Your problem is that you've lost your fighting spirit. The Maggie Simmone I used to know would have put me on my ass just for looking." Leaning closer to her ear, he whispered, "And God forbid if I'd called you scrawny ten years ago."

Maggie didn't argue.

"My Maggie Simmone would have taken any dare."

He was right.

When they'd been younger, he wouldn't have commented on her appearance just to try and get a rise out of her; he wouldn't have *dared*. And, if he'd bet she couldn't do something—even something stupid like finish a ridiculously sized meal—she would have done it just to prove that she could. Zac, who'd only just re-connected with the family after a fallout with Jake eight years earlier, remembered that. He remembered her as she had been: strong and independent. The old Maggie would have knowingly taken the bait hook, line, and sinker just to show she could spit it back out.

Now, she just sighed, resigned that she'd rather lose a dash of pride over a stupid bet than feel sick from eating too much. "What am I going to do with you?"

"I've told you a million times. Marry me. We'll elope so that Jake doesn't kill me, have a dozen more babies, and live out our days on a Jamaican beach."

"Gross, dude." This from Hudson who hadn't even managed to make it to a chair before biting into his first burger. "That's my sister," he said, around a mouthful of food.

Maggie just shook her head. Even as Zac's comment forced thoughts of Logan to the edge of her mind, pulling the breath in her chest uncomfortably tight, she felt her heart settle. There was comfort here, she realized. Her family crowding around her, filling her personal space with simple love, made her feel as if she could handle it all.

"Hey, Dad," Jake's voice pulled her thoughts back to the present. "Did you see that Hayes Somerson bought The Plaza Tower downtown?"

"I did." Phil laughed. "The goddamn kid did it."

"You always said he would, Phil," June added as she walked to the table to help herself.

Next to her, Zac asked, "Hayes Somerson?"

Maggie smiled. "One of my dad's street rats from back when he was a cop made it bigtime. He's a real estate tycoon now."

"Oh, yeah?"

Maggie nodded as the conversation continued, too wrapped up in her thoughts to focus on Hayes Somerson.

As if sensing the direction her thoughts had taken, Zac leaned closer. "You know I was just giving you shit, right?"

"I know." She sighed. "The fact that you have to add that just burns more though."

"Crap. Sorry for apologizing."

"I used to be so…resilient. So stubborn." With a resigned laugh, she added, "What happened to me, Zac?"

"Well, whereas the rest of us are committed to being juvenile delinquents, you've grown up. You have other priorities now, Mags. That doesn't mean that you've lost the fight. Just that you're fighting smarter."

"Do you think I'm crazy for letting him back into my life?" She asked him because she knew he'd be honest with her. Where her family would try and smooth the pain, Zac would just dish it out. His unfailing honesty was part of the reason they were so close.

He didn't reply right away, chose to take a huge bite of his burger as he mulled it over, his eyes far away.

Impatient, she added, "I just need someone to tell me that I'm making the right decision. I mean…I can't keep him from her forever. Can I? Because I *want* to. I want him to suffer."

Finally, he looked at her. "I think the fact that you're considering taking him back at all is…bananas."

The admission hit her hard, a fist to the stomach. "Bananas?"

"But…," he paused, "I understand too."

"You do?"

"Yeah." He looked at her, smiled sadly. "You know, when I asked Tara to marry me, she said no. She broke up with me." His voice was heavy with grief.

At the mention of Tara, Maggie hated that she'd brought it up at all.

"I felt as if my world just stopped moving. I don't even remember the first few days after she left, just snatches of time between when I'd wake up and when I'd start drinking again."

"But she came back."

"She did." He laughed. "She broke into my house because she hadn't been able to reach me for days. Turns out I'd tripped on the phone cord—back when such things existed—and yanked it out the wall sometime during my pity party. She came over to check that I was okay."

"And that's when she changed her mind about marrying you?"

"Nope. It took me months to convince her." He laughed at the memory, this time with genuine humor, then sobered almost instantly. "But that night she told me something I'll never forget. She told me that loving me would end in disaster for her. She said that I was too reckless…that she didn't want to be left alone when I wound up in trouble that wouldn't go away."

"*Tara* said that." Maggie thought back to the woman in question. Tara had been a cop too. Tough. Gritty in that way that only came from seeing a lot of bad shit. It surprised her that such a strong woman had looked at Zac and been afraid of what life with him would look like.

"She did. And hearing it…from her…it wasn't easy, Maggie."

"But she came back."

"She did."

"But?"

"I wish to God every day that she hadn't. I wake up in the morning and I relive the day she died. And my first thought is always that if she'd just loved me a little less, if she'd just walked away…she'd still be alive."

"She *chose* you, Zac. She loved you."

"I know that. *She* knew that."

"You think being with Logan is dangerous?"

"Not in the same way. Cane is a fucking savage; he'd never let anyone hurt you."

"But?"

"Don't pretend that you don't have your eyes wide open, Maggie. You know who and what he is. And—even though it hurts like hell—you're fine with it because, for you, for *both* of you, there's never been anyone else. Being in a room with the two of you is like being a dropped peanut on the kitchen floor."

"Gross and moldy?"

"Completely disregarded. Unimportant."

Maggie shook her head, thinking about Gracie. "Things have changed now."

"No. They haven't. Take it from someone who knows."

Chapter 2

Logan rolled over, turning away from the garish light that spilled into his bedroom and illuminated the scowl on his features. Unfortunately, the movement brought him face to face with his clock. The obnoxious square, red numbers screamed that it was already past noon.

He shut his eyes against the pounding in his head. Every thump was a solid reminder that he should have stopped at seven drinks instead of the ten he'd thrown back at O'Hara's the night before.

The drinking—something that he usually wouldn't have indulged in—had become a routine of sorts. A way for him to escape for just a few hours every day so that he could forget the look of cool indifference in Maggie's eyes.

The only reaction he'd seen from her at all had been the quick whip of anger as she'd flown down the stairs and slapped him and, well, he'd deserved that one. He hadn't even meant what he'd said. He'd just panicked and voiced the only thing that he could think of to get her to listen to him for a moment longer.

But now, as he lay staring blankly at the clock until the numbers merged, a blurred mash of red, he could admit that he had always known she wouldn't wait for him forever. He'd always thought she'd move on, maybe fall for someone else—a banker or a lawyer, someone who wore a tailored suit, drove a Porsche, and could give her everything she deserved.

But she hadn't met someone else.

She just didn't want him anymore.

Maggie was beautiful…smart… God, she had a heart of gold. She was a woman that any man would be stupid to let go of.

Except me. Because the picture of her with a faceless man, no, *any* man other than him, flooded his system with rage, he smashed his fist against the wall above his head. The loud crack of drywall pleased him for only a moment…right before a sharp slice of pain traveled up his knuckles to his elbow. "Mother*fucker*!"

Cradling his hurt hand, he pushed the covers back and rose out of the bed, naked.

Years of training and physical exertion had sculpted his six-something frame into something nearly robotic in its perfection, something that made women—and men—turn their heads as he stalked past.

Thick, bunched muscles and a broad, chiseled face framed by a mop of unruly, dirty-blond hair could have gotten him far in life—if it weren't for the constant angry scowl that marred his features, turning his gray eyes an inanimate gunmetal hue that made people wary. Some would even say afraid.

Logan knew the effect that he had on people. He looked exactly like someone who'd had two decades of military and private security training. He looked dangerous. Maybe even a little unhinged. And he rather liked it. The flat line of his mouth and slate-gray eyes screamed 'DO NOT APPROACH' and saved him the need to mingle with strangers.

Flexing his hand, he opened it as wide as he could before clenching it into a fist again. He knew that it wasn't broken, and didn't take anything for the pain. On principal.

Instead, he walked to the shower and turned the cold water on high, braced himself as he stepped into the frigid spray.

Fuuuuuck! The icy water lashed him, a thousand painful cuts tearing into his skin, reminding him that he was still very much alive. Spreading his big palms on the cold tiles of the huge shower, he let his thoughts drift back to Maggie.

And Grace.

Just as they had every hour of every day since the two months that he'd found out about his daughter, his thoughts whirled—astonishment, joy, regret, self-loathing; they were all there, fighting for his attention.

The last time he'd been home had been two years earlier. The last time he'd seen Maggie, they'd been engaged, planning a life together until...he'd panicked.

Again.

He'd taken one look at Maggie Mae Simmone asleep in his big bed, her long, dark hair splayed over his pillow, the ring he'd dropped a hefty sum on winking on her finger. He'd slowly risen out of bed so as not to wake her. And he'd left.

He'd told his mother that he'd landed a two-year, close-protection contract. And he had. But the bodyguarding gig had come after he'd looked at Maggie asleep in his bed that morning and he'd known in his heart he couldn't stay.

And she'd been pregnant. He hadn't known. And, although it might have made a difference at the time, he didn't let himself think about it because it didn't matter anymore.

Maggie wasn't his.

Turning the shower off with unnecessary force, he stepped out and strode to the sink, dripping water as he walked.

He looked at his reflection in the small bathroom mirror—angry eyes, a mouth set in a grim line, and a square jaw wired shut—and he hated what he saw.

He had turned out exactly as Mrs. Kamden, his high school guidance counselor, had predicted: useless.

When she'd looked at his grades, she'd told him that he was lazy and didn't try hard enough. If she'd asked, he would have tried to explain that laziness didn't begin to describe the torturously long nights he'd spent trying to decode the jumbled letters scrawled in his textbooks. Or that the homework assignment that took Lyle Simmone thirty minutes to complete took him nearly two hours to draft.

She hadn't asked.

And, in his shame, he'd never offered her an explanation. He'd sat silently in her office, a six-foot-something eighteen-year-old growing smaller and smaller with every word fired from her mouth.

It had only been when she'd said, "What Maggie Simmone sees in you is beyond me," that he'd lost his shit and stormed out. But only because in that moment, suffering under her judgment, he'd been thinking the exact same thing.

That had been the first time that he'd felt truly inadequate. He'd left Kamden's office with the weight of her judgment pressing in on all sides, and, although Maggie had forced the truth from him—and countered Kamden's every word—it had been too late.

Not even picketing her lawn with heart-shaped Tommy Lee Jones posters—courtesy of Lyle and Jake—had made him feel whole again. It had helped...a little.

Just not enough.

As he stood looking at himself in the small, bathroom mirror, he knew that Kamden had been right. He was a mercenary. He had no home and no family. He'd taken the labels that had been assigned to him as a teenager—'self-destructive,' 'anger-driven, and 'oppositional-defiant'—and he'd branded them onto his soul.

No, Kamden hadn't been wrong, he thought now. Her labels were just the two-hundred-and-fifty-thousand-dollar-education way of saying that he was shit scared and fucking angry—both of which were accurate.

Even now, only twenty minutes after waking up, he felt the simmer of rage beneath his skin. Instead of mulling on it, instead of worrying about the how and the why, he shaved and changed.

Quickly.

Efficiently.

He was a man used to being on the move, used to living out of a single rucksack. In the last two years living in the Central African Republic, he had narrowed his packing list down to:

One raincoat

Three pairs of jeans

Seven shirts

Seven boxers

Seven pairs of socks

Two pairs of boots

Toiletries

He knew that as long as he could find a tub to wash his clothes in every few weeks, he could go with only those items until they fell apart from wear.

Tucking his wallet, cellphone, and keys into his pocket, he strode from the room without a backward glance.

There was nothing to check.

Other than the big, California King bed that he had purchased at Maggie's insistence, he hadn't furnished the place with one other item since he'd bought the condo three years earlier. It was a layover, a resting place when being away from Maggie grew to be too much.

He thought he'd sell it now, try and find a place close enough to Maggie and Gracie so that he could keep an eye on them.

If he hadn't been so hungover, he would have hit the gym, taken his anger out on a few punching bags before knocking out a five- or six-mile run. But given the near-constant hum in his head and the alcohol swell that had set in his fingers, he opted for a quiet drive in search of a heart-attack breakfast instead.

It took him three minutes to get to the underground parking structure. Hopping into his SUV, he pulled out of the condo building's private parking, stopping just before he hit the street to open the glove compartment and check that his Glock was nestled where it should be.

Logan wasn't in the habit of carrying his gun when he wasn't on an active close protection assignment. But after what had happened in the Central African Republic, he'd be keeping it nearby—just in case.

Memories of his desperate escape from CAR bubbled to the surface, settling an uncomfortable itch between his shoulder blades. So he gave in to his need to scan the neighborhood from his car.

Across the street, a group of women wearing leggings and crop tops walked together, their laughter drifting to him through his open window. A young couple walked towards his truck from the right, and he watched as they subtly skirted around a homeless man who was sitting in the concrete inlet of the neighboring midrise building.

Nothing untoward or unusual caught his attention so he shifted to drive and inched onto the street. *Too goddamn skittish*, he berated himself, his eyes still scanning as he drove.

He needed to calm down, keep a clear head. Because when Charles Rue surfaced in Los Angeles, Logan had to be ready for him. He'd deal with it, he'd take back his life and protect his girls. And then—only once it was over— would he try and figure out what he could do to convince Maggie to let him stay.

This time for good.

The sharp trill of his cellphone broke through his dark thoughts, and he pressed 'Accept' on the touchscreen in his SUV. He wasn't unaware of his heart pumping blood impossibly fast through his chest at the unknown caller ID, but experience had taught him that facing homicidal assholes was always better. Walking away would more likely find you with a bullet in your back.

"Logan Cane," he answered.

"Logan!"

"Simmone?" Logan felt the grin spread over his face when he recognized Jacob's voice coming through the speakers of his car.

"Yeah, man. How's it going? I, ah…I heard you were back in town and figured we should catch up for a beer. Usually, you would have reached out by now."

Logan frowned, unsure. He liked Jake. They'd become solid friends over the years and, aside from his mother and Maggie, the older Simmone brothers were the only other people who understood him—or at least, tried to.

He didn't reply right away, still unsure if he could face Maggie's family yet, even Jake.

"Nobody except Lola, Zac, and I will know. Promise. Maggie would never forgive me if she found out, so I have a vested interest in keeping it a secret too."

"Lola?"

"I forget that you've been off-grid…I'm engaged! As of a few weeks ago actually."

"Shit," Logan said before he could moderate his reaction. "Ah. congrats."

"Yeah. She's…everything."

Even over the phone, Jacob sounded whipped, and Logan found himself grinning again. Still, he couldn't risk it. "Hey, Jake, I'm running riot this week trying to sort my life out. Mind if we take a rain check?"

"Fuck off." Jacob's reply was instant, his tone cool. "Look man, I don't see you for two years and suddenly you can't meet for a couple of beers? I smell bullshit."

Logan's instinct was to curse but a grin spread over his face instead. "Wow, Simmone. With a sense of smell like that, you should have signed up for K9 ops."

"Har. Har. You still doing the Wednesday night lineup at the Comedy Club, princess?"

"No, they bumped me to Saturdays," Logan quipped instantly. "Because I'm hilarious."

Jake chuckled over the line, but a long silence followed, filling seconds like a black hole, collecting all the unsaid things.

"Come on, Logan. I know something's up."

Logan didn't reply.

"I know you. And there's no way in hell that you would have waited this long to see Maggie again."

Sighing, Logan shook his head. "Tonight at seven work?"

"Yeah. O'Hara's?"

"Perfect. See you then." He disconnected the call, expecting to feel anger and panic.

But they didn't rise to claim him.

Strangely, he felt relieved.

Jacob walked into O'Hara's at seven on the dot. He was a creature of habit, a man who liked to find things where he left them so that he could save time in the day. He never diverted from the book…well, except that one time. And he'd met Lola, so it had been worth it.

It had been a few years since he had been in the dive bar, but he was pleasantly surprised to find that nothing had changed. The cheap, glossy pine bar top still had that sticky sheen, as if the slow-paced waitress hadn't wiped it down in a couple of nights, or worse, wiped it down with the same rag that she'd been using for the last few days.

The air was rife with beer and cigarette smoke, which in California—with its tobacco laws—could only have come in riding the patrons' clothes. The atmosphere was charged, alive with the friendly hum of chatter, laughter, and the occasional shout from one of the few single men who appeared to be watching the football game on the mounted television screens in the back.

Jake inhaled the stale scent, smiling at the tide of memories that accompanied the smell.

He, Zac, and Logan used to frequent O'Hara's a lot when they'd been younger. The neighborhood bar sat on the corner of Hope and 7th. It was far enough out of the bowels of downtown to draw more locals than tourists and just close enough to the LAPD's Central Division for it to be a convenient pit-stop for Zac and him once they signed off from work.

When he and Zac had drifted apart, and Logan had started spending more time overseas than home, they'd stopped going. But the memories of their drunken escapades together still swallowed him in a familiar haze of hops and smoke.

They used to drink for hours, sometimes until closing, but usually until one of them would find the sense to order a cab. Then, they'd stand on the pavement and take bets on whether the cab driver would stop when he saw the three of them, standing side-by-side on the shadowed corner outside O'Hara's. The drivers stopped sixty percent of the time, but always with the same 'You assholes are not going to fit in my car' expression.

But they had always fit.

Things would have been different now. Not only were they responsible enough to stay sober, but Uber's XL service had eradicated the worry for them. Correction, he thought, eradicated the worry for *him*. Zac never worried about anything, and Logan's life was so extreme in general that Jacob was pretty sure he never worried about small things like how to fit his drunk friends into a taxicab.

Turning in the bar, he scanned the room quickly, efficiently, as the cop in him had been trained to do. He noticed the three men sitting at the corner of the bar. They eyed him suspiciously and he turned away, letting them know his disinterest. He knew that he reeked of cop, and he didn't mind it as long as people let him have a beer in peace on his night off.

Not seeing either Zac or Logan, he chose a barstool on the side of the bar closest to the door and settled in to wait.

"Can I get you something, hon?" the bartender asked, her eyes raking over him.

He took in her slight figure, beach blond hair accentuated by baby-blues, real gold, hoop earrings, and flawless makeup. Expensive getup for a bartender. He wondered if O'Hara's had been bought and refinanced since he'd last been in. It wouldn't have surprised him. "Guinness, please."

Nodding, she walked off to pull the beer from the tap.

Jacob tapped his fingers in a staccato rhythm on the bar and solidly ignored the hostile stares coming from the other side of the room. He had noticed the gang tatts on the three men sitting downwind of him. Of course he had. And although tattoos—even bad ones—were not illegal, those particular ones did explain why his skin was crawling, and why the biggest of the three men kept trying to catch his eye.

He sighed. *Just one time, I want to sit at a bar in peace. One. Goddamn. Time.* Despite his resolve to stay seated, his fingers started to twitch, and he shifted on the barstool uncomfortably. The bartender placed the beer in front of him, her smile wide as the Cheshire cat's, as if she knew how uncomfortable he was and found it amusing.

Turning in his seat, he shifted his body so that he could keep a single eye on the three at the end, but only just enough so that he looked casual. They were still glaring at him with open hostility, occasionally nudging one another and nodding over in his direction.

When the door opened behind him, Jacob didn't have to turn around to know that Logan had arrived. The three men shifted noticeably on their seats. Their eyes tracked his friend's every movement. He wanted to grin, wanted to let his teeth flash in a full-Cheshire that matched the bartender's earlier one. Instead, he pivoted on the stool and grinned at Logan.

"You always make friends so easily?" Logan nodded over to the three sitting at the end of the bar, the movement of his head obvious, taunting.

Jake turned and glanced at them. He refrained from chuckling when he saw the biggest man signal to the bartender to close his tab. "Good to have you back, Logan."

Jake studied his friend. Logan hadn't changed that much in the two years that he had been gone. If it was at all humanely possible, he'd put on more muscle than the last time that they'd seen him, and the pure male in him was a little jealous of how effortlessly Logan seemed to stay in pristine physical shape. Whereas before he had cropped his hair close to the scalp, now, he had let it grow out so that it fell a little past the collar of his black tee shirt. It suited him and made him look less like a paid killer. As long as you didn't look in his slate-gray eyes, which were one hundred percent 'I wanna fuck shit up'.

Logan chuckled half-heartedly. "Yeah, I make babies cry in the store. I'm a real winner."

Jake noticed the way that Logan's shoulders were set, noticed that his eyes took in the entire bar before coming to rest back on him. Jake's skin pulled tight at the obvious scouting. "You expecting trouble?"

It wasn't like Logan to be on the watch for anything. He was the most dangerous man that Jacob had ever met— serial killers included—and the fact that he was on the lookout couldn't mean anything good.

He had meant what he'd said on the phone. He knew— by the distance that Logan was deliberately putting between himself and Maggie—that something was wrong. Unless Maggie hadn't told him about it, Logan hadn't even made an effort to meet his daughter and that wasn't true to who he was at all.

"TBD," Logan replied eventually.

"You need help?" He met skeptical, slate-gray eyes and chuckled. "I'm a cop. But I'm a friend first."

Logan looked at him as if he had grown a second head. "Since when?"

He shrugged. "Figured out that some things are more important."

"Whatever, man. You live and die by that goddamn manual. Even I can recite most of that tome." Logan laughed suddenly, his gray eyes glinting. "I remember you and Maggie studying together when she was taking the law school exams."

"Yeah." Jake remembered too. He and Maggie would stay up until two in the morning, sitting side-by-side at their parents' dining room table studying while Logan brought them takeout. Logan had been home from a tour at the time and had spent every waking hour with Maggie even though she'd been largely absent, studying for her exams.

"I can still help if you're in trouble." When Logan just stared at him, he added, "Look, you're not just my sister's ex. You're a friend and the father of my niece. I *want* to help." He shrugged again, uncomfortable by having said that much.

"I'll let you know." Pulling out a bar stool, Logan sat down to Jake's left. "Maggie won't even talk to me so I'm hoping that whatever followed me back won't put two and two together."

"Followed you back? From the Central African Republic?"

"Who told you that's where I was?"

"Ah, I'm a cop. I have resources."

"Marlene?"

Jake laughed at the expression on Logan's face. "Yeah. Before she left with Bob for Vegas, your mom and Maggie got pretty close."

"Yeah, she mentioned it when she made contact to tell me about Grace."

A little bubble of silence followed behind the mention of Gracie. Jake popped it first. "So? You gonna tell me what happened in CAR?"

"Look, Jake. I appreciate the concern…but I don't want to get you involved."

"It's too late for that shit."

Logan turned to look at him, his gray eyes calm, too calm. Jake, needing him to understand, carried on with, "If something happens to you, *my* niece will be raised without a father. *My* sister's soul will be crushed."

"Maggie…"

"Can you blame her?" Jacob retaliated, instantly stepping in to defend his sister before Logan could say more.

"No." Logan was silent for a moment, his eyes detached, far away. "I didn't know that she was pregnant, Jake," he said finally, popping the awkward bubble between them and spilling better-left-unsaid things over both of them.

Sighing, Jacob took a big swig of his beer. "I did."

Logan's head snapped up, his cold, gray eyes focusing on Jacob's face, searching.

"She told me a month before you left for CAR."

"*What?* She knew for a month while I was home and she didn't tell me?"

Jacob noticed that Logan had paled, took stock of his curled fist resting on the top of the bar. He shrugged nonchalantly despite the little tick of fear crawling up his spine. His quads shortened as if preparing to run. "I think she was hoping that she would be enough."

They both fell silent as the words hung between them, a heavy, weighted thing that pulled both of their minds back to Maggie. "She was always enough, Jake. You *know* that."

"Bullshit, man." Jake watched Logan's head whip up to glare at him again. He felt that same single chill run the length of his spine at the deadly look in his friend's eyes, so he held up his hands in a steady-goes gesture of peace. "I get it. I…know what it's like to feel inadequate, man. I do."

"Yeah. Okay, Freud."

"All I'm saying is that even if you felt that the military was your only option…hell, even if it *was* your only option, that's the first ten, *maybe* fifteen years we'll give you a pass for." Logan raised his eyebrows, and Jake wasn't sure if he was amused or just being patronizing. Still, he continued. "After that, you could have come home, found a job in security here. Fuck, dude, this is LA. With your quals, you could have a high-paying personal protection job tomorrow. You could be growing fat and out of shape looking after Lady Gaga or something. You could have joined the force…But you never stayed long enough to even look."

"What's your point, Simmone?"

"Stop using the same bullshit excuse, man. Maggie never cared about your background and she sure as hell never cared that you didn't go to college."

"Couldn't."

"What?"

"I couldn't go to college, Jake. I applied. Didn't get in. Anywhere." He laughed, and, at least to Jake, the sound was bitter. "The dyslexia was so bad. And people didn't create special classes or make exceptions back then. I couldn't even write a proper application essay. Maggie did it for me."

"She did?"

"Yeah." Logan turned his gray eyes on him. "Problem being when the standardized test results are shit and the application essay is pristine, people usually know something's up."

Jacob thought about what to say as the bartender put a Guinness down for Logan. "Look…I'm not implying that you made a bad decision when you signed up. And hell, you served for a long time, through some questionable shit. All I'm saying is that Gracie has changed the family," he admitted. "The stakes are much higher." He met hard, gray eyes. "The forgiveness bar has risen. Significantly."

"I don't think I can make it better this time." Logan took a long sip of beer, his eyes clouded, then placed his glass back on the bar before adding, "She's done with me. For good."

"Maybe," Jake replied, unwilling to lie to him. "But that doesn't mean that you have to abandon ship. So, just be there for her. As Gracie's dad."

Jake watched Logan stare into his beer for a solid five minutes before the door opened and Zac Murphy walked in. He raised his hand, waited until his friend's eyes locked on them and he made a beeline to where they were sitting. As Zac walked over, the bartender cleared her throat, her eyes looking him up and down with obvious interest.

Jake tried to hide his grin. He knew that he was passably good-looking, but both Logan and Zac had always been solid tens. They looked like athletes who could have made the centerfold of *Sports Illustrated*. But, where Logan always looked too dangerous for most women to approach without significant encouragement, which he *never* gave, Zac had a way about him that had random women leaving their numbers on the bar as they filtered out for the evening.

When Zac walked up to them, Logan turned on his stool. It took one second for Jake to see the look in Zac's eye, another for him to shift slightly to the right as Zac's fist plowed into Logan's jaw, sending him to the floor amidst a loud yelp from the bartender.

Jake held his breath as Logan's eyes changed from gray to black, and he pushed himself to his feet slowly. The room was silent except for the low-volume commentary of the football game that played on the screen in front of them. The two men faced each other, their eyes glinting, one pair sky blue the other steel gray, both murderous.

He knew that nobody in their right mind would interfere. Zac and Logan both looked dangerous, one lean and lithe like a boxer, one impossibly huge with death in his eyes. And both were clearly trained.

Suddenly, as if nothing had happened at all, Zac grinned. "I'll take a Guinness too," he said to the bartender, whose eyes were wide as an owl's. Then he plopped down on the barstool as if he hadn't a care in the world.

Logan touched a single hand to his face, rolled his neck, but didn't say anything. He knew what it was for.

So did Jake.

As much as Zac and Maggie joked about getting married and running away together, there was something there between them. Something that might have had a chance to grow had Logan Cane never existed.

"How you been, Cane?" Zac asked when Logan lifted the barstool from the floor and sat back down.

Jacob felt his heart settle as the slow chatter struck up again in the bar, and the tension level dropped with it.

"Ah, been better."

Once again, Jacob wondered what had happened to his friend in the Central African Republic, and if he'd take the help he'd offered when the time came. Jacob knew two things: one, Logan Cane was the most dangerous man that he knew, and two, whatever he was running from had him sitting down so that he could face the door with one eye permanently glued to the bar's entrance. Logan was expecting trouble.

Chapter 3

The moment she walked into the little storefront space, Maggie knew it would be where she'd put her café. From the vintage brass handle on the door to the wide front windows that bounced her reflection back at her, the small space was exactly as she'd imagined.

When she'd started looking for a location, she'd known that her ideal aesthetic was better suited to a quiet east-coast town than the churning gut of Los Angeles. But she'd also figured that in a city as big as LA, she'd find the right spot eventually.

And she had.

The building was perfect, perched on the edge of Angelino Heights, right off Sunset Boulevard. It sat between a second-hand bookstore and a taqueria.

The bookstore—to the right of what she already thought of as *her* building—was a squat, square structure made from real red brick. The bricks were crumbling off the corners to reveal patches of gray underneath, but the effect was charming, making the old store look like a modern restoration project—not a historic-aged building that had been grandfathered into the city code long before California's earthquake laws.

A big rectangular sign hung above an old door that had once been painted red. The sign was treated wood; and the words, 'USED BOOKS', were painted in big block letters.

The taqueria to the left was also square, but the plaster walls were a soft teal color that glistened in the sunlight. Metal tables and chairs in the same color were organized in a neat seating arrangement on the sidewalk, beneath a white awning. The name 'Natalie's' had been spray-painted onto the front of the building in a white and green graffitied sign.

And then there was her building, sitting quietly between them. It was small from the front, a little A-frame tucked between two squares. The façade was brick, painted white with black trim and offset by a big, painted black door. Two large windows blinked out onto the street.

She stood, just inside the door, imagining everything that she could do to make her vision come to life. Short, café-style tables nestled against the big windows, and taller, cocktail tables closer to the bar. She'd add wrought iron bar stools with emerald green seats in velvet. And, shelves for sellable bric-a-brac and a small book lending library. Plants…*tons of plants.*

The sound of the leasing agent clearing his throat pulled her from her reverie, and not wanting to appear too excited in front of him, Maggie resumed her walk around the room, taking in the scarred, hardwood floors, and the ten-foot ceilings.

He didn't seem very interested in the fact that she was looking about, so she walked through the front room, past the old, wooden bar to the kitchen in the back.

A fully functional sink caught her eye first. It was deep enamel, something that she imagined would have been useful in a farmhouse kitchen if you had six kids and just needed a tub to drown the dishes in.

There was no commercial oven, stove, or hood, which suited her fine.

A cracked four-foot-wide counter covered in white tiles ran the length of the small kitchen. Three neat rows of open shelving dropped down the wall above that.

It needs work, she thought. But that didn't stop the bubble of excitement from worming its way into her chest. Already, she could see what she'd tear out and what she'd leave in. She saw the layout perfectly in her mind and spent a minute filling the kitchen with new appliances, imagining what they'd look like in place.

Her mind reeled with the possibilities.

She took a moment to open the cupboards beneath the counter and glimpse into all the small nooks and crannies in the back.

Only once she had done a thorough examination of everything asides from the front space—the room that would serve as her seating area and bar—did she meander back through, making sure to keep her face politely detached. Neutral.

Her heart beat rapidly in her chest, fueled by her excitement over the ideas, already flowing.

"So?" Replacing his bored scroll through his cellphone with a megawatt smile, the agent held up his hands. "Is this great or what?"

She shook her head in a so-so motion, shrugged non-committaly. "It's...small. Cute."

"It's perfect for what you have in mind," he replied earnestly. "And I just heard from the owner that they're prepared to drop to two dollars a foot for the first five years."

Maggie did the math in her head, making sure to keep her smile cool.

It was a bargain considering she wanted the space anyway. "Look. I have one other location that I'm seriously considering, but I think this might work if we can come to some sort of arrangement on renovations. I mean," she sighed audibly, "it just needs a *lot* of work."

"Sure. Sure." The kid, a sweet-faced, five-ten brunette who looked like he'd rather be playing beer-pong with his other twenty-something-year-old friends grinned. "I can write you up a lease with what the owners are prepared to front by the end of the day."

"Thank you." She wanted to stay for hours and plan out every detail, but turned her back on the room and made for the door, only stopping to briefly thank and shake hands with the boy.

It was only when she was far enough down the street that she turned around and cast one more look at the pretty, little A-frame.

It's perfect. It's me. Feeling an impromptu happy dance coming on, she set her shoulders and marched to her car instead. There'd be time to dance—when she was home alone with Gracie and nobody around to watch her make a fool of herself. But the smile that flitted over her face was big and real.

Throwing her purse on the front seat of her car, Maggie glanced at her watch before pulling out into the evening traffic. Even in the rush hour, it took only twelve minutes to get home, and in no time at all, she was slipping into her driveway.

She parked, felt the first twist of need claw her stomach when she thought about holding Gracie, snuggling her to her chest, and breathing in her baby scent. Why was that, she wondered. Why could she need an hour or two to herself and still physically crave contact with her child?

She didn't know.

She didn't really care either.

Leaning over, she grabbed her purse and hefted it up off the passenger seat. "What the…?"

A glinting metal ornament lay on the seat beneath where her purse had been.

Picking it up, she turned it right and left, took a moment to study the three-pointed, rustic star. She turned it again, studied the tree-like shape and rudimentary grip.

It was about the length of her forearm, with a long, curved center blade off of which sprouted two shorter ones. One near the base and one near the top where the metal forked. It looked like a basic hand-carved tool of sorts, something from a previous civilization or…When her heart started beating in her ears, she put a hand to her chest. *Logan.*

"Asshole!"

"Maggie?"

Turning abruptly, she saw her mom standing outside her car window, holding Gracie. Both of their eyes were big and round with surprise.

Clearing her throat, she smiled at them, "Sorry. Everything is fine." The words were forced, calm over a sheen of anger.

She stuffed the blade into her handbag—grateful for the bag's unnecessary size—and got out of the car.

She opened her arms for Gracie, felt her heart settle in a steady rhythm when she breathed in her baby girl's scent. "Hi, guys," she whispered.

"Ma."

"Yeah." She nuzzled her daughter's neck right there in the driveway. "I missed you."

She had only been gone a few hours and had specifically made an evening appointment so that her mom would be free to watch Grace. But even that had seemed like an eternity.

"How was your appointment?"

Maggie looked at her mom, took in June's slender frame, greying hair, and wicked green eyes. "Perfect."

"Oh!" Her mom clapped her hands together excitedly, sending Gracie into a round of giggles. "I just knew it! The minute that I saw the listing, I knew that she was destined to be yours."

"Well, you were right." Hefting Gracie's weight onto her other hip, she asked, "Are you going to stay for a bit? I can tell you all about what I'm going to do to the place."

"Agh, I'd love to." June rolled her eyes. "Really. But I promised your father that we'd go *bowling* tonight." She said the word 'bowling' with exaggerated disgust. "I'll never

44

understand why he wants me to spend my retirement renting shoes that aren't my own. It's unsanitary."

"Yes," Maggie laughed, "but we both know that you'll continue to indulge him. I'll see you tomorrow?"

June nodded and made for her car, a secondhand Mini Cooper that Phil had picked up for her to 'zip around in'. Whatever that meant. She opened the door and turned to blow them a kiss off the palm of her hand.

"Thanks for watching Gracie, Mom."

"Anytime, baby girl."

Maggie watched her leave, stood in the driveway with Gracie on her hip and waved her mom off, then turned towards the house, excited by the prospect of snuggling on the couch.

"Maybe," she rambled to an already-dozing Gracie, "I'll watch a murder mystery while you nap?" She looked down at her daughter's flittering eyelids, "Or put you down and enjoy a long, hot bath and a single glass of wine?" *Or, flip through my portfolio and start planning out the cafe?*

Opening the door to her house, she stepped through, then gently closed them together in the quiet.

Spunk yipped and walked slowly through to her. Reaching down, Maggie ran her fingers over the old dog's head, pulling her ears gently through her fingers so the dog groaned and pushed against her palm.

Gracie didn't stir.

The house was silent but for the pad of her feet on the hardwood floor and the occasional sound from outside that drifted through her open kitchen window.

Usually, she didn't mind the quiet—she craved it. But tonight, the silence seemed to hang in the air, filling her lungs and chest with a weighted loneliness every time that she inhaled.

Strange, that her excitement could die so quickly when she had nobody to share it with. The feeling unsettled her, forced a jab of panic through the heaviness in her chest.

It had never bothered her that she was lonely before.

She'd been the steady girlfriend of an active-duty soldier. Then she'd be the on-again-off-again lover of a Special Forces weapons sergeant. Then she'd been the ex-fiancée of a bodyguard for hire. Loneliness in *all* its forms was something that she was used to.

She had never been truly alone, removed from human contact. She had her big, wild family. She had friends. It was more than that; it was the loneliness of having the one person that she longed to be with always so far away, always out of reach as she planned for the next home visit.

Thoughts of Logan turned her mind towards the little tree-knife that she'd found in her car.

So weird. It wasn't like him to leave things for her, especially after breaking into her car to do so…

She'd also have given him a week, tops, before she'd expected him to come back for round two, guns blazing. Hell, she'd spent days mentally preparing for that exact scenario, had lain awake for hours every night rehearsing the insults that she'd fling at him.

But six weeks?

She did a quick tally in her head, just to be sure. Her mind had been somewhat distracted since he had come home, and she'd hate to call fire when there wasn't even smoke. *Still…*

As Gracie dozed on her shoulder, she walked into her kitchen, Spunk on her heels, and took out a bottle of wine—a mid-range Merlot that she enjoyed.

Placing it on the counter, she rustled around in her huge handbag until she found her cellphone. Before she could change her mind, she called Jacob.

He picked up after just one ring. Maggie couldn't be sure, but she thought that she could hear a football game on in the background. "Hey!" he said, talking loudly over the sound.

"Can you talk?" she asked. Maybe he and Lola were on a date. She should have just texted.

"Yeah! What's going on?"

She heard male laughter in the background, followed instantly by a single chill that pulled her spine tight. The first she recognized as Zac, but there was no mistaking the second as Logan Cane.

The deep, dark rumble of it sent her stomach freefalling to her feet, forcing her eyes closed as she tried to recapture it. Her body stiffened and her fist clenched around the phone.

My own goddamn brother!

"*Maggie*...wait."

"Really, Jake? You of *all* people?"

"You have to hear me out!" he sputtered.

Because the tears were threatening, she snapped out a quick, "No. I don't."

She was about to hang up, aware of the fact that the tense set of her body was causing Gracie to stir on her shoulder. "Seeing as though you have him handy, tell Logan that if he ever breaks into my car to leave me his cheap, African knick-knacks again, I'll slit his goddamn throat with it."

"What? Maggie!"

She hung up on him, felt the hot tears burn her eyes. When Spunk whined, she raised her free hand to her flushed face. *I shouldn't have said that.*

But, shit!

My own brother!

Logan had broken into her car, left her a weird gift from the Central African Republic, but hadn't even bothered to try and see his own daughter for the first time. And he'd been back for *six weeks*!

Pure fury had her unscrewing the cap of the wine, even as she swayed back and forth to try and nudge Gracie back into sleep. She took a swig straight from the bottle—

nobody would know—before pouring herself a generous glass, then carried it and her sleeping child back to the lounge so that she could sit in her dad's old Laze-boy.

The chair, an old scarred leather one that her father had sat in every night for ten years, was what Maggie had preferred to nurse in through the long nights when Grace had been a newborn. Eventually, when she'd bought the house, had moved into her own home, she'd woken up one Saturday to her dad at her door, his Laze-boy in his truck.

He'd argued that June had gotten him another one, which she had—eventually. But Maggie knew that he wanted her to have it for her nights alone.

Gracie sighed and nuzzled her face into Maggie's collarbone, sending a single jolt of pure female contentment to her very soul. *You're going to be fine.* She repeated her mantra to herself as she gently rocked the chair with one foot and scratched Spunk's back with her other. The gentle back and forth motion had Gracie knocked out in under ten minutes, giving her the time to just sit.

And think.

She'd asked herself how she'd wound up the way that she had a million times before. But still, she hadn't found the right answer. She'd been a solid A-grade student in high school, even after she'd started dating Logan, who had always been a few Summer classes away from failing. She'd graduated summa from USC. Graduated top of her class from Stanford Law, found a successful law career, and lived it for nearly twenty years.

And all that time, she had only ever been with Logan. Well, either been with him or waiting for him, which really may as well have been the same thing considering that she'd never been with anyone else.

She'd never dated, had never even said yes to a date with another man, even though she had been asked plenty. At first, she'd used the, 'Oh, I have a boyfriend card'. But somewhere along the way she had stopped calling Logan her boyfriend, had stopped saying, 'My boyfriend's overseas in the military', or 'my boyfriend works abroad'. Instead, she'd just become that single woman that nobody asked out because they knew that she'd say no.

Then Gracie had come along.

She cast a look down at her sleeping child and her heart swelled with so much love.

She'd do it again. She'd go through the lonely nights a million times over, feel the pain of Logan leaving for eternity because those things had led to Gracie. If she'd said yes to dating other men, if she hadn't waited time and time again for Logan to come back to her, she might have had children… but they wouldn't have been Gracie.

They wouldn't have been *his*.

As she did when things got too tough, she rocked in the chair and imagined what her life would look like in five, then ten, then fifteen years. And because Gracie was in every fantasy, a real, breathing piece of her world, Maggie relaxed into the chair and sipped her wine, calm again.

Chapter 4

He was going to break the door down if she didn't let him in. That's what Logan was thinking as Jake pulled his SUV up to Maggie's house and he, Zac, and Jake hopped out.

As he marched across the small front yard, the trained soldier in him observed the garden and the house. Cold eyes scanned the immediate neighborhood.

A pretty row of carnations filled farmhouse window boxes. Maggie's house was a small craftsman that had been recently painted a clean eggshell white, and perfectly accented by navy trim. The windows were shut. The blinds were drawn.

It was quiet.

There were a few cars parked along the narrow road, but no through-traffic.

His heart beat a thick staccato in his chest, as it had since Jake had looked across at him in O'Hara's and passed on Maggie's message. The cold slice of fear he'd felt then had been nothing to the sick, nervous dread that he felt now as he stared at the navy-blue door, his hand raised to knock.

Although he already sensed that nothing was amiss, he couldn't bring himself to pound on the door. It was if he'd frozen under fire, too scared to make the one move that would put him face-to-face with Maggie. With Gracie. His entire body tensed when Jacob placed a hand on his shoulder and gently nudged him aside.

"Maggie!" Jacob called before banging loudly on the door with his fist. "Open up!"

The dog next door started barking, a loud, rumbling woof that had Spunk snorting behind the front door as she gave out little yips of excitement.

When he heard her soft footsteps coming down the hall, heard her placate Spunk with, "You're okay, good girl," his heart clenched in his chest. The air in his lungs solidified and for one whole moment in time, Logan thought he might pass out.

And then she swung open the door, holding Grace.

Winded was the only way to describe it; as if someone had snuck a solid punch to his solar plexus. Maggie's blue eyes glinted dangerously, but Logan couldn't tear his gaze away from Gracie, snuggled against Maggie's side.

Pale, smooth skin covered her small, chubby limbs and soft, light brown curls—somewhere between his and Maggie's color—formed a halo on her head. She was wearing a diaper and the tiniest pink tee-shirt that he'd ever seen. She was bigger than he'd imagined, but still so tiny.

"We need to come in, Maggie." Jacob's voice broke the awkward silence.

"Why?"

The single word, the clipped way that she said it, tore through his chest. It was a sharp slash through his soul that had him clenching both of his fists at his side.

"Where is the item that you thought Logan left in your car?" Jake asked.

"Mags," Logan watched her eyes track to Zac, soften perceptibly, "we need to see it. We need to check the house."

Although he didn't say anything, Logan acknowledged the jolt of jealousy that tore through his chest; heating his blood in a way that had him consciously countering the rage with a carefully blank expression.

He absentmindedly rubbed his tender jaw at the spot where Zac's fist had connected. He thought back over Zac and Maggie's interactions through the years. He couldn't remember anything, any chemistry that wasn't sibling-like. But he'd also been gone for nearly two years and he knew what time was capable of.

"What's happening, Jake?"

When Jacob looked at Logan, Maggie's eyes tracked back to him, her perfect brows raised haughtily. For some reason, he imagined lifting her off her feet and carrying her and Grace inside, slamming the rest of the world out. More than anything he'd ever felt before, right then, he wanted to be alone with Maggie and Grace.

But he didn't move.

When nobody answered, she stepped back into the house, nudging Spunk back inside with her legs.

The dog whined, and Logan, needing something to do with his hands, stepped inside first, bent down to ruffle the dog's fur. "Hi, girl," he whispered. When Spunk licked his face, he chuckled. "I missed you too."

He looked up to see Maggie, Zac, and Jake walking through to what he assumed was the kitchen. He took a moment for himself, a moment to gather his thoughts and calm his frantically beating heart.

His daughter was beautiful.

And seeing her brough all those warring emotions: Joy. Fascination. Despair. Self-loathing. Regret.

This time, fear.

Everything at once.

It was like a bucket of ice water had just been dropped over his head as he'd lain sleeping. The cold rush jarring him awake with heart-stopping finality that screamed: this is it.

Without ever having touched her or held her, he knew that nothing would ever be the same again.

He wanted to hold her, wanted to breathe in the scent of her, wanted her to look at him when she woke up.

When Maggie's face drifted into the forefront of his mind, he realized that he didn't know if he was thinking about Maggie or Grace anymore, or rather, he knew that he was thinking about them both.

He wanted to be there with them...*for* them.

He came into the tidy kitchen, felt his palms begin to sweat when he took in the black slacks and pretty white, lace top that Maggie was wearing. How had he not noticed that before?

He had noticed that she had lost weight—too much weight—and that her clear blue eyes always seemed to be tired. Every cell in his body screamed to ask if she was okay, if there was some way that he could help.

Not yet, the little voice in his head warned.

He had known that her house hadn't been compromised just from standing on the front step. He had known because if Charles Rue had stopped by Maggie's already, he would have done something obvious. Something to scare him. Something like leaving the kpinga that Jacob and Zac were examining now.

Logan *knew* that.

But knowing it didn't stop his hands from shaking with the need to decimate something. He had, after all, worked with Rue for two years, knew Francis' right-hand man as well as he knew himself. Charles Rue was the only one that Francis would trust to scout him, especially on US soil.

"What is it?" Maggie asked, turning those gorgeous blue eyes on him.

His eyes had instantly tracked down her face to Gracie, so he cleared his throat and forced himself to level his gaze. "It's a kpinga. A throwing knife typically associated with the Banda."

Maggie's eyes went wide. "Why was it in my car?"

"It's time, Logan. You have to tell us."

"We can help," Zac seconded Jacob's plea.

Glancing at Maggie, he sighed. He had brought this to her doorstep, he realized. He had brought this home to her, and now, to Gracie too.

He had thought long and hard about it as he'd been trekking through the Congo. He had wondered if coming back to the US was a good idea. His original plan, to stay in the CAR and kill Francis himself, had fallen apart when he'd found out about Gracie.

As soon as Marlene had told him about his daughter, he'd felt a strange compulsion to go home, a need to see his girls for himself and make sure that they were safe. He'd briefly considered moving south, hiding out in Zimbabwe or South Africa for a while, maybe play the American tourist until Francis gave up looking for him. But a piece of him knew that the first place that they'd look for him was Los Angeles.

So, he'd come home.

"My detail in CAR was a French national, Francis Boucher," he said, breaking the silence. "He's an older man whose family have had stakes in the CAR since before their independence from the French in 1960."

The kitchen grew eerily quiet.

"He seemed legit for the first year or so. A businessman. Sure, there were bribes and a few sketchy meetings, but…"

He thought about how to explain the inner workings of the worst parts of the world to a group of friends whose only exposure to that kind of desperate humanity was from the films that they'd watched, films that had been made a thirty-minute drive away in Hollywood.

"You need to understand that…CAR is…beyond anything you'll ever experience."

"How so?" Jake asked.

"The per capita income in CAR is four-hundred US dollars. Annual."

"So, it's poor. We get it." Zac crossed his arms over his chest.

"Four percent of the population between the ages of fifteen and fifty are HIV positive."

Nobody volunteered a comment at that.

"They've been embroiled in civil war since independence. Not even the United Nations has managed to make a dent in the civil unrest."

"The UN is there?"

Logan nodded at Jake's question. "Fifteen *thousand* personal deployed as part of the MINUSCA effort. And from what I could see, it hasn't made a difference yet."

"Okay, we get it. It's a shitty existence." Zac threw his hands in the air. "That doesn't explain why you're running, Cane."

"I stumbled into Boucher's uranium mining operation," he said, his voice calm despite the memories that assaulted him.

There was a beat of silence before Jake said, "Uranium mining is legal... Isn't it?"

"And prolific. Canada, Australia, Namibia..." Zac shrugged. "We have to get it from somewhere."

"Yeah, we do. But all those countries you mentioned are relatively wealthy. And peaceful. Their mining is heavily regulated. They have entire government bodies like OSHA, dedicated to making sure protocols are adhered to."

"He's unregulated?" Maggie asked, her voice breaking the cloud of testosterone hanging in the air.

Logan nodded. "Yes."

"So?"

"It's not just mining, Zac" Logan insisted with an impatient shake of his head. "It's *uranium* mining. It releases radioactive radon."

"And he's exposing his workers to it," Maggie finished.

"Not just the miners that we'd think of either. What I saw..."

"Desperate people with no other option," Jake supplied. "Practical slave labor."

"Women and children too." The words were whispered.

"Fuck."

"But...why come after you specifically, Logan?" Zac pressed. When Logan didn't answer immediately, he put his hands on his hips and tilted his head. "What did you do?" he asked, his tone mockingly playful.

Raising a hand, Logan rubbed his eyes. "I reported it to a friend of mine. A UN delegate. Broke my contract with no notice, and trekked through the DRC to catch a plane back to New York. Sasha, my UN lead, said that the operation had been closed down and that she couldn't find anything, but she's still working on tracing the miners, trying to find people to interview."

"Oh, swell," Zac countered immediately. "Psychopathic maniac with *literal* slaves catches you snooping, and YOU REPORTED HIM!"

"I was going to take care of it! But I fou-"

"Oh, were you then?"

"Enough." Maggie's tired voice cut through the frenzy. "Why me?"

Logan looked back at Maggie, noticed that Gracie had woken up and now stared back at him with eyes the exact color of his. "I had some pictures in my personals." He sighed. "They're all labeled and dated. Charles Rue, Boucher's right-hand man...We worked together for nearly eighteen months. He must have gone through my things."

"Okay." Zac paced back and forth. "So, he wants to kill you?"

Logan thought about the question, thought about what he'd learned about Francis Boucher in the two years he'd worked for him. "He doesn't need to kill me. I left, the operation has been shut down...It's more than that."

"What do you mean?" Jake asked.

"Boucher is an egomaniac...He's powerful. He's filthy rich. He loves nothing more than playing God. I'd hazard a guess that it's why he's stayed in CAR all these years. I mean he has the money to retire anywhere in the world—Monaco, Manhattan...anywhere—but-"

"He stays in CAR to lord it over people who have no other option than to cater to his every whim."

"Exactly."

"That's disgusting."

Unsure if Maggie was talking about Boucher, or about the fact that Logan had worked for the man, he kept his eyes trained on Jake. "It'll be fun for him," he said quietly. "A cat and mouse game deliberately intended to flaunt his cards. And Rue…Rue is worse. He may work for Boucher, but he has a streak of crazy in him that makes Richard Ramirez look like a nice guy."

"Could we convince him that it wouldn't be worth the effort?" Zac asked. "Maybe we pull some of your SF buddies to track him down?"

"He won't care. Charles is…"

He didn't know how to describe Rue's obsession with besting him, he didn't try to.

"So this…Boucher wants to get off seeing how shit-scared you are at the thought of Maggie and Grace in danger? And he's using his war dog to do it?"

Logan nodded. "Can you think of another reason he'd send someone from CAR to LA? To Maggie? And not just *someone*…Charles Rue."

Jacob looked at Maggie. "You have to go back to Mom and Dad's house. Until we can find this asshole and nail him."

"We?" Logan asked.

"*Well*, considering that Maggie and Gracie are involved. Yes. *We* are going to help you."

"Phil and June can't protect them," Zac countered, raking a hand through his unruly black hair.

"I'm staying in my own house," Maggie seconded firmly. "Jake, I will not bring Mom and Dad into this."

"You have to," Jake argued. "Or, at least come stay with Lola and me?"

"I'd offer to stay, but I'm working on a case for Kimmi Kripps and it's taking a lot of my time. I'd be gone more than I'd be here."

"Kimmi Kripps?" Jacob's head whipped up, and he squinted at Zac. "What are you up to?"

"Can't say. I have client confidentiality, man." Zac turned to Logan. "I guess that leaves you."

"What?" Maggie's voice came out a stunned whisper.

"It's the best way, Mags," Jake said, oblivious to Logan's sudden inability to breathe. "Logan knows what he's dealing with. He has all the time in the world right now…I agree with Zac. It makes sense."

He didn't want to put her on the spot, but his heart was bleeding at the prospect that she might say no. He looked at her silently, waiting.

For a moment, she just stared back, her big, blue eyes sad and uncertain.

The moment stretched uncomfortably, and Logan finally chose to break it first. "I'm not asking for anything, Maggie. Just…let me help. This is all my fault…and even if it weren't…I'm good at protecting people. It's the one thing I can do without fail."

Gracie cooed and let her head fall against Maggie's face. Maggie sighed and rested her cheek on top of Gracie's head. The picture of them like that, their heads together as they silently deliberated his value, made his heart ache in his chest. He wanted to reach out and close the space between them, fold them in his arms and shut everyone else out.

"Fine." She turned back to face Jacob and Zac, both of whom were smiling with relief.

Logan didn't know what to say. But his heart was pounding in his chest as if he'd just finished a marathon—and won first place.

The click of the front door closing behind Jake and Zac echoed through the empty hallway. To Maggie, the sound seemed too loud. It was an empty sound, one that wanted to be filled.

Logan stood silently in front of her, his body tensely set, his fists curled at his sides as if he were preparing for a fight. He wasn't looking at her; his eyes, filled with something close to shock, were locked on Gracie.

It was as if he was trying to absorb every detail. As if he were trying to commit Gracie to memory, down to her tiny fingernails and the little freckle under her right eye.

"I don't have a spare room," Maggie said clearly.

Logan flinched as her tone slapped at him, but he recovered quickly, fitting a blank expression on his face as he slid his hands into the front pockets of his jeans. "I can take the sofa."

"Okay." She took a step back, too aware of the charged space between them.

His eyes darkened when he noticed but, still, he didn't say anything. He just stood there, mute, staring at her, his expression neutral.

She wanted to ask him what he was thinking, what had run through his mind when he'd first seen their daughter. She wanted to ask him if he felt anything at all, if he noticed that she was perfect. She wanted to ask him if he wanted to hold her.

But she didn't.

He broke the silence first. "Do you mind if we talk for a minute?"

Her heart jumped into her throat, and, afraid her voice would waver, she nodded sharply.

"Until I sort this out, you can't go anywhere without either me or Jake…or Zac if neither of us is available. No grocery shopping, no running errands." He paused for a beat. "Marlene told me that you weren't back at work; is that accurate?"

But Maggie couldn't answer because, for just a moment, she'd thought he wanted to talk about *them*, about Gracie. *You're such a fool.* She bit the inside of her cheek to distract herself from the burn of tears behind her eyelids, and gave him another small nod.

She'd never been able to hide anything from him. But she'd been hoping enough time had passed that she'd, at *least,* be able to lie convincingly. When he took a step closer to her, his hand raised as if he were going to touch her, she knew that he'd read her thoughts.

"Maggie..."

"I'm fine. Just...hurry up."

"We can talk about everything tomorrow. Just...don't go." He must have realized how the words sounded because he quickly clarified with, "Don't go anywhere without telling me first. I'll come with you."

Inhaling deeply, she cleared her voice. "Is there anything else?"

He shook his head, but his eyes flitted to Gracie again. "No," he said quietly.

And with that, Maggie turned around and walked away, leaving him standing in the kitchen alone.

Usually, she would have taken Gracie—who was fast asleep again—to her crib and put her down. But, just for tonight, she didn't want to be alone.

She didn't want to lie awake, thinking about Logan in her house. She didn't want to worry about all the unsaid things festering between them. And she didn't want to be alone when her mind turned to what Logan had told them about Francis Boucher and Charles Rue because then she'd have to admit that she was scared.

So, she'd put Gracie in her bed with her—a habit she usually tried to avoid—and when she couldn't sleep, she'd turn and look at her tiny daughter and remind herself of everything she had done already, everything she'd still do to protect her child from pain.

She'd lie awake, knowing full-well that she'd lament the lack of sleep in the morning, but she'd be fine because she'd have Gracie to remind her that she'd never be alone. Ever again.

Chapter 5

Green or blue?
Green or blue?
Green or blue?

Maggie slammed her hand down on the table, frustrated by the wall of distraction she kept running up against.

Sure, the wall was a six-four-plus-change male who slept quietly in the other room, minding his own business. But that didn't matter. What mattered was that she had been trying to make the same decision for over two hours, and she had gotten as far as 'Green or blue?'.

And even that measly question had been the most productive thought in her brain since Logan Cane had moved in—sans suitcase or even a change of clothes—over fourteen hours earlier.

As if the night before hadn't been torture enough—because it had—now she would be stuck in the same house as him during daylight hours for God knew how long.

She'd lain awake for hours thinking about the surreal situation that she had found herself in. Thoughts of the strange kpinga, of the threat behind it…thoughts of Logan and the small distance separating them, had kept her up most of the night.

Her bedroom, which was right next to Gracie's, was only fifty feet from the lounge where Logan would be sleeping. The only thing physically separating them was her tidy, little kitchen with its gleaming stainless steel appliances and obnoxiously clean floor.

And, strangely, she could have handled it all if she'd just been able to concentrate for long enough to pick the damn accent color for the interior of her café.

She'd spent weeks on everything else. She already had the rustic wooden furniture, the patina mirrors, and the hanging plants. All she had left to decide was if she wanted green or blue to be the color that was dotted around the place, tying everything together. She was fifty-five percent settled on green because it would bring out the ceiling plants, but blue…blue looked good too.

Needing a distraction she switched tasks, shifting from interior accent colors to trying to decide on a name. She had been describing her idea to people as a 'café-slash-wine-bar' but she knew she'd have to pick a name to put above the door eventually. So far, she'd spent hours going down the Google rabbit hole, looking for an appropriate descriptor.

It hadn't worked. Instead, she'd found herself reading up on how to butcher a pig, which she'd found so horrifically fascinating that she'd read the entire posting before she'd even realized what website she was on and wondered how the hell she'd wound up there in the first place.

Placing both of her hands on her sides, she stretched, arching her back into the pull of muscles as she rolled her neck to relieve the tension that had set in.

She ran through the list of names that she had toyed with so far. *Piacere. Maggie's. Corked.*

Nothing stuck. Everything she tried sounded wrong. Either overused or too obscure, reminding her why she'd decided on giving the naming a rest too. She had tried a million ways to get creative, engage her inner small-business-owner and decor guru, but as of yet, nothing had seemed…right. Predestined.

Angry with herself, she pushed the sketches and catalogs aside, and tapped her fingernails over the wooden kitchen table.

It was only nine in the morning, and she still had time in the day to be productive, but that was beside the point. Maggie hated being stuck.

She was the type of woman who thrived on tasks, on scheduling time to get them done, and then knocking them out within the allotted time so that she could move onto the next thing. Only since having Gracie had she tried to relinquish some of her more glaring OCD traits. Like keeping a schedule for every fifteen minutes of the day. But it hadn't been—still wasn't—easy to completely let go.

She'd been a successful lawyer, someone who'd thrived on forcing chaos into structure, someone who'd regularly worked over seventy hours a week. Now…not as much.

More.

Scanning her eyes over the heap of crap on her kitchen table, she ran inventory on what was there and why: scrapbooks, paint swatches, magazines, and crafting supplies because she'd been planning her café for weeks and cleaning it up every night would have messed with her train of thought.

A baby bottle sterilizer because her kitchen counter was too small to leave it plugged in when she cooked.

An empty pastry bag from three days ago when her mom had brought her and Gracie breakfast. She didn't know why that was still there, but she made a note to clean it up later.

A single fork.

A rubber ducky for Gracie's bath. *That's where that went.*

An open bag of new diapers.

Gracie's diaper bag slung over the back of one of the chairs.

Her handbag on the seat of the same chair.

And that's just what she could *see.* Who knew what hid beneath the pile of crap.

Raising a hand, she rubbed at her dry eyes, trying desperately to ignore the itchy compulsion to clean.

She was so tired.

True to her own internal—and highly questionable schedule—Gracie had woken up at three in the morning, alert as a Pookie during the witching hour. It had taken Maggie two hours to get her back to bed, and now, while her daughter contentedly slept away the morning, Maggie attempted to sneak in some work while she could.

It was a routine of sorts—a terrible one. But she knew that it was far better than the alternative.

In the world where she had gone back into corporate law, she would have dropped Gracie with her mom and dad before hurrying off, still exhausted, to a ten-hour workday. Instead, now she let her baby sleep while she planned and plotted out what the rest of their life would look like.

If the café doesn't tank.

She felt the edge of her raw nerves dancing in her belly, felt the same tipsy rush of fear that she always did when she thought about going out on her own. She had quit a six-figure salary, a twenty-year career, to open a mom-and-pop passion project.

Oh, God.

If her business failed, she could always go back into law, use the, 'I took time off to have a kid' card because, well, it would have been partially true. But, after twenty years as a lawyer and one as a mom, she didn't care about the salary. Not as much as the time that she'd be losing with Gracie if she ended up failing.

Grace was already thirteen months. She was growing like a weed, and, most days, it felt like time wasn't allowing her to catch up. It felt like, soon, she'd walk through to a grumbling teenager instead of her happy baby girl.

Maggie could tell that Gracie was going to get her father's height, certainly not all six-five of it, but enough of it to overtake her eventually.

Thoughts of Logan snuck up on her. Again. She'd already spent the entire night before thinking about how his eyes had glazed over when he'd looked down at Gracie in her arms. She'd wanted him to reach out a hand and touch their daughter.

He'd kept his distance instead, and she wondered if it had to do with the fact that he was giving her the time and space that she needed. Or if he felt as shit scared as she did every time that she looked at Gracie, and realized that the game had changed and the rules no longer applied.

More, as she'd lain awake thinking, she'd *felt* the red-hot anger that had kept her going for so long leave her body in one slow seep. Each time that she'd brought Logan's stunned expression to the forefront of her mind, a little more of the rushing fury had leaked out, and by morning, there'd been nothing but a hollow ache in the space where she'd stored her rage.

Her only consolation, the thing that had kept her focused at all over the last fourteen hours, was that the lease that had come through for her café.

She hadn't waited a minute. She'd opened the email attachment eagerly, only a little surprised by how economical the offer from the owners to front the cost of renovations had been. She had known that it had been vacant for a while by the collecting dust and the musty interior.

She'd dropped any pretense of uncertainty, had signed the document right away and sent it back.

Her brothers would have called her rash, but she knew that she had made the right decision. So why wait?

Spunk's yip from the lounge had her pushing to her feet. Although she let her dog out into the small backyard first thing in the morning, it was their everyday routine to wake Gracie up together before heading out for a long, rambling walk through the neighborhood.

Padding through, still in her long, ankle to wrist, linen pajamas, she stopped in the doorway of the lounge.

Logan sat on the sofa, his long hair rumpled from sleep, his gray eyes glassy and unfocused. His huge hands enveloped Spunk's wide head as if he were trying to hold her in place while the dog shook her entire rear end back and forth in excitement.

Maggie felt the long pull in her belly, the unquestionable simmer of attraction that she had felt for him as soon as she had been old enough to recognize what such things were. Sixteen, give or take—that's the age that she had first felt that same tightening for Logan Cane.

"What time is it?" he asked, sensing her hovering in the doorway.

She didn't answer for a moment. Instead, she chose to cross her arms over her chest so that she could study him without betraying her body's response to his proximity. "Just after nine."

Nodding, he leaned forward to rest his head on Spunks. "Stop."

The dog stopped her wagging immediately.

"Sit.'

She plopped her butt to the floor.

"Kiss."

Maggie rolled her eyes when the dog licked his face enthusiastically, clearly uncaring where he had been for the last two years, just happy that he was finally home.

If only it were that simple.

"I need to stop by the condo today and grab my things," he said when she turned to walk out.

"Okay?"

"I can drop you at your Mom and Dad's for a few hours if you don't want to come, but I'd prefer if you and Gracie stuck with me until I've sorted everything."

Hearing the word, 'Gracie' from his lips for the first time made her chest tighten perceptibly. The way that he said, 'Until I've sorted everything', forced a chill from her toes up her spine.

"We'll come."

He looked at her in surprise. "Mom and Dad have an orchid fair today."

"A what?"

"A flower show, exhibit…sale." She waved her hands in the air, not entirely sure what happened at the events herself.

"Since when does Phil go to flower shows?"

"Since he forced June into retirement on the condition that she got to pick ninety percent of their activities." When his mouth turned up with the beginnings of a smile, she added, "She literally keeps a tally."

He laughed, a deep, rolling sound that tore through her. "How is your mom?"

But Maggie, suddenly very afraid of the way that her stomach had flopped over at the sound of his laugh, countered with, "Look…Logan."

She sighed when his steel eyes shuttered at her tone. "We don't have to pretend that we don't have history, or that we don't have things that we still need to talk about…"

His eyes locked on hers, sending a jolt of need through her, but she forced out the rest. "But we need to cohabitate in the meantime with as little stress as possible. For Grace."

He nodded. "So, I can't ask how your parents are doing?"

She shook her head. "You'll see for yourself over the next few weeks." She turned away, looking back over her shoulder to say, "I have to take Spunk for a walk."

"Give me five."

She took her time waking up Gracie and changing her, took the time for herself because she knew that this was a big first for everyone.

The little denim shorts and green shirt that she had chosen were one of her favorite outfits of Gracie's. The set had been a gift from her sister Emma, sent from Paris with a whole chest of other items. The adorable clothes, all from different stores and labels, were a testament to the fact that her little sister had a passion for fashion that ran deeper than her gorgeous face and killer body.

"You ready?"

She jumped at the sound of Logan's voice coming from the doorway of the nursery. She refrained from looking at him even as Gracie's head tracked to the sound and she smiled, her chubby cheeks lifting easily.

"Yes," Maggie blew a raspberry on Grace's stomach so that she giggled, "we are."

She picked the baby up, grabbed the little hat from where it sat on the corner of the crib, and plopped it on Gracie's head so that it covered her eyes as she walked to the door of the room. It was their little game. Maggie would put the hat on and pull it down low, and Gracie would laugh hysterically and yank it back up.

Grace laughed, as Maggie had known that she would, but before she'd had a chance to lift the hat up, Logan reached forward and righted it himself.

The quick movement coincided with Gracie raising her arms and Maggie watched, fascinated, as their skin touched for a nanosecond before Logan pulled away as if he had been scalded.

Everything paused.

Logan stared at Gracie as if she'd just grown wings. Gracie, her gray eyes wide, started giggling and, this time, she yanked the hat back down over her eyes herself.

Logan frowned as if he weren't quite sure what had just happened, but Maggie saw the fists that were locked at his side. "It's a game," she said, not wanting to admit that she found his confusion funny.

She tugged the hat back up, smiled when Gracie let out a peal of laughter, her big eyes smiling before she suddenly pulled the hat back down over her eyes. "See what you've done," she mock chastised him, "you've released a monster."

With her heart in her throat, she walked past Logan towards the front door where Spunk sat, patiently waiting for her walk. Bending down, she dipped Gracie, her arm snaking out for the leash, which she kept in a basket by the door.

Before she could stand, Logan grabbed her hand in his and removed the leash so that he could clip it to Spunk's collar himself.

She wanted to tell him that she could manage, that she could do it herself, that she *had* been doing it herself for over a year already, but the residual feeling of his hand covering hers, of his skin imprinting on her, overrode everything but the burning need that she'd felt for over a month.

Looking up, she met gray eyes that were dark with the same need, felt her stomach drop to her feet, and her throat go impossibly dry. Instinctively, she reached out her tongue to moisten her lips.

Logan made a sound, a small grunt that shot a ball of lust straight to her core.

Crap.

She was going to kill him. Correction, he thought, *they* were going to kill him. He hadn't had a coherent thought since he had walked into Maggie's house the night before. He hadn't managed to think of one thing besides her and Gracie through the very long night that he'd spent tossing and turning on the too-soft sofa.

When Gracie had woken up at three, he'd already been half-way down the hall before the sound of Maggie's bedroom door opening had pivoted him in place.

He'd silently padded back through to the lounge, let Spunk hop up and cuddle him around four in the morning just so that he could have a distraction from the sound of Maggie's baby talk drifting through the house to him.

Somewhere during the two hours it had taken Grace to go back to sleep, he had started listening to Maggie's words through the baby tone. An hour in, she had resorted to a gentle chant of, "Gracie Laine is so sleepy" over and over again.

It was as if she had been trying to hypnotize Grace to actually feel the fatigue, and Logan had almost chuckled out loud. He'd also had two thoughts under the humor; the first was that Maggie had given Grace his paternal grandmother's name, 'Laine', the second was that maybe he should get up and help.

He'd wanted to.

He wondered what she'd do if he just walked through and plucked Gracie from her arms.

But then he'd remembered her face when she'd told him to stay away from them and the memory had kept him rooted in place.

Soon after, the house had fallen quiet again and he had fallen into a fitful sleep somewhere close to four-thirty.

Now, he followed them out of the house, solidly ignoring the burn in his palm where his skin had touched Maggie's. Gracie seemed to have tired of the hat game, choosing instead to let her eyes wander over the morning activity in the neighborhood from her perch in the stroller that Maggie had put her in.

The late October morning was cool, as if mother nature had decided to give them some relief from the over-eighty-degree day that he knew was coming. Logan would take it, enjoy the morning walk as much as he could with Maggie walking silently beside him, and Gracie occasionally turning big, curious eyes on him.

He knew that he couldn't let himself relax, so he scanned his surroundings, made a quick mental note of the neatly parked cars along the side of the street, of the few people walking around. He did a brief tally, searched faces as he counted them off, but, seeing nobody that set off any warning bells, he kept walking.

Still, something pulled the skin on the back of his neck tight, something was…off. Because he had learned to never ignore his instincts, he guided Spunk to the outside of the sidewalk so that his body covered Maggie and Gracie from the street.

He knew it was meager protection, but any threat in a smashed-together neighborhood like this, where the houses nestled side by side, was going to come from the street. Probably from a moving vehicle.

"What is it?"

Surprised that she had sensed his caution, he glanced down at Maggie. Her body was rigid, her eyes big, blue pools of fear even though she never stopped pushing the stroller. "Nothing that I can put my finger on."

"Should we turn back?"

"No. Just keep walking."

"What about Grace, Logan?"

At the sound of her name, Grace popped her head up, turning in her stroller so that she could look at them. "Ma," she said, followed by a string of half-word, half-babbles that he couldn't make out.

"I'm not going to let anything happen to you. Either of you." He scanned the neighborhood again, did a casual three-sixty on the sidewalk.

Only one car had moved since they'd left the house a good three-hundred feet behind them. It had been a black Mercedes, an older model with a slight tint to the windows. It had been parked facing them, which is why Logan felt his blood begin to pump through his chest. The driver had flipped a U-turn and gone around the block so that he could pass them head on.

What the...Logan turned to Maggie, moved his body in front of the stroller so that his body blocked them from the car.

"Logan?"

"I'm going to inch a little to the left." He did so. "You see this black Mercedes coming towards us?"

She nodded mutely, her eyes a little glazed as she peered over the fraction of space that he left over his shoulder. "I'm going to stay in front of you two, but I need you to read the license plate as it drives past." When she didn't reply, he reached up a hand and touched her face. "Maggie. Do it."

"Eight-P-E-Z-Seven-Eight-Nine-One."

"Good." He casually moved his body as he heard the car drive past, caging Maggie and Gracie in the entire time. By the time that it had driven away, he had come to stand at Maggie's back.

He heard the car pass, knew that it had kept going, knew that if it had been Charles Rue in the Mercedes, he wouldn't be making his move today. So he didn't know why he raised his arms and encircled Maggie, pulling her back close to his chest. But he did.

His heart was beating a frantic rhythm. He could hear it in his ears, and feel it in his throat, just as he could feel Maggie's through her back doing the same.

He breathed in the smell of her. The flowery scent in her hair brought back years of memories in a flood that made his entire body tremble.

For just a second, she leaned back into his chest, relaxed fully against him, letting her head fall back against his collar bone. And then she pulled away and continued down the street as if nothing had happened at all.

Logan felt the physical distance between them. It was a growing space that was getting cold. But, not wanting her to get too far without him near, he took three big steps and caught up to her before slowing his pace and falling in at her side. She didn't say anything, didn't talk to him. But he noticed that she hadn't scolded him either, hadn't protested or cursed him when he'd pulled her close and that…he could live with that.

Spunk tugged on her leash, pulling him towards an island of grass on the sidewalk, and Logan gave her a little leeway so that she could relieve herself.

"Spuk!" Gracie shouted.

He turned to look at Gracie, felt his stomach slide about uncomfortably. How was it possible that he'd only met her yesterday, but already he'd die to protect her? He knew that a part of it was because she was Maggie's life, and he'd do anything for Maggie. But, for some unfathomable reason of nature, he knew that it was because she was his too. She was his little girl and he was intrigued, fascinated by the cocktail of emotions that he felt when he looked at her.

Pulling out his phone, he dialed Jake.

Jake picked up almost instantly. "What's wrong?"

"Had a scout in the neighborhood this morning. Can you run a plate for me?"

"Read it."

"Echo-Papa-Echo-Zulu-Seven-Eight-Nine-One. Black Mercedes, slight window tint, probably a 2015 or 2016 SL-Class."

"Will do. Everything okay?"

He wanted to say no. He wanted to say that he wasn't going to survive not being able to touch Maggie for much longer. But then she turned and looked at him, her blue eyes calm and, although cautious, smiling. "Everything's going to be fine."

"Yeah, we'll catch this asshole."

Logan shook his head, remembering that he had Jake on the line. "Yeah. We will."

"I'll have it to you in a few hours."

"Thanks, Jake." He hung up the phone and, when Maggie turned back for home, silently fell into step beside her.

Chapter 6

Logan sat in one of three chairs that were rolling around the enormous home office and studied the board that Zac had started. The display had pictures, maps, and scrawled notes tacked haphazardly over the surface. Although he had yet to read the information, Logan knew that it was for their search for Rue by the big title that had been scribbled in red letters over the whiteboard portion of the pinboard. It read: Protect Maggie and Gracie. Fuck Everything Else.

It was a sentiment that Logan himself couldn't have agreed with more.

Because Zac was clearly in no rush, Logan scanned the office again. Zac lived in a Beverlywood rendition of a country farmhouse, a big, sprawling home with a slanted, tile roof. From the street, the house took up the full quarter-acre lot, showing off a trellised wrap-around porch guarding long, rectangular windows that filled the big rooms downstairs with natural light.

The front yard and driveway had been expertly manicured—clearly by someone other than Zac. Bright patches of flowers separated the front yard from the sidewalk before a verdant lawn with paved stepping stones led up to the house.

The house could fetch three million on the low end, before renovations, which to Logan's mind meant that Zac was sitting on close to double that. Knowing Zac, his money was probably in slow-accrual stocks, nothing too risky, but not exactly liquid either. In short, leaving the LAPD seemed to have worked out for him.

Logan was happy for his friend's success. He could also unbegrudgingly acknowledge that he was slightly jealous too. Where Zac had built a life for himself and found something that gave him purpose, Logan had not.

He had money. Twenty years of high-risk, twenty-four-hour, on-call work with zero living expenses had accrued. He'd bought the Downtown LA condo in cash with a small portion of the money, but even that wasn't…home. It didn't feel right.

Always time to look around. He acknowledged the thought for what it was. The recognition that he could start moving forward, start trying to find a way to put down roots.

Maybe he'd never have Maggie again, maybe she'd never completely forgive him. But he'd be able to live close enough to her that he could see her all the time when he swung by to see Gracie.

While Zac gathered his things, pulled notes from drawers and pictures from padfolios, Logan turned to study the board again. He stood so that he could look up at the two photographs that had been tacked front and center to the board. Francis Boucher and Charles Rue stared back at him. Their casual ignorance of the camera that had been snapping shots of them made him wonder how Zac had obtained the pictures in the first place.

In the picture of Francis Boucher, his old boss stood outside of the Ledger Plaza in Bangui, the capital city of CAR. Logan recognized the distinctive building immediately. He noticed that his boss stood with his hands in his pockets, a grin on his face that lit up his blue, rheumy eyes. A uniform-clad attendant held a tray out to him, a cocktail sitting dead center, her slight bow over the tray showing her subservience.

He'd never tell Zac, but the picture was a perfect exhibit of Boucher's soul. He was a man living a life of luxury in one of the poorest countries in the world. A man who had never stopped to think that the single cocktail he'd throwback in fifteen minutes had cost him what the waitress earned for six ten-hour days during an entire week—if that at all.

When his anger began to rise, Logan banked it. Turning, he moved on to the picture of Charles.

Charles Rue, he could forgive a few vices. After all, they weren't that dissimilar. Like Logan, he was hired help, a disposable tool that could be cast away as soon as Boucher didn't have a use for him anymore. Luckily for Rue, he had proven extremely useful in his ten years with Boucher. He was useful enough that Logan still wondered about the extent of the crimes that Rue had committed over his ten-year employment period.

Even Logan, who was governed by a less-than-stout moral code and a set of firm rules dictated by his US-based protection services firm, had done things to protect Boucher that had chipped away at his soul.

He'd shot a man, a poor local, point-blank. He had watched him hit the ground at Boucher's feet with a solid thump. Worse. He hadn't said anything at all when Boucher had laughed and wiped the blood off his face with the sleeve of his white suit before stepping over the body and going about his day.

It had only been a few weeks later when nothing had come of the death that Logan had tried to follow up with the police. He had discovered that the man had lost his wife and both of his children in one of Boucher's mines.

That had been the beginning of the end for Logan. But that particular memory still followed him in his sleep, hiding in the part of his brain that he could control when he was awake but that freed the worst parts of him once he shut his eyes for the night.

He'd never done any off-the-table, uncontracted dirty work for Boucher, although he knew that the offer was implied and *very* open-ended. But unlike him, Rue was a born killer. He seemed nearly amoral in his basic human function and in the way that he went about day-to-day life. Charles Rue was the type who would kill a child the instant that the order came through, only stopping to question it if he thought that he could get an extra lump sum for his dirty work.

He was dangerous, but also the kind of dangerous that Logan was less afraid of. Rue wasn't a military man, he wasn't trained.

He was a mercenary with a gun. He was undisciplined, cruel, and impulsive, which Logan could use to his advantage when the time came.

The door opening pulled him from his morbid thoughts, and he turned to greet Jake. "Hey, man."

Jake nodded, his emerald eyes bright. "Hey." Plopping his bag on the ground, he leaned over to pull out a manila folder. "I ran those plates. On the Mercedes."

"And?"

"They didn't match. The plates were registered to a dark blue BMW Six Series. The owner hadn't reported it stolen and when I tracked her down and called she said that she was looking at the car and that the license plates were intact."

"So it's a dead lead."

"Not necessarily," Zac interrupted. Rolling his chair across the expensive hardwood floor, he pulled up a CCTV line of a street that Logan didn't recognize. But he could read, and the label on the bottom of the screen clearly said, 'Caltrans D7 CCTV 597' with the date and time.

"What am I looking at, Murph?"

"Zac!" Logan watched as Jake paled and turned slowly to stare at his best friend. "Did you...Did you hack the Caltrans CCTV?"

"*Technically*, the public has access to these CCTV logs."

"But?" Logan asked, trying to hide his amusement.

"It's not a continuous stream." Jake rubbed a hand over his eyes. "So, under *normal* circumstances, it wouldn't be helpful."

"*Anyway,*" Zac steamrolled them. "Do you want to see what I found or not?"

"Could you show me how to do that?" Logan asked, impressed.

"Sure. *If* you come and work for me. I don't share my secrets with anyone unless they serve *my* purposes." When Logan looked at him surprised, Zac shrugged, "But that's for another time."

Logan nodded slowly, then, blocking the idea from his mind entirely, he focused on the black and white CCTV camera. He shimmied his chair over a little when Jake rolled the third office chair to where they sat facing the dual monitors.

"So, this camera shows the overpass where North 101 leads to Bonnie Brae Street."

Logan knew the overpass, knew that it lead to Maggie's house just a few streets away. He took a few seconds to orient himself with the black and white screen. "You can't move it…hijack it?"

"I can but it takes time because I'd have to hack the system by tracing the individual IP address for this specific camera. But I didn't need to in this case."

Jacob grunted.

Without acknowledging his best friend's displeasure, Zac continued. "So, I accessed the automatic storage for this segment instead."

"This is a recording?"

"Yup. Now…" he used the video application on his computer to fast forward the video to six in the morning.

Logan focused on the screen. For a while, nothing unusual caught his eye, a few cars flitted across the screen, the early risers on their way to work.

Then he caught it.

Zac stopped the recording, rewound it, and paused when the car first came on screen. The video was poor quality and a little pixelated, but it was clear enough for him to recognize the black Mercedes with a single driver in the front, as well as read the license plate clear as day as the car drove past.

"Bingo," Zac said, his grin wide.

"So, this is him exiting the freeway to Maggie's house at six-ten in the morning?"

"Yes, but that's not what I have to show you." Spinning his chair around in place, Zac used his legs to propel him towards a black metal filing cabinet. He opened the bottom drawer, pulled out a third manilla envelope, and then rolled back to where they sat. "This is what I have to show you."

Taking the folder, Logan opened it. He'd been expecting a clear shot of the driver. Instead, a zoomed-in clip of a bumper sticker glared back at him. It was a silver circle, about the same diameter as the bottom of a drinking glass. Inside the circle, five pairs of lines formed a web of sorts towards a second, smaller circle that lay in the middle of the first.

"Donny Flynn," Jake said.

Logan had no idea what was going on. "Who?"

"This is the trademark signature of the biggest car thief and chop shop in Los Angeles," Zac clarified. He nodded at Jake. "Apparently, even the cops know about it."

Logan looked back at the picture again, saw that the circle was a stylized vehicle rim.

"But how do we find them?" Jake asked.

"Already done."

"You know how to trace Donny Flynn?" This from Jake.

"Yup." Zac grinned. "I called in a favor this morning. I have Donny's goddamn home address!" He shook his head. "Well, I have *one* of his home addresses. Whether he's there or not when we arrive is another matter entirely."

"Where is it? Where does he live?"

Logan watched the back-and-forth with amusement. Zac was baiting Jake, and the poor guy was so excited that he hadn't even realized it yet. Even Logan knew that Zac would take Donny's address to the grave with him. It was a golden rule when you dealt with off-grid thugs and informants: never betray your sources. If you did, you'd wind up out of information in a best-case scenario, or missing and not in need of any information in the more likely scenario.

Jake knew that too. But Logan could see by the pure glee in his eyes that the LAPD had been onto Donny Flynn for a while—and that they'd been largely unsuccessful.

"This is a job for Logan and me. *Only* Logan and me."

"What?" Jake whispered, his green eyes wide with disappointment.

Logan felt a small stab of guilt. Maggie was Jake's sister, after all. But he also knew that there were as many rules outside of the law as there were in it. And bringing a cop to any man in Donny's situation would have been game over for all of them.

"Sorry, man. You know you can't come on this one."

"Zac's right, Jake," Logan seconded, trying to play referee. "They'd spot you in under five seconds."

Jacob just rolled his eyes. "Assholes." He shrugged his shoulders one last time. "Fine. I get it. But what can I do to help?"

"Watch Gracie and Maggie for me." Jake looked over at him. "I left them with Phil and June and asked her not to go anywhere, but Maggie said something about an appointment with her consultant this afternoon." He shrugged. "She'll be pissed if I screw it up."

Jake nodded and, grabbing his bag from the floor, made for the door. "Call me as soon as you're out and safe to make contact."

"If we don't check-in by seven tonight…"

Jake just nodded his head once, his green eyes wary, and walked out the door.

When it closed behind him, Zac turned to look at Logan. "We're taking our personals only. One handgun each. No wires or taps. No trace that we were ever there."

Logan nodded. "I have my Glock in the car." His mind reeled, but in the way that he had been trained to cope with since he was nineteen years old. "We need to map our entry route and three possible exit routes, including detours between them in case we're followed or chased. We need to know each exit routes' proximity to the nearest police station and the nearest hospital."

Zac raised a single eyebrow, raked one hand through thick, black hair. "I'm going to let you do that while I call ahead." He shrugged at Logan's blank stare. "I don't usually go tactical, just try to announce my presence before I show up." When Logan nodded, Zac added, "Reconvene in one hour to go over the plan."

He pointed to a second desktop computer, also with dual monitors. The computer password is 'Cupcake' with a capital C. Printer is over there. Knock yourself out."

"Cupcake?"

"Cupcake."

Chapter 7

Donny Flynn's house was a quaint hacienda-style home, complete with a front-yard setback, a white-picket fence, and pansies growing in the flower bed beneath the square, front windows. It was located in the Studio City neighborhood of Los Angeles, north of the Hollywood Hills.

"*This* is where the biggest chop-shop operator in LA lives?" Logan asked, looking out of the windows of Zac's SUV. Turning in the passenger seat, he added, "Did you put in the wrong zip code?"

"Har. Har." Zac parallel parked and turned off the ignition. "We aren't in the Central African Republic anymore, Logan."

"That's for sure." He was feeling the adrenaline begin to kick in already. He thrummed his hands on the dash, a subconscious tick that he'd developed when faced with the prospect of death at nineteen. One he had yet to outgrow.

"These guys..." Zac paused, and Logan could feel his eyes boring into him.

"I'm ready."

"I can see that," Zac returned. "Maybe remove the ax-murderer look from your eyes before we go in though."

"What?"

"Dude, you're giving me the willies and I was a cop in LA. Donny Flynn is an operator. He's a glorified mechanic who occasionally talks big to spread his street cred."

"What?"

"He graduated from Harvard Business School."

"Why didn't we go over this in the briefing?"

"It was implied."

83

"No. It was not. Clearly."

"Jesus! His name is Donny!'

Although he would never concede that he was deflated, Logan acknowledged the point with a sigh and a single nod. "So, how dangerous is he? *Be specific.*"

"He's definitely worth watching your back over…"

"But?"

"He'll always try and think of an intellectual solution before killing someone."

"Great. Smart, controlled sociopath. My favorite."

Logan clenched his jaw and looked over at Zac, frustrated that the information was only coming out now when they were sitting in said sociopath's driveway. *This is what recon is for goddamnit.*

Logan met Zac's sharp, blue eyes. For a second neither of them said or did anything. Then suddenly, they both burst out laughing. Logan doubled over. Zac guffawed and slapped his hand on the steering wheel, his eyes filling with tears.

They laughed for a solid three minutes, each of them occasionally trying to pull back to some semblance of normal human behavior. Logan laughed harder than he had in a very long time. He laughed until his breath came in short gasps, and his eyes watered from the effort of trying to hold it in.

Eventually, Zac blew a winded breath, giving one last chuckle before saying, "So, if we're going to work together, we need to fix the communication disparity."

"Agreed." Logan shook his head. "So, play smart, not deadly."

"Be cool, not scary."

"I don't know what that means."

Zac opened his door and stepped outside. When Logan did the same, he glanced over the top of the SUV at Zac. "It means," he said, "you're not in the CAR anymore. You're in LA, dealing with a businessman who went to

Harvard and has the most expensive prison tatts that money can buy."

"Now we're getting somewhere."

Still, Logan made the switch from blasé to bodyguard instinctively, taking a few seconds to scan the neighborhood as they walked through the wrought-iron gate towards a homely front door.

Strange, that on such a perfect day, there was nobody around on the cul-de-sac. No kids playing after-school ball, no adults walking dogs, no gardeners even. *So, Flynn owns the neighborhood.*

Without so much as pausing, Zac knocked on the door. He rapped his knuckles in a standard tap, tap, tap, that had a dog barking somewhere.

He might exude cool, calm, and collected, but Logan had seen Zac's eyes running over everything as quickly as his own. The man was a fox among the pigeons, dangerous, a man wearing his charisma as a perfectly harmless disguise.

Logan felt the blood pump through his heart when he heard unrushed footsteps behind the door. He felt his fingers loosen, ready for anything.

The door swung open to reveal a beautiful redhead. She was short, with waist-length hair that fell over her shoulders and down her sides to fan curvy hips. Bright, green eyes looked at them with amusement from a freckled face, two perfectly manicured eyebrows raised in surprise, and a flashing smile gave her slight overbite the perfect amount of charm.

"The fuck?"

Logan glanced at Zac, took a moment to take in the woman's obvious delight. "Zac Murphy," she said, a slight Irish lilt in her tone. "If you don't send me that last invoice for the money I owe you, I'm not going to pay you at all."

"What are you doing here, Sarah?"

"What," she glanced at Logan, "are you doing here? And who is he?" she asked jabbing a thumb in Logan's direction.

"Logan Cane. Sarah Boyle." Zac shook his head. "Logan is Gracie's dad." He turned to Logan. "Sarah is…"

"Lola's best friend," she said, giving him her hand in a firm shake. "So," her eyes raked over him, "you're Maggie's man?"

He didn't reply. "You're best friends with Jake's Lola?"

"Do you know another one?" she countered.

"Well, I technically don't know any."

She grinned at him, that same flashing smile transforming her face to something near Titian. "I like this one," she said, redirecting her conversation to Zac again.

"That's all very good, but why are you *here*?"

"Donny is my cousin."

"Nah!"

"Yeah. Third cousin once removed on my mother's side, but you know how sentimental we are."

"Bloody hell."

Logan watched the exchange with amusement. Although he didn't pick up any sexual attraction, it was clear that the two knew each other well. The way that they communicated was sibling-like in, both its fondness and in its exasperation.

"Did you want to speak to Donny then?" she asked, stepping back into the hallway so that they could come in.

Logan followed Zac when he trudged through, stomping his feet exaggeratedly on the welcome mat although it hadn't rained in months and they'd just walked over solid, swept concrete with little chance of picking up debris.

He listened to Zac and Sarah bicker with one ear as he took in the house. There was a shoe-rack by the door that held a man's, a woman's, and two children's shoes. The long, parquet floor was accented by a pretty, red carpet that led to what he assumed was a kitchen. This was a home.

His palms began to sweat. It was one thing to show up at a man's illegal business operation and ask a few nonchalant questions. But showing up out of the blue at what was clearly his failsafe, the place where he thought he kept his family out of danger, well, that was another thing.

He would know.

He thought about how he'd felt when he'd been at O'Hara's and had first found out that Rue had left a kpinga in Maggie's car. Even the passive gesture, something intended to implant fear and paranoia in his mind, had sent him through the roof. He'd thrown Zac and Jacob in the SUV and forced Jake to put his emergency LAPD lights and sirens on. The thought of what a man would do to protect his family, of what he would do to protect his, made Logan hope that Donny Flynn was as nonthreatening as Zac seemed to think.

The sound of laughter, a deep, booming echo that traveled through the house, reached his ears just as their trio stepped through a neat kitchen and into a small, back yard. The yard had a tumble of mismatched lawn chairs strewn over a bright patch of green grass and a single barbeque off to the right-hand side.

Several people mingled about, unphased by two strangers showing up at what was clearly a family barbeque. Funny, Logan thought, that one of the most successful criminals in LA still did things as banal as schedule family gatherings.

A tall, slender woman with pitch-black hair and sea-green eyes glanced over at them from her chair and even though she smiled, Logan saw the slight shuttering of her eyes, the careful installation of a very deliberate protective barrier.

A small child with mahogany hair not dissimilar to Gracie's ran around the lawn in only a diaper. His high-pitched squeal of excitement encouraged the mixed-breed puppy that was chasing him to yip, only occasionally stalling in his barks when he tumbled over his too-big paws.

"Donny!" Sarah Boyle called to the other end of the yard, and Logan watched as one of only three unidentified men turned to wave at her.

He caught the slight pause in the gesture, noticed the quick, mischievous smile that replaced it nearly instantly. Judging by the way that Zac had tensed beside him, he had sensed the shift in the man too. *He covered up too quickly.*

"Well, that's strange," Sarah Boyle looked at Logan. "He doesn't like something about you."

"I have that effect on a lot of people."

She shook her head, her big, green eyes wide with genuine concern. "What have you done?"

"What is this, Sarah?" Zac asked.

"I don't know." She bit out the words as her cousin began a slow deliberate walk across the yard, his small frame exaggerating his agility. "Ask your friend."

Zac looked at him. Logan shrugged, confused by Donny's reaction, yet very aware of the fact that the tenor of the gathering had just changed.

Out of the corner of his eye, he could already see a few guests casually filtering out of the yard through side doors that seemed to magically open and close from neighboring properties. "Be ready," he said to Zac, unsure of what was happening.

"Sarah." Zac cautioned as he too watched Donny approach with catlike steps.

"He won't hurt me." Sarah flipped her hair over her shoulder and eyed Logan skeptically. "Can you take care of yourself?"

Nodding, he nudged her out from in front of him, felt a small ball of relief when Zac deliberately stepped in front of her.

Donny saw the gesture, and his eyes betrayed the smallest hint of surprise.

Logan watched him approach, loosed his hands by his side in case he needed to go for his weapon. He already knew, by watching the entire gathering filter through the hidden doors, that Donny would have backup in the neighboring yards. Backup that was probably already in place, waiting. But he also knew that he was fast enough to take out Flynn if need be.

"Logan Cane." Unlike Sarah's, Donny's accent was all LA, but the way that he said Logan's name made the skin on the back of his neck pull tight.

What's going on?

Logan took in Donny's pale skin that betrayed his Irish blood, met calculating, blue eyes. "I know you?"

Donny just raised an eyebrow as he came to stand three feet in front of him, a small smirk bringing up the right side of his mouth. "I heard a rumor about you recently."

"Obviously a good one." Logan indicated to the deserted yard with his head. *But how does he know what I look like?*

"What is this about?" Zac asked.

Donny turned his head for a second, his blue eyes flickering disinterestedly over Zac. "Jimmy said that you were bringing a *friend*, Murphy."

"And I have," Zac said slowly, deliberately.

"Do you know that your *friend* kills people for money in poor, African countries? Men. Women. *Children.*" He spat the last word, his voice dripping true disdain. "I had a client through my place of business a few days ago, a foreigner. Said he was on contract, hunting an animal."

Logan saw red but forced himself back to calm.

It happened in an instant. He saw the fist coming, knew that it would be a hook to the bottom-left part of his jaw. Years of training took over and he loosened his body, planting his feet to take the impact, as his hands snaked to his belt and he pulled his Glock.

Donny's fist connected with a sharp crack and Logan felt the pain instantly radiate from his jaw up the left side of his face. But before Donny could draw back his hand to pull his weapon, Logan had his drawn and pointed between the other man's eyes, the cold muzzle only a whisper away from touching the skin on his forehead.

Logan didn't need to turn his head to know that Zac had his weapon trained on Donny too.

Donny's hand paused at the waistband of his jeans as his eyes squinted down at the gun, and a bright sheen of sweat broke out on his forehead. "I have the place surrounded," he said, but his voice held none of its previous bravado.

"We know."

Logan ignored Sarah when she huffed out a disgusted, "Men," and went to sit down on one of the abandoned lawn chairs.

"Put it down, Flynn." Zac's voice was dead-calm, and Logan knew that his own eyes were probably betraying an uncanny level of comfort at the current situation.

Donny's hand hovered for a moment longer before dropping. "What do you want?"

Logan kept his weapon trained on Donny while Zac pulled Charles Rue's photograph from his pocket. "Is this the man you're talking about? Has he bought a flipped, black Mercedes from you in the last month?"

Donny's eyes flickered over the photograph, widened perceptibly when he made out Charles Rue. "Yes." Turning to Logan, he added, "He was the one who told me who you are."

"I worked as close protection," Logan spat out. "On contract with Tippenham Dunn out of New York. Run my credentials, asshole!"

Donny frowned. "I know Tippenham Dunn."

"Seriously, Donny?" Sarah shot to her feet, chose to march straight between them and the loaded gun pointed at her cousin, her hands jammed on her hips as she faced him. Logan couldn't see her face, but he knew that her green eyes were blazing. "Is it not obvious that you've been taken for a fool by the actual psychopath?"

"I don't know, Red, he looks like a killer to me."

"You're as daft as you are ugly. I know this man. He's an in-law of Lola's. He has a bloody one-year-old!"

"You know him?" He looked at her.

"Yeah."

"Why didn't you say so?"

"Well I wasn't expecting you to punch a guest in the face, now was I?" she retorted. Logan could see a red flush spreading over her pale arms as she waved them about in front of her cousin's face.

Holding up his hands in a gesture of peace, Donny looked from Logan to Zac and back again. "I think we need to fill in some gaps here."

"That would be nice," Logan said.

He didn't move the weapon immediately, but when Zac placed a single hand on the barrel and nudged it down, he didn't resist.

"Tight-strung bastard, aren't you?"

Logan didn't reply. He didn't even nod.

When Donny laughed, the big barreling laugh that he had heard drifting through the house earlier, Logan felt the first slide of relief into his stomach.

We're not going to die. Not today.

Chapter 8

While Gracie played on her donut pillow on the floor, Maggie sat at her kitchen table with Jake. She looked down at the mess in front of her—café catalogs, folders, and design portfolios—as she rifled through some of her idea folders for inspiration.

Jake had picked her up from her parents' house that afternoon and taken her to her design consultant's meeting. Not that she couldn't go by herself, but Logan had solidly refused for her to be alone at all and, well, the vehemence with which he'd asked her to listen to him had forced a slippery mass of fear into her stomach at the time, one that had yet to dissipate.

If there was a part of her that had been disappointed by the fact that he wasn't the one who'd come to pick her up, she had hidden it well, pushed it to some far recess of her mind so that it didn't rise to ruin her day.

Because thoughts of Logan often did.

"How is Lola's painting going now that she has the studio space?"

"She loves it," Jake said. "I usually have to drag her away for a few hours once I get home from work so that we can spend time together."

As he spoke, a big, goofy grin spread over his face. Maggie, who still hadn't gotten used to seeing her straight-laced baby brother be so open about his feelings, found herself grinning too.

When Jake had first brought Lola home, Maggie had been worried that they were both moving too fast. That they'd mistaken their dependence on one another through the murder investigation for something more.

She'd been wrong.

Jake and Lola might have moved fast, but it had worked for them. They weren't like her and Logan.

She and Logan had taken a long, slow walk into a relationship when she'd been sixteen and he seventeen. They had moved from friends to dating to lovers like any other hormone-crazed teenagers.

She could still remember the heart-racing, brain-vacating feeling that she'd had when they'd first kissed all those years ago. She could remember the way that his hands had trailed down her back before coming to grip her hips. He'd pulled her flush against his body, dipped his head, and brushed his lips across hers.

Then he'd taken a step away, his gray eyes doubtful.

Maggie hadn't given him time to process. She'd blurted, "I want you to be my first."

A ghost of a smile flitted across her features when she remembered the way Logan had slapped a hand over her mouth. They'd been standing in her parents' backyard and he'd whispered, "Jesus, you can't say *that. Here.*"

She'd laughed when he'd just rested his forehead on hers and said, "This is a bad idea."

Maggie hadn't thought so then.

She still didn't think so now.

Her need for Logan Cane when she'd been that young, innocent girl with undyed hair and glasses had nothing to do with him being the bad boy quarterback. Maggie had been as self-confident in herself as that awkward sixteen-year-old as she was now.

No, her need for Logan had awakened at her sixteenth birthday party when she'd felt someone watching her and turned to see him looking over with blatant interest in his eyes. Interest, which he had quickly shuttered with a cheeky wink that he'd probably meant to be friendly. But that had been it for her. That was the first day that she had felt the long, slow pull of her body responding to a man.

To him.

Just him.

It had taken her three months to get him to ask her out on a date. It had taken her three dates to get him to kiss her. The vividness of the memory of him touching her for the first time had her raising her elbow to the table, so that she could rest her chin in her palm.

"Did you two settle on a date yet?" she asked, looking for a distraction before she gave in to the tears that suddenly made her voice come out choked.

If Jake noticed, he didn't comment. "Saturday, March twenty-first."

Maggie smiled. "Not wasting any time."

"I wanted to elope, get her to marry me as soon as possible." He leaned back in his chair. "Don't want her to change her mind." Grinning, he ran a hand through his sandy, cropped hair. "But she wanted the full monty and God knows that I can't say no to anything she wants."

"I'm so happy for you two."

"Thanks, Mags." He was quiet for a moment, his face set in a somber pull. "You know, since finding Lola…"

"You can say it," she said softly, knowing where he was going by the way he rubbed the back of his head anxiously.

"I don't know how you did it all these years. Watched him leave even though it tore both of you apart every time…I think I'd have ended it if I were in your position, you know? Just ended it rather than go through that every time?"

"You say that, but could you imagine if Lola was running from something, going through life hurt and angry and the only thing that seemed to keep her going was being with you?" *And then leaving you…*

"I can't," he conceded.

"It's one thing to break up with someone and know that you'd have to pick yourself up and piece your heart back together, but it's another entirely to know that the someone you'd broken up with wouldn't have a reason to go on without you."

When the tears that had pooled into her eyes began to drip over her lashes, she bit her bottom lip. "Even then, there were a lot of times that I'd watch him gear up for deployment or pack his personals and I'd just get this sick sense of deliberateness from him."

"You think Logan's suicidal?"

Maggie shook her head, trying to quell the unease she heard in Jake's tone. "It's not that, necessarily. But...I think that other than me, the only thing that's given him a purpose in life has bee-"

"The possibility of death every day."

Maggie nodded, silently. "This was the first time I've ever turned him away, Jake. And every time that I see him, my heart stops in my chest and the memories come flooding back. I still love that idiot as much as I did twenty-five years ago. Being around him..."

Jake's big palm covered the back of her hand instantly. "I'm sorry we pushed him on you."

"Don't be." She flipped her hand over and squeezed his. "I have Gracie now, and everything is secondary to her. Even, Logan Cane."

Hearing her name, Gracie glanced up to look at them from her seat on the floor, her head of curls bobbing slightly. "Mama. Up!"

"Hi, baby!" Leaning down, she picked Gracie up and then plopped her on her knee, one arm snaking around her mid-section, as she got back to sorting through catalogs and notes.

She knew that Gracie was one, and crawling and walking about on her own already. She was spewing off strings of words that would start to be decipherable soon. But there was still something so visceral about holding her and feeling their bodies pressed close together.

Her elixir of cocaine, the coconut baby shampoo that she used to wash Gracie's hair, drifted to her as her daughter banged her little hands on the table. Maggie reached for her, but Gracie shifted and held her arms out for Jake, clearly wanting his attention instead.

Jake didn't hesitate.

Watching her brother play with her child, seeing the goofy faces that he pulled, and hearing the peel of Grace's hysterical laughter settled her. There were moments like this, moments of clarity, where the realization that Gracie would have a full life without Logan made her feel almost relieved. With the family at her side, her daughter would have the love and support that she needed wherever in the world her father ended up.

And, like Maggie, *if* and when Logan did leave again, Gracie would come to experience the heartbreak of it over and over. Until one day, she'd wake up and be okay with the fact that life wasn't easy for anyone. And that loving Logan Cane was her cross to bear. Maybe, unlike Maggie, she'd even learn to be a happy and complete person without him.

Logan let himself into the house, pausing only to bend down and give Spunk a back scratch before standing and walking towards the voices filtering from the kitchen.

"I like this one," Jake was saying.

"Yeah. I am not putting a recliner in my wine bar."

"Well, shucks," Jake grumbled in reply, clearly pulling her leg.

Logan stopped in the kitchen doorway, crossed his arms over his chest, and just looked for a full fifteen seconds. Maggie sat at the dining room table, opposite Jake. Her long mahogany hair spilled down her back, glinting in the sun of the open window, and Logan had the sudden urge to coil it around his hand. Why did he have to remember how soft it always was, or how Maggie Simmone's hair always smelled like flowers?

Her smooth, porcelain skin showed off high, sculpted cheekbones—cheekbones that she shared with her sister, that had made Emma Simmone famous. Although she was alarmingly thin at the moment, Maggie carried herself well—back straight and elongated even as she sat at her kitchen table.

His body reacted instantly, pulling out of what seemed like a long slumber. He almost turned away, but she sensed him in the doorway and turned to look at him. The smile in her blue eyes died immediately, forcing his body back to calm.

For a moment, he couldn't catch his breath through the pain. Every time she looked at him, those familiar deep blue eyes vacant, he felt as if his world stopped rotating. Paused. And every time he faced her rejection, he wondered if the impending sense of permanent loss was what she had felt every time that he left her for some dangerous corner of the world.

"What happened to your face," she said suddenly, pushing to her feet and coming to stand in front of him, her arm under both of Gracie's as their child's long body dangled down her torso.

Gracie, clearly unfazed by her current inelegant position, smiled up at him. But Maggie's blue eyes were wide with concern as she lifted her free hand and cupped his left cheek, placing her cool palm at the spot where his cheek met his chin.

He closed his eyes, and let his face rest there for a second, absorbing the feeling of her skin against his. God, her hands were the softest that he'd ever felt. "That feels good."

The scraping of a chair on the tiled kitchen floor had Logan looking back through at Jake. Maggie dropped her hand suddenly and took a solid step back, although he could still feel the exact imprint where her skin had touched his.

"I'm going to head on home. Gotta convince Lola that she can put down the paintbrush for long enough to go on a date with me."

"Tell her I say hi. Oh, and that I'll text her about that wine tasting next week. I really do want to go."

"Will do." Jake walked past them as they stood inside the doorway, stopping to give Gracie a smacking kiss on the cheek. He shouted, "We'll check-in about that shiner tomorrow, Logan," over his shoulder as he opened the front door.

"Are you okay?" she asked once the door slammed shut.

She was looking at him, her eyes narrowed in confusion, but all he could think about was how he'd always loved her eyes.

She was in all his favorite memories, those eyes looking at him as if nobody else had ever existed. From the moment he'd spotted her at her sixteenth birthday party and realized that, suddenly, she filled out a bikini real nice, he'd been hers. But it hadn't been the bikini or the way Maggie's willow-frame filled it that had stolen the air from his lungs. It had been the knowing look in her eye, the way that she'd sized him up as if he were everything she'd been waiting for.

His throat closed with the memories, but he managed to nod and choke out a quick, "I am."

"Here, let me…" Walking over to her old refrigerator, she yanked open the top freezer compartment, using her one hand to rummage around through the ice chest, her other scooped around Gracie.

He hadn't even seen her shift Gracie, but the position that his baby girl was in now gave her the perfect window through which to stare at him, and she did. As they eyed each other skeptically, Logan felt his heart stammer when gray eyes exactly like his own studied him with open curiosity, never wavering despite Maggie's hurried movements. When he raised one eyebrow, a wide grin split his daughter's face, and she giggled. *At him.*

The sound went straight to his heart, a javelin through the center of his chest that tore a hole that he knew he'd never be able to fill with anything else.

When Maggie angrily said something that sounded like, "Fudgesicles," he moved forward. He could look for his own damn ice.

"Here," he said, stepping up to her side, "let me."

"Thanks." She stopped her rummaging long enough to turn and plop Gracie in his arms.

His arms came up instinctively, caging her in so that he didn't drop her considerable bulk. She was heavier than she looked. Logan froze in place, petrified, as the baby smell of her drifted up to him. His heart raced in his chest and he hazarded a glance down at her.

Gracie was still looking at him, her pretty eyelashes fluttering over heavy-lidded eyes. Petrified that he'd drop her, he tightened his arms around her. *Oh, boy.*

"Okay, found it."

The sound of Maggie closing the freezer was enough to have him bringing his gaze back to her guiltily. She was frowning at him, her blue eyes wary as she held out a bag of frozen peas for him.

When she took a step closer, he assumed to take Gracie back, he turned around, taking the peas and his daughter to go and sit at the kitchen table. His heart beat a frantic rhythm in his chest, but he solidly ignored it as he said, "Thanks, Maggie."

Sitting down, he shimmied Gracie around so that she was facing him and brought the peas up to his aching chin. He grinned down at her when she tried to make a grab for them. Curious, he let her touch them, laughed when her hand gripped the cold plastic and she yanked it back, crinkling her nose in displeasure.

"Ah…"

Logan looked up at Maggie, still standing by the fridge. She had wrapped her arms around herself and, for a moment, he felt guilty of having deprived her of her shield. "Why don't you go take a bath, Mags. Relax. Gracie and I will be fine."

He felt her hesitation. It came off her body in strong waves that charged the air between them. But when Gracie flopped forward to rest her head on his chest and let out a small, contented sigh, Maggie nodded. She walked past them towards her bedroom, pausing once to add, "Just call if you need anything."

Logan waited until he heard the water running, then pushed to his feet, taking Gracie with him. He walked through to the lounge, shook his head when Spunk wagged her tail from the sofa that she was not supposed to be on.

Resigned that he was the world's biggest softie when it came to anything female, he sat down by the old dog. He stroked her head when she rested it on his thigh next to Gracie.

Gracie faced him, balancing on his legs, and mimicked his slow stroke over Spunk's head. When she grabbed one of the dog's ears in her little hand, he caught her wrist between two of his fingers. "Gentle," he whispered.

He unfastened her hold. Spunk, clearly used to being baby-handled didn't bat an eyelid but continued to snore quietly. Placing the dog's velvety ear in his open palm, he stroked Gracie's hand over it, trying to get her to stroke, not grab. When she followed his movements, the dog groaned contentedly and repositioned her head for better access.

Gracie threw her head back and laughed. *There it is.* Even though he knew what to expect now, the sound of her giggle filling that little reserved place in him made him smile even as his chest constricted.

He wondered what she had looked like when she had first been born, all wrinkled and alien from nearly ten months in amnion. Had she fussed and cried? He wondered how Maggie's heart had broken when she'd looked at their daughter for the first time and realized that she had no way of contacting him. No way of letting him know.

He had wanted to stay with her, even now, he wanted to build a life with Maggie, have more babies with her—the full hooligan. But every time that he had tried to tide over the anxiety of failing her, he had ended up packing his bags and hopping on the first flight to the worst shithole he could gain access to on short notice.

His job was his purgatory for wanting something that he didn't deserve: Maggie Mae Simmone. And now, Gracie Laine.

He knew that a part of it was fear, an overwhelming sense of insecurity that reminded him every day that Maggie was too good for him. That she could have anything that she'd ever wanted. She was a drop-dead gorgeous *lawyer*. And he was the no-college-degree son of a carpenter. A man whose claim to fame was the speed at which he could disarm and neutralize an enemy.

He was white trash Los Angeles and she was blue-blood America.

"Mama!" Gracie said loudly, tearing him from his thoughts.

"Mama is in the shower," he replied in a tone that he had never used before.

She let out a string of sounds that could have been a whole sentence or a volley of cuss words for all he could deduce. But she seemed content to sit on his lap and play with Spunk's face while he watched her, and that was enough.

Everything.

And while he watched her, he thought about what Donny Flynn had told them. Charles Rue was on American soil fulfilling a contract—a contract to kill him.

Chapter 9

The cool evening air was a welcome relief from the near-ninety-degree day that had forced Lola to open all the second-story windows in the new house. For some reason, the cloying heat made everything about painting worse. The paints off-gassing was worse. The turpentine seemed to wrap in the air as if it was not brave enough to drift through the open windows and into the outside heat.

Worse than all that combined, her mood had kept plummeting with every hour of the day, resulting in a mediocre patch of ocean in a Maine coastline landscape that she had been commissioned to paint. A patch of ocean that she knew she was going to end up painting over anyway. So, technically, she had done nothing all day except brood about the heat and breathe paint fumes.

Currently, the only two things that were forcing her mood back to the green zone were the facts that she was in Phil and June's backyard with the entire Simmone gang, and that the godawful day was finally cooling off.

Sitting in one of the garden chairs, her feet bare, her toes in the freshly mowed grass, Lola listened to the conversations swirling around her. She still hadn't gotten used to the Simmone's, with their big, rambunctious family gatherings, and their loud, no-personal-space way of communicating. But God she loved it.

She was from a small family. An only child adopted to academic parents who'd hoped that she'd grow up to share their love of long, quiet nights filled with focused research. Instead, probably courtesy of her birth parents, she'd grown up a creative, an artist who'd left her parent's house at eighteen to try and make it as a painter in Los Angeles.

Every time she thought back to those first few years alone, those first few months when she hadn't been in touch with her parents and had felt completely abandoned, she ended up comparing her parents to June and Phil. And no matter how hard she tried, she couldn't imagine either of the Simmone's disowning one of their children, especially over something as benign as a career choice.

She sighed and looked down at her sapphire engagement ring, twirled it on her finger with her thumb. It was so perfect, so…her. *Just like Jake.* He'd made everything fall into place. It had been that way since the first time she had opened her door to him.

"What are you thinking about?" June looked at her as she sat down in the chair next to hers. "You had a faraway look in your eyes just then."

"I was just taking this all in," she said, using her arm to gesture to the yard. "I can't believe how lucky I am."

Zac, Hudson, and Jake stood a little off to the side with Phil. They sipped beers as they prepped for what Lola knew was going to be a serious family gathering.

They were just waiting for Logan, Maggie, and Grace to arrive before they talked about how they were going to keep them all safe.

"We'd say that Jacob is the lucky one," June replied with a small wink.

Lola chuckled, grateful for the camaraderie.

"What's really eating at you?"

Lola glanced at her soon-to-be mother-in-law in surprise. "What makes you think that there's something else?" *Shit.* Her mind reeled.

"Other than the fact that I've done it five times?" she asked with a small laugh. "Then, because I saw you turn green when Phil was marinating the steaks, and because your hand hasn't left your pancake-flat belly since you sat down."

Lola stared at June for a full five seconds, then moved her hand off her stomach, her movements robotic. "I only found out yesterday," she whispered, horrified that June had figured it out so easily. She cast a glance at Jacob, just to be sure that he wasn't watching the exchange. He could read her emotions like a book.

"And why aren't you dancing a hole in my yard? This is the most exciting time of your life. You only get to have one first pregnancy, Lola."

She quickly glanced back to check that the boys were still wrapped in their own little world. "Please don't say anything yet. I...I haven't told Jake."

June stared at her, her brow furrowed. "Well, why on earth not?"

Lola felt a small stab of guilt. She'd wanted to tell him, wanted him to feel the huge burst of happiness that she had felt when she'd looked at the stupid pink plus on the test. She wanted to be held by him when the enormous ball of fear at the prospect of having a child wormed its way into her mind. But, more than that, she wanted him to focus on Maggie and Gracie now.

"I...He only proposed two weeks ago. And then Maggie started talking to Logan again. And now...I don't want him to be distracted from helping them. Maggie and Gracie *need* him right now."

The words came out a little fast; it were as if someone was wrapping their hands around her throat and she had to say them all before her breath ran out.

"Honey..." June covered Lola's hand with her own, making her jump at the unexpected contact. "Jake would want to know. And you know that between him, Phil, Zac, and Logan, nobody on earth can get to Maggie, let alone Gracie."

"I know that, but...I don't want to take any attention away from their situation right now." Nerves made her carry on. "I'm also so early. I'm seven weeks...Wouldn't mind waiting a few months. Just to be sure. And by then everything will be back to normal again. Right?" She didn't give June time to answer before rushing on with, "I mean, they're going to figure this out soon."

June squeezed her hand, pulling her gaze up to meet kind green eyes so similar to Jake's. "Have you been speaking to someone?" she asked. "About…well, that little incident with a serial killer trying to off you and all?"

Lola giggled at the candor, just before her chest closed with panic. "Not yet." She rubbed her forehead. "Jake keeps trying to get me to go…but, I think I'm doing okay."

"Really?" June raised one eyebrow, clearly unconvinced. "Still having nightmares?"

She nodded because she had learned over her long recovery that June was a living, breathing lie detector. "Not as frequently."

When a bustle of noise turned her attention to the back door, Lola saw Maggie and Logan come through the house and into the yard. She was surprised to see that Logan was carrying Gracie, her bottom planted solidly on one of his huge arms, her little hands resting on his chest. She had never seen the man before, had only heard the stories. She sighed, "Well, isn't that a picture that needs to be painted."

"That boy has always turned heads. Add a baby to the mix and it's borderline antifeminist. We're not biologically equipped to cope."

Lola chuckled, completely in agreement. Angling her head in the other direction, she looked back at Jacob. He wore blue jeans that rode low on narrow hips, and a plain, black tee-shirt that hugged a barrel chest and big biceps. Her stomach fluttered in the way it did every time that she looked at him, and for just a moment she imagined a baby, *their* baby in *his* arms.

She had already seen him with Gracie, knew that he loved his niece beyond reason and that he'd love their kids beyond reason too. She wanted to have his kids…was going to have his kid. *So, why am I still so scared?*

Feeling her gaze, he turned to look at her, his emerald eyes smiling when their eyes met. After only a moment, he angled his head, frowning at her. *Shit.* She realized that she had probably looked a little panicked, so she smiled back quickly.

"Honey, I can feel the anxiety rolling off you."

By the door, Logan put Gracie down and she hobbled straight over the grass straight to where June sat, before trying to pull herself into her grandma's lap.

Laughing, June plucked her up and snuggled her. "What are you really worried about?" she asked, her voice low so that only Lola could hear.

"Ah…everything. Absolutely everything." Hands around her neck cut her air supply again, a quick jolt that trapped the air in her lungs. "The world is so…dangerous."

"That it is."

"Gama," Gracie said before going on a tangent of baby-talk that Lola didn't understand.

"Yes, baby?"

"Look." Gracie pointed to her shirt, to the pink unicorn printed on the front.

Lola felt her heart trip. "That's a new word!" she said, reaching forward so that she could run her hand over Gracie's downy head.

Gracie looked at her for a moment, her little eyebrows raised as if she was thinking about something, then she quickly turned on June's legs and started trying to crawl over to Lola's.

Instead of waiting for her to navigate the space between them, June picked Grace up and plopped her onto Lola's lap.

When Gracie made a beeline for her big, beaded necklace, Lola let her rattle the string. "You are growing like a weed," she said, feeling the solid weight of Gracie on her thighs.

"Life goes on, Lola." June looked over at her kindly, and when their eyes met she nodded towards Logan and Maggie. "Terrible things happen all the time. And, still, people fall in love, women fall pregnant, babies get born." June looked at Gracie even as her head angled towards Maggie. "Everyone on the outside can see that if they just stopped running, everything would turn out okay."

Turning slightly, she looked at them. Even now, she could see the long, loving glances that Logan and Maggie snuck when they thought that the other wasn't looking. She could see the way that Logan's eyes kept darting back to Gracie as if he wasn't quite sure if she was okay to be on her own yet. From where she was sitting, the solution seemed so obvious.

When Logan glanced towards Maggie, she turned to look at him, and Lola watched, fascinated, as identical smiles bloomed on their faces. "God, their love is so hard to watch."

"But it seems so obvious from the outside," June added. "I think it's the only reason that Phil and I could never hate him. The reason that we always welcome him back without causing a fuss."

Lola sighed. "I'll talk to someone."

"Thank you. And don't wait too long to tell Jake. It's his first baby too."

"I won't. Promise."

June nodded, clearly having accomplished what she'd intended. "Shall we get this family meeting started?"

"Absolutely."

Without further prompting, June stood and clapped her hands, a quick rap, rap, rap that had everyone looking up, and then slowly realigning their bodies to face the small woman who commanded their attention.

"Now, I know that we all have a lot of questions," she began in her no-nonsense tone, one that clearly everybody present knew meant no interruptions. "But I think that we should start with Logan telling us a little more about what we're facing, and what we can expect. Logan?" June nodded her head in his direction.

Lola watched, fascinated as Logan stepped forward, his impossibly huge frame drawing everyone's eyes even as his held Maggie's.

As he recounted his story, spoke about his two years working in the Central African Republic, and about the work that he had been doing protecting Francis Boucher, Lola listened with rapt attention. She didn't understand the job that he did, didn't understand how one man could go from eighteen to forty-three living so dangerously. Heck, she'd had one run-in with a psychopath, and it had very nearly destroyed her. *If it hadn't been for Jake…*

She hadn't realized that she had pulled Gracie close to her chest until the baby grunted and slammed the beaded necklace against her collarbone. "Sorry, honey," Lola whispered and lessened her pressure on her soon-to-be niece.

"If I know Rue at all, he'll be biding his time," Logan continued, "waiting for me to get lax."

"Will he actually hurt Maggie or Gracie?"

Lola looked at Phil when he spoke, then shifted her gaze back to Logan. He bowed his head slightly, unsure of how to answer. "If he thinks that it'll draw me out, then yes."

Lola felt her chest squeeze tight, and bounced Gracie on her knee, needing to do something.

"Despite what Donny heard from Charles Rue, I don't think that this is a contract. Or, at least not *only* a contract. If it was-"

"You'd be dead already." All eyes shifted to Zac. He shrugged. "He would. Rue drove past them walking the dog in broad daylight. Why didn't he just plug him there while he exposed his obnoxiously broad back protecting Maggie."

"What is it then?" Phil, his bushy eyebrows meeting in a scowl of displeasure, asked.

"He wants me to be scared," Logan said. "He knows that Maggie, and now Gracie, were the only evidence of my personal life. As much as I hate to admit it, me coming back here was my first mistake."

"So, it's a game to him?" Jake asked.

Logan nodded silently. "He wants to compete with me, wants to play cat and mouse, probably at Boucher's insistence. Francis…likes to play God. And the fact that I up and left, the fact that I sold him out, the fact that Charles and I are almost equally dangerous…"

"Pistols at dawn."

All eyes shifted to Zac again.

"Exactly," Logan corroborated. "He wants to take the shot, but he wants to draw me out, to challenge me. It's how he operates. It's…who he is. Except, unlike a duel in a Western, there'll be no law to intervene."

"So what can we do?" Maggie broke the all-male conversation. "Asides from strapping a six-chamber to your hip and sending you out of the saloon at sun-up?"

Lola saw Logan's lips twitch and, not for the first time, she wondered how the two of them survived being separated.

"We wait him out. It might take a few weeks for the plan to work, but he'll bait eventually."

"Bait?" Lola squeaked. Considering that she had just come out of a cat-and-mouse game of her own, she did not like the word. Not. One. Bit.

All eyes turned to her.

Lola felt her heart hammer in her throat and swallowed, the sound loud to her ears. When Jake placed his hand on her shoulder from behind, she jumped a little in surprise, then leaned into him, drawing comfort from the contact.

"Nothing quite what you went through." Logan smiled kindly at her.

"We asked Donny to keep feeding Rue from his chain of resources—at least those that Donny has an in with."

"What does that mean?" June asked, clearly speaking for her husband and for Jake, both of whom stood listening with identical expressions of appalled disbelief.

Lola wanted to smile. Jake was such a good man. Just like his dad, he was a cop, an idealist who believed that no man was, or should be, above the law. She loved it about him, but she also knew that he was going to need her help turning a blind eye to the illicit conversation happening in his parent's backyard. Just as Phil was.

"It means," Logan picked up the conversation, "that while he's in LA, Rue is going to have access to cars, guns, and other resources."

"But?" Maggie asked.

"Every time that he so much as moves we'll know where he is. We have the tracker from the chopped car that he's currently driving. And Donny will inform us when he makes a purchase or talks about his plans."

"It seems that Charles Rue is quite prepared. But I don't quite see *your* plan yet," Phil finally said, his tone tight, tense.

"We can't actively go after Boucher without doing anything illegal," Logan said firmly, but quietly. "Yet."

"So, what are we waiting for?" Lola piped up again.

"My friend with the UN, Sasha Riley. She's compiling the evidence against Francis Boucher and Charles Rue. Once she's got enough to approach the UN with…we'll be able to go after Charles, bring him to the LAPD so that they can contact the feds who'll begin the extradition process."

Lola felt her stomach slide. Whoever Sasha Riley was, she must be a fearless woman to behold if she was taking on Boucher with nothing but the protection of the UN. She hoped that she'd get to meet her one day.

"Sasha is smart, but still…this could take months."

Logan fisted his hands at his sides, clearly frustrated. Lola knew that his preferred course of action would have been to scout and flush Rue himself, take him out before he dared touch Maggie or Gracie. But the thought didn't scare her. *He* didn't scare her. There was a corner of her mind that knew she would have been relieved if that had been the plan instead.

She wondered why that was. Was it the absolute love that shone from his eyes when he looked at Maggie or Gracie? Or, was it the strong honor code that she felt he lived by? Cold-blooded killers didn't risk their lives to expose a man who was abusing the rights of poor people in devastated countries, especially when the rest of the world was content to stay ignorant. Lola herself hadn't even known that the Central African Republic was its own country before Jake had told her as a precursor to the family meeting.

"So, in the meantime," Zac finished for him, "we monitor Charles Rue through Donny and make sure that we have Maggie and Grace protected twenty-four-seven. It's going to be a long couple of months here, but we have to stay sharp."

If anyone had any doubts about the plan, they didn't speak up and a long, quiet spell fell over the group before everyone started getting back to what they had been doing before.

Jake dropped to his haunches next to her, his hand moving from her shoulder to her cheek. "You okay, baby?"

She nodded. Her heart skipped in her chest, just once, but hard enough that she felt it in her stomach.

The sudden tears in her eyes had more to do with the fact that the word 'baby' coming out of Jake's mouth had taken on a whole different meaning in the last twenty-four hours. But, at least for now, until the family had dealt with keeping Maggie and Gracie safe, she'd bite her tongue and keep her news a secret. Well, a secret between herself and June Simmone.

"I reckon we stop moping and cook some dinner," June stated, breaking up the group's wariness.

"Sounds good. I'll cook, Dad." Hudson's forced calm tone had Lola's mouth lifting at the corners.

At her side, Jake chuckled. "Subtle." He rubbed his hand over Gracie's hair, before giving them each a quick kiss and standing to his feet.

"Jake and I have it, Dad," Lola heard Hudson say, loud enough to have Jake wandering off to prove his little brother's point.

She watched the negotiation with open interest, chuckled to herself when, finally, Phil handed the barbeque tongs to Hudson and moved exaggeratedly to the side with a flourish of his arms.

"It still overwhelms me too."

The voice had her turning her head, then looking all the way up into Logan Cane's flint-gray eyes. She smiled and reached out a hand. "Lola."

"Logan." He shook her hand, then gestured to where the Simmone men were still squabbling about who was going to cook. "The family is a lot to take in at first. Just give it time, then you won't know how you ever got on without them."

When she smiled and patted the chair next to her, he sat, eyeing Gracie the entire time. Lola sensed that he needed her in that instant, so she unclasped her niece's hands from her necklace. "Want to go to Daddy?"

"Da!" Gracie mimicked the sound she'd made as Lola hefted her into Logan's big hands, which took her weight as if the solid one-year-old weighed nothing at all.

"Thanks," he said, placing her gently on his lap as if she were breakable. "I'm so scared I'm going to drop her, or accidentally elbow her or something. Figure the only thing that'll help is practice. Huh, Gracie?"

Lola remembered the feeling because Gracie had been the first baby that she had held too. *Only eight weeks ago.* It was a weird feeling, to have something so fragile but so resilient in your arms, especially when that something was a tiny human being who belonged to someone else.

"Congratulations, by the way," he said, sending her a smile while he rocked his knees up and down, sending a delighted Gracie into a fit of giggles. "I'm really happy for you and Jake."

"Thank you, Logan," she said. "It still feels…surreal most days. I'll be driving home to my old apartment before I remember that I don't live there anymore, that I'm not alone anymore. I have missed a lot of exits in the last two weeks."

He laughed, a deep, rolling laugh that made her smile and made Gracie start laughing too. Looking up, Lola saw Maggie glance their way at the sound. She caught the way that her eyes lit up before she quickly turned away to hide her response.

Judging by the way that Logan's eyes glazed over a bit, he had seen her turn away too. Because she didn't know what to say, she changed the subject entirely with, "So, how does it feel to be back in the US?"

"Good. It's never easy being away, but those first few months back on home soil are always the best."

"I can't imagine doing what you do," she said, shaking her head.

"To be fair, I can't imagine doing what you do either." When Lola glanced up at him, he smiled, "I nearly failed my art elective in high school. The only reason that I got a C was because I begged Maggie to do my homework assignments for me."

"Maggie cheated for you?" Lola asked, not quite believing it.

"She did. In more than that one class." He chuckled, but the sound resonated as hollow to Lola. "I wouldn't have gotten my high school diploma if not for Maggie cheating for me."

"Only because he was seriously dyslexic and only because he needed his high school diploma to get into the Military," Maggie added, closing the distance between them.

"God," Logan laughed, looking up at her. "I can still remember Mrs. Dexter's comment on my final report for that art class."

"'If Logan applied himself more instead of having Maggie Simmone do his homework, he'd be proficient at anything he put his mind to'," Maggie recounted, smiling back at him.

"She knew the entire time?"

"Oh yeah. The difference between in-class and homework was...noticeable."

"What did your mom say when she read your report card?" Lola's parents would have grounded her for eternity. Good grades were something to be achieved, something to strive for.

"'Thank Jesus for Maggie'."

"She did too," Maggie confirmed with an easy laugh. "I was there."

When they looked at each other, Lola felt like she was intruding on a private moment. She knew that they had their reasons, but God their need for each other was palpable. It was almost physically painful to be between. June's words came back to her, and not for the first time Lola wondered if she was doing the right thing.

"Mind if I take her for a moment? She needs to eat."

Logan looked down at Gracie, ran one huge palm over her head. "Sure."

"Unless you want to try?" Maggie said. Before he could respond, she added, "Let me just go and get her food," and walked off into the house.

Logan looked at her, his eyes wide with worry. Lola smiled encouragingly. "It's really easy. Just spoon goop into her mouth. She loves to eat."

Any protest he was about to make died on his tongue when Maggie brought the little jar of baby food out and put it in Logan's huge palm with the tiny, thick-lipped, plastic spoon.

He hesitated for only a moment before popping the top and taking the lid off. Lola felt her mouth water at the apple smell. She took one solid gasp of air before dashing for the house as bile filled her throat. *No, no, no.*

She made it just in time, burst into the Simmone's guest bathroom, and slid to the toilet bowl before throwing up a liquid mess, probably tea—the only thing she'd been able to stomach all day.

"Lola?" Jake's concerned voice carried down the long hallway nearly immediately.

Shit. Closing her eyes against the nausea, she flushed the toilet and shifted away from the bowl. "In here."

He pushed open the bathroom door, came to where she sat, taking her clammy hands in his cool ones. "Are you okay?" he asked, raising one hand to touch her face.

She nodded, felt her stomach heave again at the small gesture, and stilled immediately. *Here goes nothing.* Because she knew that Jake might not put two and two together, but because June already had, and Hudson—the family doctor—most certainly would, she said, "I'm pregnant."

He was quiet for a long moment, long enough that she risked opening one eye to look at him. He was grinning ear to ear, his emerald eyes bright with joy. "I know."

"What?"

"I was throwing out the bathroom trash this morning…"

"What?" she repeated. "Why didn't you say anything?"

"Because I knew that you'd need time to come to terms with it." He sighed. "You've had so much going on the last two months, and I didn't want to make a big deal out of it until you'd processed."

Tears choked her throat, and she let her head drop to his shoulder when he sat by her side. She breathed in his scent, felt her heart settle when it wrapped around her heart. "I want you to focus on Maggie and Gracie right now. I just…I didn't want you to be distracted, or worrying about me when some…psycho is out there, watching them."

"I love you so much," he said, placing a kiss on her head. "I love that you still think about them when you're going through the most exciting experience of your life. I love that you're trying to be strong even though I can feel you panicking."

She laughed a watery chuckle that had her snapping her mouth shut. Her throat burned, but she managed to add, "I'm really freaking out about them. About this," she waved over her stomach.

"I know," he sighed. "But…you also need to acknowledge that this is an entirely different situation from the one that you were in."

"They're still in danger."

"They are. But unlike you, who just had one lame LAPD Lieutenant and his best friend looking after you, Maggie and Gracie have an ex-Special Forces soldier, three ties to the LAPD, and the LA criminal underworld. *And,* although I have yet to see it with my own eyes, people tell me that Hudson is a really good doctor…You know, in case things get really bad."

She punched his arm gently, unconsciously heartened by the fact that he felt confident enough to joke about it. "I am trying to work through it. I swear." Sighing, she said, "I already promised your mom that I'd go talk to someone…"

"You did?"

She nodded. "I thought it would just go away…but it hasn't. Other than when you're home, I still feel like I'm being watched…"

She felt him tense beside her. "Why didn't you tell me?"

"I didn't want you to worry. You…" She thought about how to explain. "You already have enough to worry about."

"Nothing means more to me than you." He rubbed his hand on her thigh, sending a jolt from her leg to her center and up to her heart. "Nothing."

"I know. That's why I was going to wait."

He was quiet for a moment before asking, "Can I come with you?"

"Where?"

"To the shrink. Therapist," he corrected, instantly. "I meant therapist."

She chuckled. "Yes, you can come. But only because I don't want to do it by myself."

"You don't have to do anything alone. Ever again. I'm prepared to keep saying it until you believe me: you're my person."

His words, the simple honesty with which he said them, burrowed into her mind. They made Lola feel so safe that her secondary thought was that she'd been silly not to tell him all along. "I love you."

"I love you too." He kissed her forehead, as his hand moved to her flat stomach. "Both of you."

Chapter 10

The week after Lola broke her news to the family passed by in a blur. It had taken three hours after the initial shock of another baby in the Simmone clan for everyone to settle down. And that had been about the time Hudson had blurted, "You're so skinny anyway, so at least you'll still look good in your wedding dress."

That had led to an entirely different flurry because exactly five minutes from when Hudson had dropped that bomb, Lola had convinced Jake to move the wedding to January second, giving them all *ten weeks* to plan.

Maggie didn't mind.

The schedule was a little rushed considering that she had her own business to get off the ground, but Lola and Sarah were taking the brunt of the stress. All she had to do was show up to the scheduled bridesmaids' appointments—which already included two dress fittings and the bridal shower, both of which had been neatly penciled into her calendar. The rest she'd have to deal with as it cropped up.

Her landlords, true to their word, had agreed to meet her halfway. She'd already sent them conceptual designs of the renovations that she wanted for the two single-user restrooms, the small kitchenette, and the front room.

Over the next two months, she'd be working with them to get the café ready for her first furniture shipment. As soon as that was in place—precisely thirty days after renovations were done—she'd officially be paying rent. She, Margaret Mae Simmone, would be a small business owner in exactly ninety days.

And the thought scared the shit out of her.

Some nights she'd wake up from lucid dreams where she was wearing an apron, her hair a mess, running around cranky patrons while a fire was actively being put out in the kitchen by a faceless man who always had Logan's build.

Those nights, where she dreamt about the space and the faceless, Logan-shaped man putting out fires, she'd sit up in her bed and run her hands through her hair as she tried to calm herself down.

Unfortunately, the only thing that seemed to distract her from her midnight bouts of paranoia was thinking about the man who slept on her sofa fifty feet away. She'd lie back down, her mind drifting to what she imagined he'd do if she slipped through the lounge and straddled him on the sofa.

And that wasn't entirely accurate because she knew exactly what he'd do. She knew what his hands would feel like on her body and where his eyes would gravitate. She knew the feeling of his skin on hers as he hovered over her, and she knew the way they slotted together: perfectly. Her memory, something she'd always cherished for its perfect recollection, had become increasingly burdensome with every day that passed.

And because caving to her body's need to be touched by Logan Cane was the absolute last thing that she wanted to think about, Maggie had started counting the days that she had resisted him instead. So far, she was fifty-four days in from the moment that he had shown up on her doorstep with the African Violet.

And after fifty-four days, she knew beyond a doubt that whoever had said that it took twenty-one days to break a habit had been talking shit.

The small beep of her phone pulled her thoughts back to the present. Glancing up from her mound of décor research, she reached for it, unsurprised when Lola's name popped up. She opened the message, read:

Lola: Hiya! Are you still going to make Grand Cru tonight?

Lola: So excited! I can't believe it. This is happening so fast!

    Sighing, Maggie took a moment to think about it. She wanted to go, wanted to drink wine with the girls, wanted to relax for one night, and help Lola plan her wedding. And even though they had become fast friends, Lola was also marrying her baby brother, which meant that she felt some small obligation too.

Maggie: Can I get back to you? 🙁 I don't know how I'm supposed to navigate the bodyguard...

Lola: Duh. Bring him!

Maggie: And Gracie?

Lola: Come on! Jackson is a total pushover. And Logan can watch Gracie while we drink, gossip....oh, and plan my wedding.

Lola: ????

Maggie: Let me check with the man in question and get back to you? If you don't hear otherwise, see you at 7 pm!

Lola: Yay! I can't wait!

Smiling at the last text, she meandered from her dining room table to the lounge where Logan had been playing with Gracie.

Although she'd never admit it aloud, he'd stepped into a father role as naturally as if he'd been there the entire time. He had gone from holding Gracie to changing diapers in the space of a week—she hadn't even seen him struggle with his gag reflex the first time he'd changed her solo. And, sure, he still had moments of panic when he didn't know how to do something. But he'd just stand aside and watch, his eyes sniper-focused, as she showed him then attempt to do it on his own the next time.

A small part of her wanted to resent that he had swooped in and taken over so naturally. Already, Grace was comfortable enough with him that she'd hold out her arms for him when he walked into a room. Or run over to where he stood and demand, "Up!" and every time that she did, Maggie would feel that same little pinch in her chest.

For nearly two years she'd imagined what it would be like to have Logan home, to watch him navigate fatherhood after getting no warning at all. She'd expected him to flounder and panic, maybe, even run away screaming. But nothing could have prepared her for how easily he'd adapted...and how quickly she'd come to rely on him. Again. Because no matter how scared she was that he'd be leaving as soon as Charles Rue had been taken care of, she also just couldn't deny the fact that it was...nice.

It was nice to have someone else to pick up the slack, change a diaper, feed Gracie, entertain her—because God knew that her daughter required *a lot* of entertaining.

It played Russian roulette with her ovaries, sure. But unsteady nerves and a jumpy stomach seemed like a fair tradeoff if it meant that she could get the help, especially *now*.

The café was a done deal. It was happening and she was woman enough to admit that having Logan help with Gracie was a Godsend.

Walking towards the lounge, she strained her ears, wary of the quiet.

It was too quiet.

Turning into the room, she came up short, taking a moment to silently study them. Logan was spread over the sofa, his long legs resting on the arm of the chair, feet spilling over. Spunk lay between him and the back of the huge couch, her head resting on his shin. The dog gave a half-hearted tail wag when she opened her eyes and saw Maggie. *Traitor.*

Gracie, her little arms folded under her, her mouth half-open, slept belly-down on Logan's chest.

She swallowed down the sigh that rose to her throat at the sight of them. *Shit.*

The curse didn't do anything to calm her frantic heart because she had imagined this scene exactly. As well as dozens of different iterations of it. But seeing him—*them*—like this, his impossibly large hands caging Grace in place on his chest as they both slept...It hurt. It felt as if every flood of fresh blood through her bruised heart was as excruciating as it was healing.

But at the same time, she wanted to take a picture. She wanted to have something that she could look at to be reminded of this moment once he left.

But then he stirred, opening his eyes as if he had sensed her watching. His gaze scanned over her, pausing for a moment at the look on her face. Maggie replaced it with a calm mask without missing a beat.

"Hey," he whispered, looking down at Gracie. "What time is it?"

"It's nearly six."

"I don't even remember lying down."

Coming up into a sitting position, he brought Gracie with him, his big hands easily transferring her weight so that she barely moved. She didn't stir at all, just let her head loll to the side when he placed her on her back over his knees.

"How long has she been out?"

"Probably an hour or so," he replied, his voice hoarse with sleep.

She cringed internally, already thinking of the early morning to come. If Gracie had been asleep for an hour, she probably wouldn't sleep through to her three-a.m. wake-up time. But right now, looking at them, she tried not to think about how her body would protest when she had to wake up in the middle of the night to her restless child.

"I was supposed to meet Lola and Sarah at Grand Cru to help with wedding stuff..."

Before she'd even suggested that he tag along, he said, "We'll come with you. Just give me five to get changed."

Nodding, she moved forward to take Gracie. "Here, let me change her at the same time."

He didn't move, and Maggie reached down to wrap her hands around Gracie's waist. *Mistake.* The movement brought her face to face with Logan.

Her gaze tracked to his lips of their own volition, then guiltily shifted back up to his steel-gray eyes, which had darkened perceptibly. He didn't move, didn't even breathe.

She swallowed. Loudly.

She wanted to pull back, she really did, but his gaze held her in place, welding her to the spot. Her stomach dropped low, and she felt every cell in her body pull tight, collecting in a throbbing weight between her thighs.

She knew exactly what his lips would feel like on hers, knew the exact drop-and-swing motion that her stomach would travel in when his hands ran the length of her body. Her mind summoned memories of their bodies melding, and she sighed, feeling the familiar swell of emotions clog her throat.

He leaned towards her as if he were going to kiss her, and the movement broke the magnetic pull. She stepped back first, broke eye contact, and, heaving Gracie off his lap, took two big steps away.

She didn't look back down at him, didn't trust herself to. Her entire body was alive, charged full of static awareness that brought a physical ache. Scared by her reaction, and by the fact that all she wanted to do was close the distance between them, she turned and walked away, Gracie in her arms.

Maggie had changed her clothes and it was driving him crazy. For some reason, even though she was only meeting Lola and Sarah for a glass of wine, she had slipped out of her casual blue jeans. She'd changed into a white skirt that fell in soft waves to her ankles and a silky, purple top with thin straps that highlighted the smooth, soft skin of her shoulders.

She had left her hair down, and it tumbled in a rich, cascade down her back. Her blue eyes, usually so bright and clear, were all sultry and sexy, painted with the faintest pink eyeshadow and mascara.

He had half a mind to refuse to let her go out looking so...

So...what?

Beautiful?

And *that* was exactly why he hadn't said anything at all. He had no right to tell Maggie Simmone anything, let alone how to dress to avoid turning every male head in the establishment.

Which is exactly what she was doing.

From the moment that they had walked into Grand Cru together nearly two hours earlier, he'd counted five men craning their necks to get a better view. And Maggie didn't even notice. She'd just handed him Gracie before wandering off to Lola and Sarah's table, and she hadn't looked their way again. He'd know because he hadn't taken his eyes off her.

As he watched from the sofa on the opposite side of the room, a tall, thin man with a mustache approached the girls' table. He enveloped Lola first, then Maggie and Sarah in a hug. He said something, and they all laughed. Lola swatted his arm playfully.

Logan clenched his fists at his side and glared at the group, not unaware of the fact that Gracie was eyeing him skeptically, as if she knew that something was wrong but hadn't figured out what. "Does she always go out looking like that now?" he asked her, his voice naturally coming out in what Jake would have called 'gaga' tone, which was just exaggerated baby talk.

"Da!"

"Is that Russian for 'yes', or are you trying to say something else?"

"Mama, look," she added, pointing in Maggie's general direction.

"Mama's busy talking." He didn't want to tear his eyes away from the man talking to Maggie, but, needing the distraction, he picked Gracie up off the sofa next to him and plopped her on his legs.

Taking the gesture as a sign that he must be interested in her toy, she held it up for him to inspect. It was a sloth, with soft, gray fur and fabric touchpads that were labeled on different body parts. Logan squeezed the sloth's 'Hand' label, cringing when a creepy voice burped, "hand" back at him.

He wasn't quite sure why, but Gracie found the sound hilarious. The moment that the voice blurted out its respective body part, she threw her head back. Her baby giggles—loud and high-pitched—went straight to his heart.

She calmed quickly, looking up at him with big, gray eyes. Logan held the toy up, and when she smiled, he pressed the label that read 'Foot'. A different voice squeaked "foot," sending Gracie into another fit of laughter.

"This is another game, huh, kiddo?" he asked, smiling at how simple her joy was. "Can you say 'foot'?" he asked, grabbing her entire foot in his hand.

Laughing, she kicked out her foot from his hand and, grabbing it with her own hands, said, "Da!"

"Ah...almost." On a roll, he picked up the sloth again, pressed the button that said 'Leg', and repeated, "Leg."

She giggled again and although she didn't give him a word, her big smile was enough to sink him completely.

"What are you guys doing over here?"

Logan glanced up at Maggie, smiled when he noticed the wine-drunk, sleepy look in her eyes, and the gentle sway of her body. *Oh, she's plastered.* He wondered if she'd realized that she'd lost a good twenty pounds and probably couldn't hold her booze like she used to. But because he didn't want to ruin her night of fun, he said, "We're playing with Mr. Sloth."

She came to sit on the sofa next to them, laughed when Gracie crawled over onto her lap, snuggling up to her chest. "His name is Sid."

"Sid the sloth?"

Cocking her head, she looked at him, her blue eyes heavy-lidded. "Yeah, like *Ice Age*."

"What?"

"Come on!" Angling her head slightly, she added, "The kids movie? About the prehistoric creatures who survive the ice age together..."

"Haven't watched it."

"We'll have to remedy that. Won't we baby?" she asked, kissing Gracie's cheek.

Logan's chest constricted at the sight, and he took in one long, silent breath.

"I'm almost done with my last glass," she said, breaking his reverie. "Jackson didn't know that Lola can't drink anymore so naturally, I had to have her complimentary tasting too. I feel *good*," she said.

"I'm glad." And he was. He enjoyed the way that she was smiling at him unhindered—even if her smile was a little bit lopsided.

"Give me twenty more minutes and then we can go home?"

Nodding, he took Gracie back, tucked her into the crook of his arm so that Maggie could stand and wander back to the table.

As he watched her go, something...settled, something that he couldn't name fell into place. "It's going to take me a lifetime," he whispered to Gracie. "But I'm going to make it up to her."

Because he couldn't linger on the thought, he leaned down and kissed Gracie on the head before picking up the...Sid once again.

He played with Gracie for another fifteen minutes before Maggie wandered back, this time with a glowing Lola and near-stumbling Sarah at her side.

"Ready?" he asked.

Nodding, she smiled and yawned loudly before turning to give Lola and Sarah a hug goodbye. "I'll start working on my list of things to do."

Lola smiled. "Thanks, Maggie. I just..." She glanced at Sarah. "I don't know what I'd do without you two. I love you all so much."

When tears filled her eyes, Logan shifted from one foot to the other, eyeing Lola warily. He had never been good with tears. At least when Gracie cried it was because she was tired or hungry. Hell, even Gracie's grumpy tears were safer than any grown woman crying in front of him.

"I love you guys too," Sarah said, her eyes brimming.

"Don't you dare," Logan whispered when Maggie's lips started to tremble. "I can handle one woman crying, but not three."

"Oh, shush!" Sarah laughed. "We're not crying. We're...leaking."

Logan grinned at Sarah Boyle's weak argument. Something told him that she wasn't one to cry easily under normal circumstances "How about a ride home, Sarah?"

"Nah! I came with Lola...Because she's knocked up...And can't drink," she stated facts, her words slow as if she were focusing on enunciating each one.

Turning his attention back to Lola, he asked, "You okay to get home?"

"Yes. Thanks, Logan." Reaching up on the tips of her toes, she enveloped him in a hug. "Thanks for bringing my girls...and for keeping them safe," she whispered.

When she let him go, he smiled. He had known from the moment that he'd met Lola that he'd like her, but seeing how she looked after her friends even though they were out celebrating her wedding and baby, solidified his respect for her.

She'd fit in well with the Simmone's, he realized. She'd slot in as if she'd always been there, whereas he'd always been the one welcomed in but never really belonging. Or, never really *feeling* like he belonged. Somewhere in the back of his mind, he knew that there was a difference.

"Ready?" Maggie asked, hefting the baby bag full of toys off the sofa.

He nodded, taking the bag off her shoulder. "Text us when you're home," he said to Lola before following Maggie out of the door.

It took them ten minutes to get back to the house, and by the time that he had pulled into the driveway, Gracie was fast asleep in her chair on the back seat of the car. "I envy her that," he said, opening the back door so that he could gently undo the buckles of her car seat.

"If only she'd stay down until dawn," Maggie replied sleepily.

Picking Gracie up, he cradled her on his chest as he leaned in to grab her bag with his other hand.

"Here, let me," Maggie leaned in past him, her hand reaching for the bag too, her body brushing the full length of him as she did so.

The feeling of her body touching his sent his system into overdrive and he exhaled sharply, struck by the jolt of lust that traveled from his stomach to his groin.

"Are you okay?" she asked, momentarily confused as she looked up at him from her position leaning over the back seat.

"Yup," he replied, forcing his tone into a believable nonchalance, and standing quickly so that she wasn't so close.

She's drunk. Just keep your distance. You'll be fine.

He would not make a move when she had been drinking. *No way in hell.* It would snap that tiny thread of trust they'd just established again.

Focusing all his attention on placing one step in front of the other, he moved towards the door, Gracie asleep on his shoulder and Maggie at his side.

"Thanks for taking me tonight," she said, swaying as she leaned forward to try and open the door.

"Of course." Shifting Gracie onto his other side, he pulled out his phone and turned on the flashlight. "Here."

Holding the light over the keyhole for her, he watched as her slender hands fumbled with the lock. For some reason, seeing her hands—all smooth skin and slender wrists—brought back *very* vivid memories of just what those hands were capable of. *Fuuuuck. No.*

Not wanting to be an asshole, but in desperate need to add some distance between himself and a very tipsy Maggie, he nudged her aside. "Here. Let me."

She took a step back, which was really a mistake because she ended up side-by-side with him. She stared up at him and he felt the air between them thicken.

Quickly turning his attention back to the lock, he slid the key in, satisfied when a clean 'click' sounded, and the door slid open.

"I'll let Spunk in from the back. Can you put Gracie down?" she asked, entering the house behind him.

Because he had already intended to do just that, he said, "Sure," and kept on to Gracie's room, moving fast.

He didn't turn on the light when he entered the small second bedroom that Maggie had done up for Gracie, but even in the dark, he knew that her carved, white crib sat against the pink accent wall.

Walking slowly to the far side of the room, he reached into the bed and pulled back the big, fluffy blanket, which memory told him was pink as well. It felt so small in his hand, yet he knew that it all but drowned Gracie's tiny body when she was underneath it.

Cradling her head, he leaned over the rails of the bed and placed her gently on the mattress before pulling up the covers. He loved the way that it felt under his calloused palm, so he stroked a hand over her downy head once before turning for the door.

Maggie was standing just out in the hallway, her mahogany hair shimmering in the light. Logan smiled when he noticed that she was leaning against the wall, supporting her weight. He'd bet money on the fact that she didn't even realize she was doing it. Her eyes, although smiling, were half-shut.

He was two steps from the door, his eyes on Maggie, when he stood on something that let out a loud squeak. The sound reverberated through the small room.

He paused, frozen to the spot. His heart leaped once in his chest before quietening. In the crib, Gracie sighed in her sleep.

Looking up, he met Maggie's eyes, which had gone from nearly closed to wide with dread. Her hands were spread in front of her as if she were trying to balance on a ship or stop an imaginary dog from jumping on her.

Logan stood still for another ten seconds, then when no sound came from the crib, he lifted his foot off the offending toy and exaggeratedly crept the last three steps towards a grinning Maggie.

"That was close," he whispered.

"You have no idea how many times I've done that." She reached past him to close the door to Gracie's bedroom, and the flower scent of her hair hit his system like a slap in the face, forcing the blood from his head to his groin. He held his breath, too afraid that another hit would send him overboard.

"She should be down for-" Her voice trailed off when she glanced up at him and saw the look on his face.

He knew that his need was painted openly there, knew that it would have been easier for both of them if he'd had more self-control. But it was Maggie and she looked like a forest nymph and smelled like paradise.

Just take a step back. He was about to do just that, add distance between their bodies so that he could think straight, but then she leaned forward and wrapped a single, cool hand around the back of his neck.

Logan felt the touch, her palm at the back of his neck, like an electric shock that traveled from that single point of contact to his toes. He met her eyes, saw his raw desire reflected back in big, blue pools, felt her warm breath against his face. She didn't move for a moment, just looked at him as if she were thinking through her next move. Then she pulled his head down so that she could brush her lips against his.

He didn't resist. He couldn't. He had wanted this for so long, had missed her for what had felt like a lifetime.

The small contact, the casual touch of her lips burned through his blood, sending his heart racing in his chest. Nothing had changed. He was still as hopelessly in love with her as he'd been since he was seventeen years old. Still as intoxicated by the ripe, floral scent of her, by the sound of her breath humming in her throat, and by the feeling of her hands, whisper-light, on him.

He wondered if her skin would feel as soft as he remembered under his hands. The thought brought a rush that had him stifling the groan in his throat and shifting his body so that he didn't give in to his sudden urge to rub against her.

She was looking at him now, her eyes wide with shocked need. He knew that she had been drinking and that it wouldn't be fair, but the thirst for her was a physical ache, a searing drive that overpowered his body and paled everything else.

And then she kissed him again, rose on her toes, and slipped her tongue into his mouth, and he was lost.

He met her desperate mouth with his own even as his arms snaked around her so that he could grip her perfect ass, and pull her body against his body.

Her tongue tangled with his until their breath mingled in heavy pants for air. She roped her arms around his neck, locking him in place, and her body pressed against his, branding his skin everywhere that it touched.

"Maggie," he choked out once before succumbing to his urge to taste the perfume-scented skin of her neck. He was unsure what he was going to say. His mind screamed that he needed to stop, that she wasn't sober, but the way that she was rubbing against his erection stopped the flow of blood to his brain, shattering the warning. And the way her skin tasted under his lips scattered all the pieces, leaving him reeling with lust-filled confusion.

He pulled away suddenly.

Sensing his hesitation, Maggie stepped back to him, trailed kisses down the column of his throat, each feather-light touch of her lips as visceral as a solid punch to the gut.

"Please, Logan." Her voice came out breathy. "You know that I want this. You."

He let out a strangled sound that sounded like a dying animal's whimper. The throbbing weight in his groin felt unbearable, nearly painful. He needed her like a dying man needed a savior.

Leaning forward, he lifted her off her feet, let out a quiet groan when she hiked her skirt up and wrapped her legs around his waist.

I'm going to die. That's what he thought as he carried her through to her bedroom. Although he doubted that any man had ever died from a hard-on, he knew that if it were at all biologically possible, he might be the first.

Placing her on her bed, he kissed her once. A quick, hard melding of lips that left him choking for air.

Then he took an abrupt step back, hating himself already.

"What's wrong?" she asked, pushing herself into a sitting position.

The movement inadvertently exposed the smooth, slender skin of her inner thighs—thighs that he'd die to be buried between at that moment. He closed his eyes. Just for a moment so he could collect his thoughts. "I want you more than air, Maggie." Raking a hand through his long hair, he sighed. "But you've been drinking, and I don't want you to do anything that you'd regret tomorrow."

"Logan, I-"

He held up a hand to silence her. "When we're together again, and we will be as soon as humanly possible," he ground out, "I want you to be sure. I..." He met her eyes then. "I don't want to hurt you again, Mags. I want to stay. For good. And I need you to believe that."

When she sighed and looked away, he felt a small part of his heart die. She still didn't trust him.

"I know that I'm going to have to spend my life proving it to you. I *know* that."

"Can't we just have tonight?" she asked.

"It's not enough for you, Maggie. You...you deserve everything."

"Don't say that!" Suddenly she was standing in front of him, her fists at her side, blue eyes snapping with fury. "Every time that you start talking that bullshit, you're up and gone within a month, and quite frankly Logan, I don't want to hear it!"

Flinging her hands in the air, she paced back and forth. He'd never say it, but he thought she looked beautiful, her blue eyes fiery, her hair a tumbled mess down her back.

"I'm going to stay," he said lamely.

"That's fine and well. You're entitled to live where you like. You're a grown man! But you need to stop with the 'you're too good for me bullshit'. I am *so sick* of that crap."

Her eyes were filling with tears, so he took a step towards her, intending to wrap her in his arms. She held up a hand, halting him mid-stride. "I never wanted anyone else. Ever. Do you know that you're the only man I've ever slept with?"

He didn't say anything. He didn't know what to say.

"Logan...It wasn't only about sex. It...it was about you. About *us*."

"Maggie..."

"No. I've loved you for *so long*. I always will. But until you realize that you're good enough, that you're it for me...I can't give my heart back to you. It's nearly dead as it is. A quick jaunt is one thing, but actually getting back together..." She laughed, a sad half-sob that stuck in her throat.

"I want to try. I just...I need help."

"Well then get help! Because clearly, I can't make a difference."

She pushed him back with both hands so that he was standing outside her bedroom. "Maggie, please. Just give me a chance."

134

"If you want to stay, then fine. I won't ask you to leave. For Gracie's sake. And for selfish reasons, because I do like having you home."

"But?"

"Don't ask me for more when you're the one incapable. I'm tired of always giving myself wholly to you and coming out battered and bruised…" She shrugged, "At least if we're just having sex I'll scratch an itch and not have to worry about you being a flight risk."

He hated how cold her voice was, hated how quickly they had fallen from simmering lust to cold facts. "I don't want it to be just *scratching an itch.*"

"Easy for you to say. I haven't had sex in two years! So, I have a *serious* itch that needs *serious* scratching!"

Neither have I. He didn't say it aloud because he didn't want to undermine how she felt, but he knew that it was important that he told her eventually.

He had touched Maggie Mae Simmone and everything, rather, *everyone,* else had ceased to exist for him. Since that first time he'd inched inside of her, he'd spent his life trying to figure out how he'd be able to keep her.

Because he hadn't been able to afford college, and because she had been prepping for USC, he had enlisted in the military. Then he'd come home after four years and she was suddenly a…woman—a woman with stars in her eyes and the world at her feet.

When she'd told him that she was going to apply to Stanford Law, he'd freaked out and re-enlisted. Only the second time around he'd pursued his tap for Q Course so that he could join the Special Forces.

And after that, he'd come home but…things had changed.

Maggie was a lawyer, earning a shitload of money and working her butt off trying to make it big. And he was a military man, a lifelong career gun who'd never be home enough to make it up to her. Never be around enough to eventually stop some rich, educated shmuck from moving in on her.

He'd eventually retired from the SF—and not because he didn't enjoy it. God, he had loved being in the United States Army Special Forces. He had felt proud. Important. But he'd seen the writing on the wall. He had known that sooner or later Maggie would move on, find someone to have a family with, to build a life with. So, he'd quit after nearly fifteen years.

At the time, his idea had been to find a temporary job in private protection in LA, but the war in Afghanistan had been in full swing. There had been a lot of foreign nationals that had been prepared to pay through the teeth for seasoned close protection. So, he'd gone on what should have been one last stint away from Maggie.

It was supposed to have been a transition, a period where he could pick up the skills to come home and start a private security outfit. And he'd followed the plan. He'd done five years, only coming home for two months every Christmas. And when the five years were up, he'd got down on one knee and asked Maggie to marry him.

He could still remember the heart-stopping fear when he'd looked up into her eyes, could still remember the stomach-lurching anxiety he'd felt when she'd stared at him in shock for a solid fifteen seconds. He could also remember the entire world pausing the moment that she had smiled at him and said yes.

He'd bought a goddamn condo.

Opened a pension plan.

Settled on a wedding date.

And then he'd screwed it all to hell one last time when he'd lost his nerve and run back to the only thing he knew that he was good at. Hurting people.

He had been so scared of falling short of his own bar that he'd screwed any real chance that he could have had with her. But it would have been unfair to try and explain it to her now, when she needed to vent. And, worse, when he deserved everything that she said to him.

So, he didn't.

"I don't want it to just be casual, Maggie. I love you." When she snorted, honest to God snorted, he rolled his neck, stupefied about what he was going to say next. "I'll make you a deal."

"What?"

"I'll make you a deal," he repeated.

She eyed him skeptically, her arms crossed over her chest, hip cocked. Her entire body posture read, 'Do not fuck with me' but her eyes narrowed. "What kind of deal?"

"One year."

"What?"

"One year from today *when* I'm still here and I haven't left, you have to marry me."

She sputtered, but he was pleased to notice that her eyes were wide with shock. "That's ridiculous," she said, finally, but there was no anger behind the words.

Shaking his head, he took a step closer to her, felt a laugh bubble up in his chest when she took a step back. "Come on, Mags. You said so yourself. I'm a flight risk. So, what's the harm?"

"I'm not going to marry you because I *lost a bet*!"

"Then marry me because you love me," he countered.

"You're so missing the point here."

"No. You said that you love me but that you can't give yourself to me because you're worried I'll leave again. Affirmative?"

She nodded, begrudgingly, but she nodded.

"So, if in a year, when I still have no intention of going anywhere, then you won't have an argument against it, and you'll have to marry me."

Placing her palm on her forehead, she closed her eyes and shook her head. "This is absurd."

Oh, I know your weaknesses, Maggie. She'd never been able to resist a good dare or a harmless gamble. Underneath the corporate lawyer, Maggie Simmone was all street smarts. Which is how he knew that she'd agree to the deal before she looked up at him and asked, "What's the pot?"

"Other than my dazzling company for the rest of your life?"

"Har. Har. I'm serious, what's in it for me when you're back in CAR in six months?"

The casual way that she said it hurt more than he cared to admit. "Double or nothing." He swallowed once the words were out.

"You don't come back again?"

He shrugged. "It doesn't matter because I'm going to win."

"No deal."

For a moment, he felt deflated, as if she'd sucker-punched him. Then she grinned. "I can't deprive Grace of future contact with you when you lose. So I'll take your deal but when *I* win, I get a lifetime of bragging rights and the single condition that you never touch me. Ever again."

He hesitated. Not being able to touch Maggie again if he messed up was very-near a dealbreaker. *And she knows that. Won't be a problem if you stay.* When *you stay.* "Deal."

When he held out his hand, she looked down at it in surprise for only a moment, then reached out her own and shook it. "Deal."

She turned to walk away. "Wait," he said.

Looking over her shoulder, her eyebrows raised, she asked. "Yes?"

"Do you still have the ring, or do I have to buy you another one?"

"Of course I still have it." Never one to back down, she added, "I'll mail it to you if you leave an address this time."

He felt a bubble of joy unravel in his chest but smothered it with a cocky grin. "Do I get to touch you in the interim?"

She laughed. "I gave you your chance, Cane. Tonight I'm going to bed with something small and battery-powered."

He let his head fall back against the wall. The image of Maggie touching herself, even if it was with the little, pink vibrator that he'd bought her years ago, drained his blood to his crotch instantly.

"I'll think about you when I come though," she said, then turned back into her bedroom and closed the door in his face.

Chapter 11

Logan pulled his SUV into the driveway of the ramshackle house and took a moment to just look.

Nothing had changed since he'd last been there to visit his dad almost two years earlier. The house, a small square structure with faded yellow slats and chipped white trim sat on the back of the small lot, its little windows staring straight ahead at the small, crowded neighborhood.

The front yard, a patchwork quilt of faded greens and browns, hadn't seen much water, and the dirt was packed where a path led up to the front door. A coiled garden hose lay in a tangled knot by the corner of the house, the head bent at an angle like a snapped neck.

To the left and across the street, houses in similar states of exhaustion huddled together like schoolchildren in a playground. They had been built similarly, with efficiency. Their squat, square frames were intended to provide the most use per-square-foot of the little space inside. Still, each one had been slightly customized by its inhabitant through the years. The result, a colorful array of tiny, well-lived-in homes was one he'd always thought of as homey. Welcoming.

Cars, some of which were caked in dust, crowded either side of the street even though it was noon on a Wednesday.

When the front door opened and his dad stepped outside, his arms outstretched, Logan turned off the engine and climbed out.

His father, Mike, looked older, thinner. He had always been a big man, someone that people assumed worked physically by the size of his broad shoulders, thick forearms, and huge, rough hands. He looked what he was: a retired blue-collar worker. A carpenter who had been lifting, sawing, and heaving his work around with him for most of his adult life.

The full head of hair that he usually kept tied back had been cropped close to his skull, emphasizing a face that was not so different from Logan's. His dad's eyes, the same gray as his and Gracie's, were bright and alert despite the faint smudges of fatigue beneath them.

"Dad."

His father broke into a grin. Pulling Logan into a hug, he thumped him on the back. "It's good to see you."

"You too." And it was. He hadn't realized until that moment how much he had missed his parents. And his friends. Thinking of them, missing them, had always taken a backburner against thoughts of Maggie. When he was gone, *she* was who he thought about. She was who he missed.

She was who he came home for.

When Mike released him and started for the house, Logan followed behind, keeping on the packed dirt path.

"Your mother called me a few weeks ago to tell me you were coming home," he said, looking over his shoulder as he opened the front door.

Logan found himself frowning. "You speak to Mom now?"

"Yeah. We've been...cordial since we ran into each other in the hospital when Grace was born. Maggie told us that she was giving the baby your grandmother's name." He laughed. "I guess Marlene and I figured there were more important things that could connect a couple other than a failed marriage."

Logan didn't know what to say. His parents had always had a rocky relationship, neither one quite happy with the other and neither one willing to change. When he'd come from his first tour and they'd told him they were getting a divorce, he'd felt…relieved. He'd always imagined they'd be happier apart.

"I was expecting you sooner," his dad continued.

"Yeah, sorry. I…I brought some trouble back with me. I…I've been trying to keep a low profile."

Mike raised his eyebrows as they came into the kitchen, but he didn't say anything as he opened the fridge and rummaged around inside before pulling out two beer bottles. He handed one over and Logan took it, grateful to have something in his hands that he could fiddle with.

The inside of the house looked exactly as he remembered too, a near-perfect match for the tired exterior. Everything was a little chaotic. Old newspapers were stacked by the microwave. The coffee pot, a Mr. Coffee from the fifties, sat on top of it. And, although the cracked-linoleum kitchen counter was small, there were two toasters on top of it. One was an antique, with yellowing plastic around the base and on the lever. The other was a pastel blue Oster that looked like it had never been used.

"Mine broke," Mike said, following his gaze. "Maggie bought me a new one before I could fix it."

"Why don't you throw the old one?"

"Because I fixed it." He shrugged. "Besides, it's too old to sell and I hate throwing things away. It's bad for the environment."

"So sell the new one."

"No, because the old one isn't going to last much longer. And then I would have consumed three appliances instead of two."

Logan smiled, unwilling to fight the logic. "Is your newfound concern for the environment why you haven't been watering the lawn?" he asked, taking the first sip of his beer.

"Partially." He shrugged. "Mostly, I couldn't be bothered. Never found much enjoyment in gardening. And

I have too much goddamn pride to hire someone to do it for me."

"There's that," Logan said with a small laugh.

"No HOA to complain about it in this neighborhood. Although, Crystal does keep bitching about it. Goddamn woman never shuts up. About *anything*."

"Crystal is still alive?"

Mike's neighbor to the right, was a bird-like old lady with a big, belly laugh and crude sense of humor. The last time Logan had seen her had been at her ninety-fifth birthday party, nearly two years earlier.

"Yeah. Still in charge of her faculties too. I go over there every couple of days to check that she's still alive."

"Ah...what?"

"Yeah. Blame the Crime Channel for that. Watched a bit about an old lady who died and nobody found her for *years*. She was partially mummified."

"*How* does that even work?"

"Don't know. Still gross. Keeps me up at night."

Logan nodded in his father's direction. "And you, Old Man? Maggie told me you were sick."

"Agh," Mike waved his hand, "got pneumonia."

"You okay now?" Logan couldn't help but worry. His dad had never taken care of himself. Ever. It was probably the biggest fight between his parents when he'd been a kid. Marlene didn't want to watch Mike die from long-term, soda-related complications and Mike thought she was exaggerating. Like most things, Logan knew that the truth lay somewhere in the middle.

"Never been better. Gracie's got me on my toes."

"Glad to hear it." He rubbed the back of his neck. "Thanks...for being there."

There was a beat of silence, a small pause where Logan thought about what else to say. He didn't have a chance to make up his mind before Mike said, "So...how does it feel to be a father?"

"Terrifying," he admitted instantly. "I find myself seeing danger...everywhere. In the most unusual places."

Running a hand over his head, Mike laughed. "When you started walking, I taped all the sharp corners with painter's tape to soften the edges. Marlene came home and had a fit when she saw the blue everywhere. Apparently" he waved his hand in front of his face, "they make gizmos for that."

"Yeah. The other day I stood and watched my bathwater drain for six minutes because I realized once I was out that she could drown if she fell into it."

"Wait until she's old enough to start using appliances."

"Oh, God." Logan didn't even want to think about it.

"Yup."

"What am I going to do?" It was intended as a joke, but he realized the moment that the words were out of his mouth that he meant them. He had no idea what he was doing when it came to Gracie. Mostly, he just mimicked Maggie and hoped for the best.

"You let her do things herself. Let her ride a bike and use a toaster. And if and when she hurts herself, you deal with it."

"It's not enough."

"It never has been. For any parent. But there's more danger in being over-protective than not. Show her, let her try, and for God's sake, let her make mistakes."

"Shit," Logan said, leaning his hip against the kitchen counter. "I'm so unprepared."

His dad just grinned. "You have only yourself to blame for that. Maggie had nine months to read, to learn, to think and panic and wonder. If you'd been here..."

"I know." The words were barely whispered.

"Please, Logan," the tenor in his dad's voice changed instantly, laced through with panic, "enough now."

"I..."

"What?" he asked suddenly, throwing his hands in the air. "What is wrong with you? Why can't you see what's right in front of you."

Logan stared at the condensation on the beer bottle, trailed his thumbs over the frosted glass. "I see her. Them. I see them and I know exactly what I could have. But..."

"Is it not...enough for you?" Mike's words were choked. "Is the killing, the...adrenaline...more? I won't judge you if it is. I've heard of men who struggle when they come home from fighting. I just need to understand."

Logan didn't know how to say what he needed to.

"You know," his father continued, not waiting for him to find the words, "I never thought that Maggie would stay with you."

His head snapped up at that.

"I thought she'd get tired of waiting. Hell, I thought she'd end up ditching you for one of her lawyer friends first chance she got."

Logan felt his blood heat with rage. Just the thought of her with someone else made him want to hit something, anything.

"But that little girl stuck around through all your shit. And, honestly, Logan...I don't know why she did. You haven't done a thing to deserve her."

"I know." Tears burned the back of his eyes and, because he was ashamed of them, he didn't look up when he added, "I always knew that I was never enough for her. Maggie's...everything. And now it's worse because there's Gracie. And I'll definitely never deserve her. Not in a million lifetimes." Needing to tell someone, anyone, he carried on. "I see the way Maggie looks at me. She *sees* me." His voice rose with every word. "And all I can think is that I'm not enough. Fucks sake, I have to concentrate when I write my own name!" he roared. "I can't compete with *any* other man."

Mike was staring at him, his eyes wide with surprise at the outburst. He opened his mouth, snapped it shut again.

Snatching his beer up from the counter, he spun around, only pausing to issue a quick, "Come with me," as he walked towards the garage door.

Logan ground his jaw against the fury and grief that was still surging through his blood and collecting in a knot in his stomach. But he pushed to his feet and followed, too embarrassed by his outburst to ask where the hell they were going.

His dad opened the door and walked through, pausing to flick the light switch. The moment he did, the workshop flooded with bright light, layering the gleaming carpentry equipment win a soft, yellow glow.

A gleaming band saw nestled next to a planer. Against the far wall, dozens of shiny tools hung in a custom cabinet, all perfectly maintained and polished. A big work table had been pushed against the wall on the other side of the room, and Logan could just make out a set of hand-carved figurines, each about the size of a cellphone. Unlike the rumpled house, the workshop was pristine, everything clean and put back in its place at the end of the day.

Mike walked to the far corner of the room where a blue tarpaulin covered something big. Before Logan had a chance to ask what it was, his dad pulled the covering off, revealing a small bed.

It had been perfectly joined out of a dark wood that Logan couldn't identify. Two half-moon rockers formed the base instead of legs so that the bed would rock gently from side to side when Gracie—for it could only be hers—rolled over in the night.

The headboard was an ornate semi-sphere carved from the same wood, and, when he looked closely, Logan could make out an intricate fairy world carved into the surface. "For Gracie?"

Without waiting to see his dad nod, he walked forward so that he could run his hands over the details in the wood. "Dad…" Logan's voice hitched, but he cleared his throat and said, "This is incredible. Gracie will love this. Maggie will love this."

"They will," Mike said, too proud of his work to be humble.

"How long did this take you?"

"Six months so far. And I'm not done yet. I'm embedding fairy lights into the forest scene—you can see the drill holes where they'll be placed." Walking forward, he crouched down by Logan. "You see these cutouts here?" His hands glided over a series of intricate shapes carved into the side of the bed.

"The figurines." Logan could see exactly where the little wooden toys on the workbench would slot into the bedframe.

Mike smiled and Logan could see the love pouring out of his features. "The figurines," he confirmed.

"It's beautiful, Dad."

"It is." He rubbed a hand over his head again, suddenly awkward. "I am not a lawyer or a doctor, Logan."

"Thank God."

Mike didn't laugh. "I didn't graduate high school and I haven't read anything asides from Stephen King since the day I dropped out at eighteen. I watch too much television. I drink soda with breakfast. I eat pizza six nights a week."

He stroked the bed like he might have a favorite dog. "I'm not successful by society's standards. But…I can make things with my hands that lawyers and doctors will pay me a fortune for. I can show Maggie and Gracie that they're the most important people in my life with something as simple as making a big girl bed for my granddaughter. And…it's enough. It's *more* because they know that this is the best I can do. This is how I tell them when I can't find the right words."

147

Guilt like he had never felt before washed over Logan, filling him with desperate need. He wished that other people could understand that every time Maggie smiled at him, every time that she studied him when she thought he wasn't looking, he felt...decimated. Unworthy. He couldn't even make her pretty furniture. "I've done terrible things, Dad." He didn't know why he was bringing it up now; the words just slipped out, looking for an escape.

"And you think that adds to your undeserving?"

"Doesn't it?"

"Countries need armies, Logan. And armies need soldiers. A soldier's job is to follow orders." He placed a hand on Logan's shoulder, squeezed. "In my opinion, you're just an instrument for a poorly run government. It's not your fault that you just happen to be a goddamn good weapon."

He was quiet a moment. "I should never have let you go that first time. You were a kid. You knew nothing about the world, about the other options you had. I could have found you a goddamn construction job or...shit, I don't know...Anything else. But...there comes a time where you just run out of painter's tape."

"I had to go. To prove to myself that I could do something..." Logan touched the wood of the bed again, hoping to ground himself. "I still remember the moment that I realized I was *good*. I saw the way my team looked at me, looked *up to* me, and...suddenly I wasn't just the high school quarterback who'd peaked at seventeen and couldn't read a paragraph out loud. I was a leader. I was a soldier...I was someone that Maggie could be proud of."

"She's always been proud of you. *We've* always been proud of you."

"I know. It makes no sense. But I know. I just...I needed to know that I deserved it. That I deserved *her*. She's all I've ever wanted."

"I understand. I do." Pushing to his feet, Mike dusted his jeans even though there was no dirt on them. "I never resented you for signing up. But, Logan…"

Sensing that he needed to say what was on his mind, Logan prompted with, "What is it?"

"You're not a soldier anymore. And Maggie and Gracie might forgive you for leaving again, for putting yourself in danger to protect someone who doesn't deserve protecting. But I need you to know that I won't. I can't condone it. Not anymore. Especially now that you have Grace."

"Okay." And what else could Logan say? The line had been drawn, and, strangely, at that moment, Logan felt as if he knew which side of it he stood on.

Chapter 12

Another two weeks passed without incident. The days slowly bled into the holiday season without any of the usual fuss.

Nothing had come of Charles Rue.

Yet.

But Maggie wasn't encouraged by the radio silence. If anything, the lack of motion scared her more. It was as if every time she relaxed, found herself smiling or laughing or thinking about Thanksgiving, she'd suddenly remember that he was out there, nearby. Waiting to make his move. And then she'd feel the sick anxiety all over again.

Even Logan's near-constant presence hadn't been able to ease the sense of impending doom. She knew that he could protect them, but she understood that something terrible would have to happen for him to need to.

Looking for any distraction, she threw herself into her work. She spent most of each day working on her plans for the café; even though she'd had most of the details sorted before she'd signed the lease. Going over everything again and again grounded her, gave her something solid to grasp onto, something to look forward to.

And, most importantly, obsessing over the café gave her a distraction from Logan Cane.

The kiss that they'd shared had shattered the illusion of restraint she'd been trying so hard to front. She thought about him constantly. When she woke up in the morning, refreshed from having a full night's sleep, her first thought was that if she was quiet she could catch him napping on the sofa with Gracie. More than once, she'd found herself creeping to the lounge, Jacques Clouseau-style, in the hopes that she'd be able to watch them nap.

And from that first moment in every day through to when she fell asleep thinking about him, wanting him, thoughts of Logan filled her head. Sometimes they'd jump out at her, like a child hiding behind the door waiting to give her a fright. Sometimes they'd sneak up on her quietly. But usually…usually, she'd look up from her portfolio, her eyes blurred because she had been staring at the same page for twenty minutes while she daydreamed about him, completely unconscious of when she'd let the first thought slip through her barricade.

Worse, when she looked at him, she could see in his eyes that he understood her need.

And that he felt the same way.

For the thousandth time since she'd initiated the kiss, she berated herself for letting her guard down. But she still blamed *him*.

She'd been minding her own business, drinking wine and planning Lola's wedding. She'd just happened to glance up and see him across the room. He'd been holding Gracie's foot in his hand and talking to her, his expression exaggerated in that way that most adults unconsciously did around babies.

She'd made the mistake of kissing him once they'd been home. But she'd made up her mind to make a move as she'd sat in Grand Cru, only half-listening to what Lola and Sarah were saying, all the while sneaking glances of Logan and Gracie.

The lie that she wanted to tell herself was simple: You were drunk and made a mistake.

But the moment the excuse flitted into her mind, she felt ashamed. She *had* been drunk. But she'd wanted Logan Cane since she'd been sixteen years old. He wasn't a mistake, he was a habit. A bad one.

Now, agreeing to marry him was another matter entirely—a mistake she wouldn't have made if she'd been sober.

Loving him, giving herself to him again was completely different from marrying him. If they were lovers and co-parents, she could pick up the pieces of her life again when he moved on. If they were married, it changed things—for *her*.

Her entire life up to that moment had been surviving Logan Cane leaving her, and she had developed a tough, independent shell to cope with that eventuality over the years. It hurt like hell every time, but…she could do it. She *had* done it, numerous times.

But now, with the *small* possibility of him staying, Maggie was terrified that she wouldn't know who she was with him always around. Or, worse, she wouldn't know who he was. And that, the slow creep of doubt in her mind about how well she knew Logan, had scared her more than her dread of him leaving had in the past.

A lot more.

Being friends with him her entire life, and being his lover for over twenty years didn't constitute *knowing* the person that he had become. Logan had spent ten months of every year since they had been eighteen away from her. He wasn't the boy she'd fallen in love with all those years ago. And she certainly wasn't the same girl.

So, as much as she'd wanted to, she hadn't followed her previous theatrics with a follow-up performance.

Even when the lust in her belly, an unwelcome yet constant companion, flared whenever he stood too close or looked at her with his burnt metal eyes, she'd taken to ignoring it and immediately adding distance between them.

Shouldn't have taken the bait. Logan had deliberately turned their relationship, their *future*, into a bet because he'd known that she wouldn't be able to back down. Especially when she'd been fueled on by a little too much wine.

Had she just been sober, she would have had the common sense to back down.

Probably.

Maggie's windmilling thoughts scattered when Gracie's high-pitched wail tore through the house.

Pushing to her feet, Maggie ran through to the nursery, her heart galloping in her chest. She could hear the sound of Logan cursing and Spunk yipping.

"What happened?" she asked, slightly out of breath, as she came to a sudden halt in the doorway.

Before he could answer, her eyes absorbed the scene.

Logan stood cradling Gracie in his arms. His eyes were wide with fear, his huge hand covered her tiny one as he rubbed it between his fingers. Gracie's gray eyes were scrunched shut and, although she no longer screamed, she whimpered as if in pain.

Spunk had obviously run through at the sound of Gracie's scream but had no clue what was going on. She sat at Logan's feet, looking up at him excitedly as if waiting to be initiated into the game.

"I…I accidentally jammed her finger in the crib's side-rail," he said, his voice uneven, his face pale.

Maggie's heart slowed its pounding. She looked at his bunched shoulders, at the rigid set of his arms holding Gracie, and the spread stance on his legs.

"Here, let me look." Stepping up to them, Maggie gently pried his hand away so that she could take Gracie's in her own. Deliberately ignoring the tremble that ran through him, she studied her daughter's fingers.

She could see the bruise that ran the length of Gracie's tiny index finger and could see exactly where the crib had pinched her. The skin wasn't broken and when she gently bent the little finger through its normal range of motion, Gracie didn't react at all.

Maggie's heart slowed in her chest the moment she realized that nothing seemed to be badly hurt or broken.

But she could see the tight set of Logan's muscles and the stormy anger in his eyes. "Oh, no." She shook her head sadly.

Both Logan and Gracie stayed stock still, looking at her as if she were about to deliver end-of-the-war news. She sighed, shaking her head solemnly. "We're going to have to take it off."

Logan paled even more and turned to stare at Gracie, sending his shoulder-length hair forward into his eyes.

She wanted to reach out and smooth it back, but Maggie looked at Gracie instead. While Logan seemed too shocked to notice, her daughter knew the tone that she was using, so Maggie focused on her.

Taking Gracie's hand, she made a show of tucking her little fingers into a fist, leaving only the hurt one sticking out, pointing upwards.

Gracie stopped whimpering and looked at her with big, round eyes right before Maggie stuck the finger in her mouth and pretended to bite it off, quickly folding it into her little fist with her other fingers before she said, "There. All gone."

Gracie laughed, her mood instantly righted, and poked her finger back up out of her fist before waving it in front of Maggie's face in a 'You're not so smart' gesture.

"Oh, look! It grew back good as new," she said, sending Logan a small smile.

He didn't react, just stared at them as if they were a little unhinged.

Needing the contact after hearing Gracie scream, Maggie opened her arms and took her daughter's weight when Logan released her.

Gracie leaned her head on Maggie's collarbone, and the normalcy of the gesture calmed them both.

"She's fine," Maggie said, looking from Gracie back up to Logan.

"I hurt her." His voice was cold, quiet.

Ah…okay.

Standing there, looking at his pale face and clenched jaw, it dawned on her that he hadn't been initiated into the dealing-when-shit-went-sideways faction of parenting.

She should have walked away.

She didn't.

Reaching up a hand, she placed it on his cheek and turned his head to her, ignoring the tendrils of awareness spreading up her arm. The sad look in his dark, gray eyes was enough to send her pulse racing again. "She's fine, Logan. She just got a fright." To prove her point, she held up Gracie's finger for him to look at.

His gaze dropped and he studied the finger in question for a moment. Maggie saw the flicker of self-loathing in his eyes before he cupped Gracie's little hand in his and leaned down to place a single kiss on the bruise. "Sorry, baby," he said, before placing a second kiss on Gracie's forehead.

"Kiss," Gracie said, holding her finger back up to his lips for a third kiss.

Maggie's stomach swirled uneasily. Her blood seemed to thicken and pool between her thighs. Her heart vacated her chest entirely, choosing to tick away in her throat instead.

She cleared her throat, trying to relieve the itch, afraid that her voice would betray her raging need. "Are you still good to come with me to the café today?" she asked, deliberately drawing his attention away from the moment.

"Of course." He ran a hand through his hair. "I just need to call Sasha at some point."

"Are you worried that Rue hasn't made a move yet?"

He nodded his head in a so-so motion. "A little. Donny says that he hasn't purchased anything else, and Zac swears that the car hasn't moved from the motel in nearly ten days…"

"But?"

"That doesn't mean that he hasn't been working. Planning. Hell, he could have ditched the car and been following us around the neighborhood for the last week."

"Unlikely."

He raised his eyebrow at her confident tone.

"You would have spotted him if he was hanging in the neighborhood. Even I know that."

"Probably. But that doesn't mean he hasn't been planning."

"Agreed. So, let's get going and you can call Sasha from the café?"

When he nodded, she turned on her heel and walked out of the room, ignoring the thick thump of her heart in her chest.

When it still hadn't settled by the time she'd strapped Gracie in the car, she made up her mind to focus on keeping a solid two-foot radius between herself and Logan Cane going forward.

He was too close.

And she was losing what remained of her objectivity.

He looked around what would be Maggie's place in less than three months and felt a real sense of awe. She had chosen the perfect spot for the business concept that she had described to him, and standing inside the spacious, sunlit front room, Logan could see what the space would be with a little TLC.

Already, he could imagine the stressed, wooden tables that she had ordered dotted around the room. He could imagine the luscious, hanging plants that she had shown him online, dangling from the ceiling, dripping fronds of green throughout. He wasn't even much of a wino, but he could imagine that a lot of people would want to filter in and gossip over a glass of wine or grimace over an espresso.

It would work because she had chosen the perfect spot, and already, even he could see her vision coming to life. It would *keep* working because the Maggie he knew was as hardworking and determined as a carthorse, and as long as she wanted it to thrive, it would.

"What do you think?" she asked nervously, her eyes taking in the space with what he would have called unaffected love.

"I think it's perfect," he replied. "I think it'll be a hit."

"Right? Can't you just *see* the layout?" She twirled on the spot.

Gracie, seeing the impromptu dance from where she sat on the floor in the center of the room, laughed and wobbled her body back and forth, clapping her hands.

Maggie chuckled at Gracie's performance, her eyes lighting with joy, and Logan felt that same kick low in his belly.

He had been ignoring his burning need for her over the last few weeks. He had been trying to give her space to think over the fact that she had agreed to marry him. Again.

But he knew that the truth was somewhere in between. He had also been giving himself the space to figure out how he could do things properly this time. There was a ton to do, but he had started a running list in his head:

Sell the condo.
Get a job.
Convince Maggie that I should move in permanently.
Find out where she keeps the engagement ring.
Steal it.
Plan an actual proposal.
Get married.
Have at least two more kids.

In theory, it was a simple enough list, and already he had retained a local realtor to view, stage, and list the condo. The other items would take time and a shit ton of finesse considering that he'd have to convince Maggie to play along too.

And even though thinking about her was taking up a dangerous proportion of his thinking space, he hadn't forgotten about Francis Boucher and Charles Rue.

In the three weeks since Charles had left the kpinga in Maggie's car, she hadn't been out of his sight unless he had dropped her with her parents or had Jake come over to the house while he'd run errands. And even then, he might have left her and Grace alone a total of five times. Once or twice when he'd had errands that couldn't wait and a few times when he'd gone to visit his dad and Maggie had an appointment she couldn't reschedule.

And although Jake has said that they could lean on him more, Logan didn't want to. It was more than the fact that he knew that they weren't safe with Rue in the US—it was that he was the best person to be protecting them.

He had worked with Charles Rue for two years; he knew how Rue thought, how he operated. He knew which weapons he preferred, as well as his strengths and weaknesses in hand-to-hand combat. Logan knew just about everything about Rue, short of his favorite color and *that's* why he was doing everything possible to stay with Maggie and Gracie rather than pull someone else to watch them, even for short periods.

"I've got to make a list of things I need to bring next time, so if you want to call Sasha…"

Maggie's voice broke his reverie, and he glanced up. She was standing in the center of the room, dressed in simple black jeans and a white top that tied in the back, leaving her bare shoulders exposed. She held a clipboard in her slender hands, and a look of intense concentration masked her face as she stared at the bar, ignorant of his desperate perusal.

He imagined she was trying to picture what it would be like once it was done to her specifications, and as much as he didn't want to interrupt her, he found himself wanting to ask. Then again, he found himself wanting to do a lot of things when it came to Maggie Simmone and that was basically where his problems began and ended.

Gracie stood on her wobbly legs and was walking over to him. He closed the distance between them in two steps and leaned down to pick her up from the waist. "Wanna come talk on the phone with me, baby?"

She nodded absent-mindedly and continued to tug at the bottom of her white, frilly shirt, clearly dissatisfied with the lace trim that snaked around the bottom hem.

He could feel Maggie's eyes boring into him, so he turned to look at her again. This time, she was staring at him, her blue eyes drawn. Wary.

His heart sank in his chest, leaving him feeling hollow, but he forced his face to display a calm façade. "Everything okay?"

She shook her head as if trying to dislodge an unpleasant thought, then smiled at him. "All good. Just…distracted." She shrugged and turned away, back to the bar.

Taking Gracie before Maggie could think of a reason why he shouldn't, he stepped outside onto the sidewalk, making sure to close the door behind him. He had already checked the building and knew that there was no back door. So, Maggie would be safe inside with him on the phone right out front.

Pulling his cellphone from his pocket, he dialed Sasha's number, switched Gracie to his other hip while it rang.

He checked the small street running past the café, made sure that there were no unusual vehicles parked nearby or suspect pedestrians meandering past.

On the fourth ring, an unfamiliar, male voice answered the phone with a quick, breathy, "Hello."

Logan felt his heart slide into his stomach at the unknown, clipped, British accent, and bit back the panic clawing at his throat. "Who is this?"

"This is a friend of Sasha Riley's. Who am I speaking to?"

There was a long pause in which neither man said anything. Logan wouldn't disclose his name on the off-chance that Sasha had been hurt...or worse, and whoever had tracked her had taken her phone.

"Is..." the man paused as if thinking through what he was about to say. "If this is Logan Cane, tell me what Sasha's favorite contraband from home is."

Twizzlers.

US goods were hard to come by in CAR and he had once seen her pay an American UN volunteer a ridiculous price for her stash of the long, licorice candy. It had become a joke amongst those who'd known her after that.

"If you don't know the answer, then you don't know Sasha and I have no business talking to you."

Logan sensed that the man was about to hang up, so he breathed a quick prayer for luck and said, "Twizzlers."

"Mr. Cane?"

"Affirmative. Who is this?"

The man paused. "I can't give my name over the phone...but I'm a friend."

"Where is Sasha?"

"On her way home." There was another long pause before the man eventually added, "Via the same route you took."

Logan's heart rate picked up perceptibly. Sasha was on the run, moving south through the Congo. This could only mean that she'd run into trouble asking questions about Francis Boucher and was scared enough to believe that the UN couldn't protect her.

When Gracie squirmed against arms that had unknowingly caged her tightly against him, he loosened his hold. He kissed her on the forehead, unsure if he was trying to reassure himself or her.

"Did she find anything?" he asked. If the man was who he said he was—a friend—and Sasha had trusted him with her phone, then he might know where she had left off her investigation.

"Yes. She said to tell you that the case has been filed and that by the time she finds you in America, you'll have the green light. Although I...I," he stammered, "I'm not too sure what she meant by that."

"That's okay," Logan said. "I do."

"She also told me that as soon as you'd called, I should dispose of the phone. So...I guess this is goodbye."

"Thank you," Logan said, just as the line went dead.

He let out a rush of air, one long pent-up breath that did nothing to relieve the additional reason he'd just added to his list of things he should be shit scared about.

Sasha was on the run.

You idiot. His heart accelerated as anger, a familiar friend, rose in his chest. He could have just taken the goddamn pictures himself and run, turned them over to the UN when he'd arrived back in New York.

But no.

Instead, he had handed the case to a friend—a friend who had no means of protecting herself. And then he'd come home, bringing Francis Boucher right to Maggie's doorstep.

So stupid.

He felt sick to his stomach. He took three quick, consecutive inhales, then released them in one long exhale that instantly calmed his mind.

With his mind reeling over what to do next, he had completely forgotten Gracie, but when she puffed out her cheeks and mimicked his exaggerated exhale, he smiled down at her.

The muscles in his shoulders relaxed. The suffocating rage in his chest dissipated.

Sasha was coming back to the States to find him, and she'd told her contact that by the time she was back, he'd have the green light—meaning, he could track and hunt Charles Rue like the animal that he was.

The door opening behind him pulled his attention. Maggie poked her head outside. "You ready to go?" she asked, her eyes searching his face.

"Yeah."

She disappeared inside, only to pop out a minute later with her handbag and the clipboard. When she led the way to the car, Logan followed with Grace.

"What's wrong?"

Logan grunted. He had never been able to hide what he felt from Maggie. Just as she had never been able to hide what she felt from him. "I'll tell you at home. We need to call Jake and Zac."

Nodding, she leaned over to take Grace so that she could strap her in her car seat. When she plopped her on the back seat, waiting for her to climb into her chair, Gracie shimmied to the other side of the car.

"Gracie Laine," Maggie warned, her tone so maternal that it sent a shiver of fear down Logan's spine.

"Da!" Grace said, pointing at him.

"Yeah, Dad is coming too. Get in your chair." When Gracie just shook her head, Maggie looked at him. "Your turn."

Logan stood there for a full five seconds, staring at her over the top of the car.

"Logan?"

"Yeah."

"A little help?"

"Sorry." He leaned back into the car. "Gracie. We're going home to see Spunk."

She eyed him as if she wanted him to know that she knew what he was doing.

"Look." He closed the door and climbed into the driver's seat. "We're going home."

Silently, she crawled back over to the other side of the car and climbed into her car seat, all the while keeping an eye on him—just in case he decided to abandon ship. As soon as she was nestled in, Maggie leaned forward and clipped the buckles into place.

With Gracie strapped inside, she opened the passenger door and slid into the car herself. "Let's go," she said. "Before Houdini decides she'd rather ride freestyle."

Logan snorted, but he felt like he could take on absolutely anything.

He kept quiet because the word still hovered in the air between them. But as sure as he knew he'd heard it, he knew that Maggie had said it deliberately too.

Dad.

Chapter 13

Hudson followed Jacob up to Maggie's house and waited as Jake knocked before pushing open the door without waiting for a reply.

When Spunk came trotting up to them, he leaned down and enveloped her head in his hands, rubbing the top of her skull as he massaged her ears. The dog gave a satisfied groan and wagged her entire rear end in excitement.

"Hey, girl. How are you doing?" he asked, lifting her lip at the side so that he could peak at her gums. *Still pink.*

As if she knew what he was doing, she peeled her lips back, grinning at him, and the smile made him chuckle. It was their little routine, something that the doctor in him couldn't help but do.

But who could blame him? Spunk had been in his older sister's life for thirteen years. Hudson had been seventeen when Maggie had adopted Spunk, which meant that he and the old dog had a whole lot of secrets between them.

He had told Spunk more than he'd told his entire family over the same period of time.

Dates gone wrong.
Dates gone right.
School stress.
Work stress.

When Maggie had first given birth to Gracie, and he had taken Spunk for six months, he had shared every single thought with the dog. Spunk knew it all.

It wasn't that he didn't have a human ear to listen to his woes, because he did. He *chose* to confide in Spunk because, where his siblings would have jumped in and told him—the baby in the family—what to do, or how to fix whatever

164

problem he might be having, Spunk just wagged her tail and looked at him with understanding in her eyes. And, unlike his siblings, who would have called one another the minute they got off the phone with him, Spunk *never* divulged his secrets.

When the front door opened and Zac stepped inside, Hudson grinned from his crouched position. "Hey, man."

"This scene brings, 'Girl's slobbering over you' a whole new meaning," Zac said, laughing as he skirted past.

Hudson nearly replied, nearly let loose the retaliation that his quick mind had processed before Zac was halfway done with his jab. But he didn't.

Two older brothers, two older sisters, and their hordes of older friends had taught him well over the years. And somewhere in the chaos, he had fallen into being the laidback sibling.

He wasn't exactly sure if it was one hundred percent him, but he enjoyed being nonchalant. Enjoyed being the casual jokester, the calm and collected flirt. The one that nothing ever bothered. It was a low-stress approach to life—one that kept his siblings' overzealous attention off him and on bickering with each other instead.

When voices from Maggie's kitchen filtered through, he rose off his haunches and moved through the hallway.

He wasn't supposed to be at the meeting. He hadn't really volunteered because, unlike Jake, Zac, and Logan, he wasn't equipped to protect Maggie or Gracie in any way. He was a doctor, someone who had taken a vow to help and heal—not hurt.

That wasn't to say that he wouldn't take a crowbar to the face of any man who tried to go after his big sister and niece—because he would. But until he had to, he'd let the professionals deal with Charles Rue, and *if* and *when* they needed his help, he'd stitch their wounds pro bono.

"Hudson?" As if proving his train of thought, Maggie frowned at him when he came into the room, surprised that he'd tagged along. Judging by the way that she looked at him, she wasn't happy about it either.

"Maggie," he said, pausing only to shrug at her before making a beeline for where Gracie sat in her donut pillow on the floor.

"His car is in the shop, so Mom and I are giving him rides to and from work this week," Jacob answered, used to filling in Hudson's silences.

Hudson wanted to mention that he'd been perfectly happy to catch an Uber until his car came out of the shop. He was, after all, a grown man. And *a doctor*. But he knew there was no point when it came to his family, so he took the lesson instead: Don't tell Mom when your car breaks down.

Plopping on the floor, he heaved Gracie into his lap and leaned against the kitchen wall as he waited for the meeting to start. His niece, used to being manhandled by everyone, leaned back against his chest and settled in for the show. She occasionally wriggled to grab at her little, pink dress so that she could tug it down in frustration.

Maggie filled water glasses for everyone. She passed Zac a soda without asking because she knew that it may as well have been water for him.

When Logan walked into the room, Hudson saw the way that her spine stiffened, even though she had been facing away from the door, talking to Jake.

Unbeckoned, Hudson's mind shot him a memory of the last time that Logan had left. He remembered it well because he'd been the one to find Maggie after.

They were supposed to go shopping for their mom's birthday. When she hadn't met him outside or answered her phone, he'd gone up to the condo thinking she'd be fussing with her makeup. Instead, he'd found her alone, crumpled on Logan's bathroom floor. Her eyes near-shut from prolonged tears, her engagement ring glinting on the floor.

He'd picked her up and carried her back to the bed, hugged her as she'd cried and told him that Logan had left. Again.

At the time, he would have sworn that it'd be the last time any of them ever saw Logan Cane.

He'd have been wrong.

Sure as summer, Logan had come back and, already, there was a general sense that everyone was holding their breath, watching as Maggie took her inevitable slide closer.

Although he'd never say it, Hudson didn't understand what all the fuss was about. Sure, Logan had some major insecurities, and, sure, his sister had been put through the wringer because of it. But God, if someone looked at him the way that Maggie looked at Logan or the way that Lola looked at Jake, he'd do everything in his power to keep her at his side. He'd go to the moon and back to make it work.

He would know.

He'd had one failed relationship after another. He was always looking for something that wasn't there with women who didn't want the same things. He was only thirty years old and, already, he'd had four live-in girlfriends, women who had loved playing the part as long as it suited their needs.

His brothers called him a pussy, his sisters called him a romantic. It had become such a routine that his mother had made a Christmas stocking with a Velcro name patch. That way she could add his current girlfriend to the Christmas festivities without spending money on a custom stocking— something which the rest of the family found hilarious and that he'd never admit hurt like hell.

It wasn't that he *wanted* to be a bachelor. Zac was the bachelor, the ladies' man. Hudson wanted to find someone who'd stick around despite his work schedule. Someone who'd rough and tough through the hard times with him, through the long nights and all the other shit that life had in store.

"Let's get started," Logan began, his voice pulling everyone's attention towards him.

Hudson watched as everyone settled immediately. Even Jake and Zac, both of whom were leaders in their worlds, fell quiet. Their huge bodies blocked the light that had been filtering in through the small kitchen window just a moment before.

Logan had always had that kind of presence. A heavy, solid mass of confidence that commanded attention.

As he watched, Logan glanced towards Maggie and when she smiled at him, he continued. "My friend with the UN, the one that I tipped off about Boucher, is on the run."

"What?" Hudson watched as Zac raked a hand through his shoulder-length black hair. "Is she okay?"

"She's a tough nut. Sasha is an investigative journalist who enlisted with the UN in CAR to get her stories out of northern Africa while evading suspicion."

"But?" Jake asked.

"The fact that she's on the move when she had UN protection is not a good sign. She's spooked."

"Where is she now?" Maggie asked. "Can we...can we get to her? Help in some way?"

"She's on her way south through the Congo. She has no phone, and if I know Sasha, no way of tracking her whereabouts. She's a pro and if the man I spoke to on the phone was an actual friend of hers, then she should be arriving on US soil within a few days, a week tops."

"Do you think she'll make it?" Zac asked, his blue eyes dark, dangerous.

Hudson didn't have to know what had happened to Zac's girlfriend, Tara, to know that he was personally invested in seeing Sasha Riley safe and back on US soil. The violence in his clenched fists, rigid shoulders, and bunched muscles made it clear enough to everyone.

"If I'd bet on anyone, I'd bet on Sasha Riley. She's...wily." Logan continued, "But we need to prepare for when she's here. We need to come up with our POA for once we have the green light on Boucher." Logan looked at Maggie, held her gaze when he added, "This needs to end."

Jake, oblivious to the magnetic pull between Logan and Maggie said, "As soon as he's listed for extradition with the FBI, I can open an official case, use Department resources to help out considering that we have evidence of him in our jurisdiction. But it sounds like that won't be for another few days." Jake homed in on Zac. "Anything you can do in the meantime?"

"Does a bear shit in the woods?" Zac grinned when Maggie rolled her eyes. "I've been meaning to check-in for the last twenty-four, but I've been…busy."

All eyes focused on Zac.

"So, I've been watching the tracker since we got it from Donny."

"We know this," Logan said, his jaw clenched.

Zac held up a hand. "After the first two days of the Mercedes not moving, I added surveillance to the motel."

"You *did what?*" Jake sputtered.

Zac ignored him. "I thought that Rue must have abandoned the car and moved home base. But he hasn't."

"He's still there?" Logan asked, his brow furrowed with confusion.

"Yup. The motel is within a half-mile of Whole Foods and other than the store and a little gym called Dino's, the guy has barely moved in ten days."

"He's been told to sit tight. It's the only reason he wouldn't have tried something."

"A well-trained dog," Zac seconded Logan's point.

Jake added, "If Boucher got wind of Sasha Riley looking into his operation, he may have told Rue to lay low for a few weeks. It makes sense, especially if Boucher was worried about the UN monitoring his movements."

Logan paced back and forth in the small kitchen, his caged-animal movements crowding the already small space.

As if sensing his angst, Gracie reached her hands up and said, "Da!"

Without flinching, Logan plucked her from Hudson's lap. Maggie didn't bat an eye, but Hudson noticed that Jake's eyebrows raised instantly, and Zac's face broke into a loud, obnoxious grin.

"But the mine operation had been shut down when she arrived." Logan plowed forward, ignoring his friends' reaction. "The last I heard from Sasha, she was trying to track down a few of the miners to interview them."

"She must have succeeded if she said she'd already turned the case to the UN." All eyes turned to Hudson. He fidgeted for a moment, uncomfortable by the attention. Shrugging, he added, "She's a journalist. She wouldn't turn something in without substantial evidence. And she sounds like the type who wouldn't run unless she knew that her evidence would land a very dangerous man in a lot of trouble."

"The kid's right," Zac said.

Hudson took no offense to the casual ribbing. He had known everyone present for nearly twenty years. He had actually been a kid when Zac and Jake had met in the Police Academy. Hell, he couldn't even remember his earliest memory of Logan. He'd always just been there. A neighbor, a friend of his older brothers, then his sister's boyfriend.

"I agree with Hudson's reasoning," Logan ceded. "Especially if she thinks that we'll be allowed to legally trace Boucher by the time she's in the US."

"So?" Zac asked.

"Plan?" Jacob seconded.

Hudson had known Logan Cane for a long time, as long as any of the Simmone's had. Logan had been the one who'd taught him how to talk to girls, how to lay on the moves when he'd barely been thirteen. Hudson knew that Logan would never hurt anyone who didn't deserve it.

But seeing the dangerous glint of excitement in Logan's eye when Jacob and Zac casually mentioned tracking down a trained killer, made him want to get up and run. It sent a chill from the base of his spine to the tips of his ears. And when Logan handed off Gracie to Maggie and rolled his shoulders, his gray eyes focused and lethal, Hudson felt exceptionally glad in that moment.

Glad that he was not Charles Rue.

Chapter 14

By the time that everyone had left, Maggie felt a bone-deep weariness that reached into the depths of her soul. It was a sucking, hollow vacuum that pulled everything she had been trying to balance to the surface of her mind.

Instead of calming her, and making her feel like she had three qualified, loyal men watching her back, the meeting with Logan, Jake, and Zac had left her feeling cold and exposed. And violated.

Charles Rue was a faceless man who, try as she might forget, wanted to hurt Logan. And Gracie. Unease, heavy and ripe, slid into her stomach at the thought, leaving her anxious and…lonely. It was as if she were walking through a room filled with people who she knew intimately, but none of them could see or hear her.

For the first time in her entire life, Maggie felt completely isolated. Even the solid weight of her child sleeping on her shoulder, and the warm whisper of Gracie's breath against her neck couldn't detract from the chill that had settled, like a river stone in her stomach.

"Do you want me to put her down?"

Glancing up at the voice, she saw Logan standing in the doorway. He wore jeans that rode low on narrow hips and a plain, black tee-shirt that pulled slightly over his thick shoulders and biceps. His hair was pulled back in that little bun that she hadn't quite gotten used to seeing on him and his eyes, usually so cold, warmed as he watched her.

Every time that she looked at him, the blood in her body seemed to heat and move faster through her system, forming a consistent thrum, a constant awareness for him that plagued her peace of mind. Her mouth felt bone dry and her stomach took a slip-n-slide down to her feet.

Pushing to a stand, she shifted her weight so that she didn't disrupt Gracie. "No, I've got it."

As she walked through to the nursery, she was aware of the fact that he followed her through. It wasn't the near-silent padding of his footsteps that gave him away, it was the live nerve that ran along her spine. The one that seemed to be reserved solely for alerting her as to when Logan Cane was in proximity.

Stifling it, Maggie leaned over the crib and placed Gracie down on the covers, gently loosening her tiny hand where it had fisted her top before lifting the blanket out from under her and pulling it up to her waist.

The routine, the simple act of covering her child, tucking her in for the night, made her feel centered in some small way.

She knew that he was behind her, watching. But she placed her hand on Gracie's tummy so that she could feel the gentle rise and fall of her daughter's breath when she whispered, "I don't know what to do."

When the first tear fell, she slowly lifted her hand, afraid that she would wake her.

His arms wrapped around her instantly, gently pulling her back against his solid chest.

Slowly, she let herself relax into the embrace, felt her mind and body give in to her own need to touch him, to be touched by him. His breath warmed her neck, even as the rapid pumping of his heart in his chest beat against her back, forcing hers to hurry to catch up.

"I would never let anyone hurt you or Grace," he whispered, his deep voice sending a welcome spike of heat down her spine to her center. "If I thought there was the remotest possibility that I couldn't protect you, I'd have shipped you off somewhere safe already." He sighed. "Maggie…I…"

173

She knew what he wanted to say, knew that there were a million unsaid things between them still. But she couldn't help but think that she didn't want to hear them. Not now, when the electric current of lust in her blood was offering the distraction she so desperately needed.

She knew what she *should* have said:

How long will this go on?

Will we be okay?

What if Charles Rue hurts Gracie?

What if Charles Rue hurts you?

What are we going to do?

What am I going to do?

What am I going to do when this is all over?

What am I going to do if you leave?

What am I going to do if you stay?

All of the questions and more traveled through her head, merging in a thick ball that caught in her throat and carved a path down to her stomach. She couldn't. Couldn't speak the thousands of thoughts that had wracked her brain since he'd come home. She couldn't speak the hundreds of emotions that she felt bottled up inside of her and couldn't ask the dozens of questions that had no answers.

"Maggie...what is it?"

Letting her head fall back on his chest, she placed her hands over the thick, corded muscle of his forearms. "I just..." Struggling with the words, she exhaled one long breath that opened her ribcage, making it possible to breathe again. "There's just...so much to think about."

His arms tensed around her, but he didn't pull back. Instead, he simply said, "I know."

"I don't know what to do, Logan," she repeated. "I...feel so helpless."

"You've done enough." Turning her in his arms, he touched a hand to her face. "You've done everything up to this point, Mags. Let me handle it."

She could see the self-loathing turning his eyes from gray to near-black, and she knew what he was going to say before he whispered, "This is all my fault. Please...just let me fix this. I *need* to fix this."

"I trust you. Implicitly. But...I can't just sit around while that...that *animal* is out there."

The sound of Gracie tossing in her sleep brought her back to the present and, nodding her head, she indicated for Logan to follow. He did, stopping only to flick off the light in Gracie's room and close the door behind them.

The naturalness in which he did it, the ease in which he had fallen into being a father in general did not go unnoticed. Every day, she picked up on some small thing that he had learned and started helping her with.

The first week it had been diapers.

The second week it had been feeding.

The third, convincing Gracie to go to sleep.

Now, he practically did everything that she did, and he had become the perfect complement to her routine. Nearly four weeks since he'd moved in, Logan—who was used to a grueling schedule—had started taking the three o'clock wake-up calls. Twice, Maggie had woken up at six in the morning completely panicked because she'd slept through Gracie's pre-dawn rants, only to find her and Logan sprawled on the sofa, catching up on the sleep lost from their witching-hour socials.

More times than she could count, she had glanced up from her stack of paperwork and design material to find that hours spent elbow-deep in her café plans had passed without her noticing. But it hadn't mattered because Logan had been in some small corner of the house entertaining their daughter. Or napping with her cuddled against his chest.

Things had fallen into such an unusual load share that Maggie wondered what on earth she'd do again when he found a job. Or left. And that thought always pulled her back from the brink before she let herself become submerged in the fantasy.

It was safer to assume that he wasn't going to stay.

For all of their sakes.

He led her through to the lounge, and she sank into her oversized couch next to Spunk, letting her head fall back against the ridiculously large cushion. "It's going to take me a while to get used to sharing," she spoke her thoughts as she looked up at him towering above her.

"Understandable." He sat down too, on the other side of the dog.

Spunk wagged her tail furiously, thrilled by the fact that Logan had effectively sandwiched her between them.

Chuckling, Maggie rubbed the small dip between Spunk's eyes until the dog groaned and shimmied onto her side to expose her belly. Complying with the obvious play, Logan stroked one big palm down the dog's side.

Maggie watched his hand, fascinated by the size of his palm, mesmerized by the play of muscles in his thick forearm. How was it even possible that something as benign as watching the man's hands turned her on?

The obvious answer was that she knew what they were capable of, and that forced a hot blush into her cheeks. *Get up, leave the room, and go back to the two-foot radius rule.*

"Are you okay?"

No. Her mind played back the sleepless nights that she'd had since he'd been back in town. She'd tossed and turned more and eaten less in the sixty-one days that he'd been home.

And if it had been bad before the kiss, her sleep patterns had been shot to hell after she'd thrown herself at him after the wine bar. Instead of falling instantly asleep, exhausted from her day, she'd found herself lying awake, staring at the ceiling as she remembered what it had felt like to have Logan's lips on hers, his hands moving over the length of her body.

He cleared his throat and she jumped a little. Shifting slightly, Maggie tried to dispel the weighted need in her belly, a heavy bunch of swollen nerves that had been collecting for months. One that not even her vibrator had been able to relieve.

"Maggie?" He reached up a hand to touch her cheek.

She let her face rest against the calloused skin of his palm for a minute, sighed when he rubbed his thumb gently over her cheekbone. The sound, a half sigh, half groan, came out a quiet mewl. *What was that? Oh, God!*

Embarrassed, she hazarded a glance up at him, noticed that his eyes had darkened. Her breath caught in her throat. Goosebumps rose on her arms.

It's time. Surprisingly, the thought settled that tremor of anxiety that had been in her system…it calmed her. As much as she'd thought she'd be able to brave the storm, she'd known that she'd eventually give in to her own need for him. That she *wanted* to give in for her need for him.

They sat there, frozen.

Neither one of them said anything for a full thirty seconds.

Maggie was the first to move. She stood and walked towards the door.

When she came to the doorway, he hadn't moved to follow, and she looked back at him. He sat on the couch, his hands gripping above his knees as if he was afraid of what they'd do if they weren't glued there. His jaw was clenched. Near-black eyes looked back at her.

"You coming?"

He paled, raised one hand, and ran it over his head before looking back at her. "Only if it's what you want."

"You know I wouldn't have asked if it wasn't what I wanted."

He nodded once. Pushing to his feet, he came to stand in front of her, his eyes never leaving hers.

Her breath caught in her throat as predatory need radiated off him and ran along her skin, pulling all her nerves to attention. But she reached out a hand and touched his chest, encouraged by the tremor that rippled through him at the contact.

He looked like he was about to change his mind, or worse, run in the other direction, so she stood on the tips of her toes and brushed her lips over his. At the small contact, the bundled nerves in her stomach seemed to unfurl at once, releasing snaps of pleasure that traveled through her entire system and back again before collecting between her thighs.

When he didn't reciprocate, she cocked her head to the side, confused. "Your turn."

He didn't need any further prompting. With a rough groan that sounded more like a growl, he gripped her hips and pulled her up against him. His mouth met hers in a hungry kiss that stole the breath from her lungs.

His tongue melded with hers, forcing all coherent thought away and replacing it with need. The need to touch, grope, squeeze, kiss, lick, and nip.

Breaking the kiss, she panted slightly and angled her body so that it rubbed against the hard length of him. She swayed the tiniest bit, moving from side to side, slowly increasing the friction between them.

When his hands tightened at her hips and he let his head fall back, she felt a lick of power travel through her. Riding it, she lifted the bottom of his shirt, only pausing when it reached his armpits so that he could raise his arms, allowing her to remove it fully.

Standing in front of her, stripped to the waist, he looked like something that Michelangelo would have carved out of stone for the Medici. Although she had seen him this way hundreds of times, her eyes traced the contours of his chest, followed the taper of his waist over defined abdominals, down to the thick bulge of him under the fabric of his jeans.

Her body pulled tight, coiling towards her core and collecting in that same central ball. The physical symptoms of being without anyone, without *him*, for so long felt almost painful. Her hands shook ever so slightly, so she clenched them into loose fists in the hope that he wouldn't notice. Her breath glued to the back of her throat, making it hard to breathe. The little white thong that she had thrown on earlier—with no intention of this happening—was already soaked.

He didn't say anything, but he had read the emotions of her face because he was smiling. Just one corner of his mouth slightly upturned in the same half-cocked grin he'd had since they'd been children.

Needing to feel him, skin-to-skin, she reached for the buttons of her shirt, but his hand snaked out, gently stopping her. "I want to."

She stared at him, her body aware of the way that his gaze traveled the length of her before coming back to her face. She dropped her hands to her sides.

When he reached forward, she tensed in anticipation, waiting for him to start on the small buttons. She would have given anything in that moment to feel the cool air against her skin as he ripped her shirt to pieces with his bare hands.

Instead, still without touching her, he placed his palms flat against the nearby wall, hands on either side of her head, caging her in.

Maggie's heart gave one solid thump in her chest before falling into a rapid patter that ticked against her ribs.

Leaning forward, he brought his face close to hers then slowly, so slowly that her body ached for more, he trailed small, light kisses from the sensitive skin at the bottom of her ear, down her throat, ending at her collarbone. When she shivered, he followed the same path on the other side.

She closed her eyes as she wallowed in the torturous sensation of his lips on her skin. The thought that he hadn't even used his hands yet sent a jolt of pure, pagan lust to her core, forcing a quiet moan from her lips.

Logan froze. "Maggie," he whispered, his voice hoarse, raw. "I've missed you every hour we've been apart."

Afraid that he would bring up everything that she was trying so hard to forget, she reached up and slapped her hand over his mouth, "Please. Don't. Not now."

His eyes clouded, but he nodded and nipped her fingers playfully. When she removed her hand, he bent down and picked her up.

She yelped, surprised by the sudden tilt of the earth, then grinned when he moved towards her bedroom.

He placed her on the bed, but this time he didn't turn away.

Maggie shimmied up onto her elbows so that she could watch him.

He didn't move at first, just looked down at her with such intensity that she felt her skin prickle. Then, he lowered himself down beside her.

The bare skin of his chest, only inches from her, radiated heat. His leather and pine scent wrapped around her senses, making her feel lightheaded. He trailed a single hand down her fully-clothed body in one smooth stroke. Maggie wished that the movement had shed her clothes like snakeskin.

With one hand, he started on the tiny buttons of her blouse, nimbly unfastening them despite his huge hands. *Oh, thank God!*

By the time that he had opened the top half of her shirt, he had added small nips and kisses, his mouth following the trail of exposed skin. When he finally unfastened the last button, her breath was coming in small, frantic pants and her entire body vibrated.

Impatient, she rose to sitting and pulled the blouse off. She hesitated at the button of her jeans, but when she glanced up and saw the wolfish gleam of humor in his eyes, she unfastened them and peeled them off before kicking them to the side, leaving herself naked to his gaze but for her underwear.

His smile faltered, just for a moment.

In one fluid movement, she straddled him, forcing him to lie flat on his back as she aligned her hot, heavy center with the shape of him. She kissed him, took his mouth in a frenzy as her hands fisted in his hair, pulling it loose.

She ground her pelvis slowly over him as she took his mouth again. The friction of his denim-clad erection against her pulling her nipples tight. He groaned, breaking the kiss as his hands moved to grip her hips so that he could hold her still.

"You're going to kill me"

"Fair's fair."

He sat up, forcing her upright so that they were heart to heart, center to center, her knees folded under her. "I've been a dying man without you, Maggie. I…I don't know who I am when you're not with me." Reaching one arm behind her, he unclasped her bra and threw it aside.

Maggie's arm rose instinctively to cover herself.

Usually, she wouldn't have been self-conscious with him. He had seen her naked more times than she could count, seen her naked at seventeen and at forty. But he hadn't seen how carrying a child, how breastfeeding, had changed her. He frowned at her, so she whispered, "You haven't seen me…in a long time."

His eyes softened, warmed. "You're the most beautiful woman in the world, Maggie. You always have been." He shrugged. "You always will be to me." He looked as if he wanted to say something more, but then the moment was gone and he pried her arms away, exposing her to his hungry gaze.

Moving his hands down to cup her ass, he shifted her forward a little, and taking her left nipple into his mouth, gently used his lips, tongue, and the slightest graze of teeth on her until the pleasure became unbearably intense. When he switched sides for a repeat performance, Maggie threw back her head. Gripping his shoulders as sensation after sensation shredded her tightly-strung body.

She could feel the orgasm building, and, *needing* him, she pried his grip off her curves. She brought his right hand back to the front of her body. Lifting her hips, she raised herself off his lap, then guided his hand to her so he could feel how aroused, how wet, how ready she was for him.

"Fuuuuuck," he said on a long exhale, his fingers sliding over her.

"I want you, Logan. Please," she bit back the desperation in her tone and added, "I'm ready."

"I want you to come for me first, baby."

Shifting her lace thong to the side, he began a torturously slow exploration of her, only one finger rubbing soft circles over her clit. The feeling of him touching her was enough to derail her.

"Do you know how many times I've woken up hard after dreaming of finding you wet like this? For me?" His voice was rough. "Most days I would tell myself that it was an illusion, that I'd built up this fantasy of you in my head that wasn't real."

"Maybe you did," she whispered before she ground her hips, rubbing herself against his fingers. "But this...this is real."

"It is," he replied before removing his hand and tipping her off his lap so that she lay on her back.

She had been turned on moments before, in need. But, this time, when his fingers found her, her body drew in on itself, rising, pulling, striving for release.

She arched her back, pressing herself into his hand and he dipped his head, gently drawing her nipple into his mouth.

The feeling of him, of his fingers sliding over her clit and his tongue circling her nipple, battered her with sensation. Feeling as if she might shatter into a million pieces, she gripped his shoulders again, used her short nails to anchor herself to him, to earth.

As aware of her needs as she was herself, Logan gently spread her with his hand. Then, using his thumb on her clit, dipped his index finger inside of her, gently curling it forward slightly each time.

Maggie shifted her hips, forcing him further inside of her, and whimpered his name between moans. When he felt her body tighten he quickened the pace. "Logan…"

"I know, baby." On the last word, he bent his head and drew her nipple back into his mouth.

Maggie's world exploded, and she cried out, arching her back as the orgasm decimated her body, tearing through her mercilessly.

Her body pulsed around his finger, and she let her head fall back. She closed her eyes to the residual sensations traveling from her core, outwards to her head and feet. In that moment, she let it all go, let her body take over, and gave herself completely to the feeling of being with Logan again. Finally.

Her breath was labored. Her body relaxed. But her mind was clear when she met Logan's eyes and smiled shakily as her trembling calmed again.

Reaching out her hand, she palmed him through his jeans. "Are you going to take these off?"

He pushed to his feet so that he could pull off his jeans and boxers. Maggie watched as he stripped, swallowed with a dry throat when he came to stand naked in front of her.

She'd seen him hundreds of times. More. But that didn't stop the pure female purr that rose in her throat. Or the steady pulsing of her body begging him to fill her, begging him to bring her back to the brink of ecstasy.

He climbed back onto the bed so that their bodies were aligned, the steel length of him pressing into her hip as he pressed a gentle kiss to the side of her mouth. He shook his head, his gray eyes stormy. "I love you, Maggie. Only you. Since before I understood what it even meant."

I love you too. The words spilled into her mind unhindered, but when she opened her mouth to say them, they clogged her throat, refusing to come out.

"It's okay." He touched her face, his thumb brushing the spot he'd just kissed. "I know."

She nodded, aware of the tears that had gathered in the corners of her eyes.

He kissed her, chased away the demons with his tongue and lips. Maggie returned the kiss, pouring everything that she couldn't say aloud into the moment. Because although she couldn't say it, she wanted him to know. She wanted him to know that she could be angry and confused but still only ever want to be with him, love *him*.

The press of him, hard against her leg, sharpened the hollow need clawing back into her stomach, center, and thighs. Sensing that he was giving her time, she reached between them, gave him one long, firm stroke from root to tip.

He bit off the kiss, groaning as he closed his eyes and let his head fall onto her chest.

He didn't move, didn't dare move as he clenched his jaw and quietened his mind so that he could focus on not coming in her hand. Since Maggie had looked over her shoulder and invited him into her bed, he had been rock hard, and now, only fifteen minutes later, the smallest touch from her was like water to a stovetop.

"Are you okay?" she asked, her voice wavering.

He wanted to say, 'Hell yes', but even he knew that the response probably wasn't what she had been looking for. So, he told her the truth. "It's...been a while for me too."

"Oh." The surprised tone of her voice wasn't enough to hide the cat-ate-the-canary look in her eyes, but she moved her hand away. She tilted her head and looked at him, her blue eyes big and round with awareness. "How long is 'a while'?"

Exhaling on a long breath, he moved over her, brushed his lips against hers as he reached down and spread her legs wide with a single hand. Touching the head of his penis to her slick warmth, he answered, "Two years," then slid inside of her with one smooth movement that took him to the hilt.

She gasped, and he wondered briefly if it was because she was surprised by his celibacy or because they fit as perfectly as they always had. She bucked her hips once and started moving under him, and everything—his pain, his fears, his need for her forgiveness—was swallowed with the need to consume her.

Her body was liquid in his hands, pliant and soft. Every time that he touched her, ran his calloused palms over smooth skin, she shuddered, sending a ripple of pleasure through his own body.

Her small, rosy nipples were peaked and when he took one in her mouth in that way he knew she loved, she moaned and raked her nails down his back. Logan buried himself in her. He breathed in her flowery scent as he thrust, each movement long and slow so that he could prolong the feeling of her squeezing tight around him.

His entire body was begging him to let go, to bury himself, and just give in. But he knew that he couldn't.

Pulling out of her briefly, he knelt on the bed between her legs before gently stringing her legs over his thighs so that Maggie was on her back, her legs draped over him, their centers touching.

When she raised her hips in welcome, he slipped inside of her again, gripped her tightly, and gave in to the animal need that had been eating away at his resolve since the first time that he'd seen her again. *Longer.*

With every thrust, her body coiled more tightly around him, and when she moaned the sound traveled straight to his dick. Biting back a dozen curses that he wanted to loose, he lifted his hand instead and ran his thumb gently over her clit.

Knowing that he couldn't hold on much longer, he looked down at her again. Maggie was beneath him again, her hands gripping the sheets, her eyes half-closed, her breasts moving in time with his thrusts, begging him to touch, to taste. He branded the image of her into his brain.

Every cell in his body screamed, 'Mine!', and when she shut her eyes, welcoming the second orgasm, he said, "Look at me, Maggie."

She opened them, stared at him as he matched the desperate speed that she had set. When she arched her back off the bed, raising her hands to grip his biceps, he swore, and, tightening his grip on her hips, held her while she rode out the second orgasm.

The feeling of her warm, wet body tightening, pulsing around him, nearly drove him over. But he steeled himself and waited until she finally loosened around him, then pulled out of her and let himself go before collapsing on the bed beside her.

Chapter 15

Maggie opened her eyes slowly, blinking against the bright light that filtered into her bedroom window. As her mind woke up and began processing, memories of the night before had her raising a hand to cover her face.

The sheets were cold beside her, so she let the groan that she felt bottled up in her chest loose in one long, slow whoosh.

She'd done it.

She'd caved and slept with Logan and now everything was ruined. Again.

Before last night, she'd been able to keep up the ruse of having moved on, of being able to live without him. But now that he'd touched her…everything came flooding back.

Just like it always did.

Tears welled in her eyes, and she blinked furiously to try and clear them as she stared up at her white ceiling. *Why? Why do you do this to yourself every. Single. Time?*

The answer was simple. It had always been simple. She loved Logan Cane and the thought of being with anyone else…Well, she *didn't* think of being with anyone else. Ever. Even though she'd been asked out by other men in the past, she'd only ever thought of them briefly—and usually regarding how she could reject them without hurting their feelings.

She pushed into a seated position, letting the white linen comforter fall to her waist. *I slept with Logan.*

Panic came alive in her chest, spreading fast, and she closed her eyes against the wave of anxiety it brought with it.

"There's Mommy!" His voice, coming from the doorway had her eyes snapping open.

Maggie hadn't even heard them, but when she looked up and saw him standing there, Gracie perched on one huge arm, her pink pajamas bright against his grey shirt, she forced a shaky smile.

She hadn't been looking for comfort and she didn't believe in signs. But at that moment, with him standing there, holding their daughter, with cautious longing in his eyes, she felt the first shimmer of hope replace her fear.

It flowered in her heart, smothering the panic that had been there only moments before. And with the flowering hope came the realization that she would do it. She would love him, only him, always. And she could live her life waiting for him to come home to her—because pretending otherwise was a waste of her time.

She'd wait for him for Gracie's sake. And for hers. And if he needed to go again, she'd do her best to remind their daughter that he loved them every way he knew how.

When Gracie reached out her arms and said, "Mama," Maggie smiled and held out her own.

Logan walked in and deposited their daughter in her lap.

With the solid weight of Gracie sitting on her, acting as a barrier, she found the courage to glance back up at him. He stood off to the side of the bed, but he didn't move closer.

Strangely, as they looked at each other, her mind kept going back to the night before when he'd told her that he hadn't been with anyone else while he'd been away.

He was watching her, searching her face for some sign of how she felt about what had happened the night before. He was waiting, giving her space to process.

So she patted her hand on the bed next to her.

He looked startled for a small moment, then exhaled on a short breath. Lowering himself onto the bed, he stretched out his huge body so that he lay next to them. After a moment, he said, "She slept through to six this morning."

"What?" Maggie rubbed a hand over Gracie's full head of soft curls, chuckled when Gracie nodded as if she were interested in their conversation.

"Yeah. I nearly had a heart attack when I woke up and she hadn't made a sound. But she was still sleeping when I walked through. Only woke up when I was about to leave the room."

When Grace looked up at her, gray eyes wide and round with curiosity, Maggie said, "Wow!" Smoothing down Gracie's pale eyebrows with her fingers, she asked her, "Did you sleep all night?"

Gracie nodded solemnly, drawing a deep chuckle from Logan. The combination spiked Maggie's estrogen by a thousand, and she welcomed the shiver of pure female ecstasy that traveled over her skin from the tips of her ears to her toes.

When Logan reached an arm behind her, pulling her close, Maggie acquiesced. Nestled under his arm, with Gracie on her lap, she felt like nothing could ruin the moment. "She has never slept through the night before," she said, letting her head fall back on Logan's shoulder.

"*What?* Like ever?"

She shook her head. "Not once. The latest we've ever gone before today was four in the morning."

"Shoot, that's a lot of sleepless nights. Huh, baby?"

Hearing his voice, Gracie smiled and said, "Da," before vacating Maggie's lap so that she could crawl the space, over to Logan.

He didn't hesitate, took her in his arms as naturally as if he had been doing it the entire time, not just the last weeks. "What?" he asked, noticing her raised eyebrows.

Shaking her head, she laughed. "So easily replaced."

His eyes clouded, his eyebrows drawing together. "Maggie, I...I didn't mea-"

Placing a hand on his arm, she smiled. "I'm kidding." When a flicker of relief passed over his features, she added, "I'll never begrudge you having a relationship with her."

"I...I appreciate that, Mags. More than you'll ever know."

"I was thinking about it this morning," she said.

"About me? And Gracie?"

She nodded, taking the time to frame her thoughts. "I think I'm done. I can't do it anymore." Turning to him, she saw the blood drain from his face, leaving him pale. "I can't live my life pretending that I'm ever going to move on, so...I'm not going to."

"Maggie..." He looked confused. "What are you saying?"

"I want to be with you. Only you." She shrugged. "Always."

"Christ, do you think you could have lead with that?" Laughing, he pulled her closer, crushed his mouth to hers. "I thought you were asking me to leave again."

"No."

"I promise that I'm going to work every day to make it up to you." His eyes tracked to Gracie. "To both of you."

"Just be here when you can, Logan. It'll be enough. It has to be."

He opened his mouth as if he wanted to say more, but then he paused and closed it without a word.

When she met his eyes, eyes that were happy and sad at the same time, she felt her stomach knot, felt her mouth water as blood pooled in her cheeks.

Memories from the night before, of his hands and mouth on her, brought a welcome flush of awareness. Logan leaned over and brushed his lips against her temple. To Maggie, it seemed as if the world sparkled just a little.

"Ma!" Gracie interrupted the moment.

Logan drew back with a deep chuckle. "I, ah, guess that's our cue."

Maggie pushed back the covers and stood. "You hungry, baby?" she asked Gracie. "I could eat a horse myself." And it was true. She was *hungry*.

Moving forward, she grabbed her pajama bottoms so that she could slip them over the boy-cut underwear that she'd put on with her tank top the night before. "You know...I'm *genuinely* ravenous. Maybe I'll make a full American breakfast? Or pancakes?"

Turning around to face them, she paused. Logan's eyes studied her body with dark, greedy need. Swallowing the lump that had formed in her throat, and conscious of her daughter in the room, she leaned over so that she could pull her pajama pants on.

"Pancakes sound...really good," he said, his voice hoarse.

As if sensing that something was happening, or maybe that both of their attention had wavered from her, Gracie tapped her hands on Logan's cheeks, bringing his attention back to her.

"What?" he asked, exaggeratedly furrowing his brow.

Gracie giggled. "Da da da."

Maggie watched as Logan grinned, and her heart stuttered a little in her chest, pulling her ribcage tight. Because she needed the distraction, she slipped her feet into her slippers and said, "Alright, you two. Breakfast time."

Chapter 16

Sasha Riley cast a quick glance up and down the pretty residential street before crossing the quiet road towards the neat white house.

Her nerves were raw, her stomach queasy from weeks of too much coffee, too little sleep, and a whole horde of fear. Even now, back on US soil, she couldn't quite shake the feeling that she was being watched.

She'd arrived home from CAR three days earlier, and, still, every strange man that looked at her on the street forced her muscles to tighten in case she had to run. Every car that drove by made her spine pull tight and her eyes track nervously. Every shadow that danced on the streets of LA held the possibility of someone lurking there, waiting for her.

She was a mess.

She approached the small house. Her steps were quiet as her eyes scanned the neighborhood, taking in the details. Small custom homes lined either side of the street, only ten or twelve feet separating each house from the next. Front yards, picketed with knee-high fences, boasted small irrigated lawns of verdant green while the few weeds sprouting from the cracks in the pavement struggled with the arid Los Angeles' climate.

Logan had left her with no way to contact him once she left CAR. She had called Tippenham Dunn once she'd arrived back in New York and, after some sweet talking— and one promise for a return favor—she'd managed to convince one Ralph Bowman into rifling through Logan's employment file.

His address had turned up an empty condo in downtown LA. But his listed next of kin and emergency contact had returned one Margaret Mae Simmone, and Sasha knew that if he could be found anywhere asides from his condo, he would be at Maggie's.

Logan had told her about Maggie one drunken night in CAR when she'd tried to lay the moves on him, and he'd very sweetly turned her down.

It had been disappointing. And, not because she'd anticipated anything more than a quick roll in the hay.

Logan wasn't her type in general. He was too 'lethal mercenary' for her taste, which tended to run more towards starving artists with distasteful tattoos and meta insight into their own attitude problems. Hell, the only reason that she'd made a move was because he had been a good friend. He had been around during one of the loneliest assignments of her life.

And he has a great ass. She would not lie and say that Logan's looks hadn't played a part in her poor attempt at seduction. Because they had, and she was woman enough to admit that Cane being a total dish had made the decision to try and sleep with him that much easier.

It had been disappointing because while she'd been aiming for a night or two of no-strings-attached, sweaty sex, and an outlet for the loneliness of CAR, he'd somehow managed to trick her into breaking down and having a heart-to-heart about why they were so messed up.

The end result of their drunken confessional had not been five-star orgasms, it had been sniffles—at least on her end—and the promise that if and when they made it home, they'd do their best to not be fuck-ups.

As she came up to the door and she raised her hand to knock, she wondered how Logan was doing with his attempt at non-fucked-uppery. She knew how she was doing—not so good.

She was just about to issue a swift tap when the door swung inwards, revealing none other than Logan Cane himself. Grinning at the shocked expression on his face, she turned her eyes to the gorgeous baby on his hip, then to the old mutt frolicking on the end of her leash. "This a bad time, Cane?"

"Sasha!" With a shocked laugh that somehow managed to settle her stomach, he pulled her into a one-armed hug. "I'm so glad to see you."

Casting a look down the street, he receded into the house, nodding for her to follow. "We were really worried about you," he said as he walked down a short hallway.

The dog walked at his side, glancing back at her with intelligent, almost accusatory, eyes.

Sasha followed, her years of working as a journalist being put to good use as she took in the small, but cozy house.

Tastefully framed photographs lined the white hallway walls. They were all filled with a swarm of very attractive people that grinned openly back at her. She assumed that they were Maggie Simmone's family. Correction, her *big* family.

Stopping by a single photo that caught her eye, she slapped a hand to her mouth. "Holy shit. Dude, is this you?"

Logan frowned and backtracked to where she was standing in the hallway. He leaned forward to glance at the photo. His face instantly changed when he realized that the picture was, in fact, of him. "Huh. I never realized she had put this up."

The photo was of a young Logan, his hair cropped short, military-style. His back was ramrod straight, his big arms caging who could only be Maggie Simmone as she stood in front of him. Her gorgeous long, brown hair flowing down either side of a shimmering, lake-blue dress.

He hadn't changed. Sure he'd grown into a man, gotten bigger and, if at all possible, better looking. But he was still the same boy with the lopsided, shit-eating grin.

Seeing the picture of Maggie instantly made her feel better about being rejected by Logan. Maggie Simmone was…gorgeous, with a long, willowy frame and big, blue eyes set perfectly above a wide mouth with full lips.

Sasha couldn't hold the nub of a candle to her, with her pitch-black, monotone hair, black eyes, and five-two body that looked built for a live-action reenactment of an anime. Sasha worked what she had—short legs, wide hips, a generous ass, itsy waist, and boobs that had earned her a plethora of unnecessary nicknames in high school.

…Okay, well, she'd earned *some* of the nicknames in high school.

"It was Maggie's prom. I actually got leave to come home for that."

He didn't offer more, just turned and walked through to the kitchen where the clatter of utensils could be heard, accompanied by a heavenly smell that made her mouth water.

Sasha followed closely. She noticed that the baby had craned her neck so that she could follow her movements around Logan's arm.

Not really one for children, she waved. The little girl grinned and waved a small, chubby arm back at her. Her big, Logan-gray eyes wide with humor. *Grace.*

She'd been with Logan when he'd found out that he had a kid. She remembered the dazed look that had frozen his face once he'd hung up the phone. Remembered the glimmer of excitement that had followed, then the earth-shattering fear that had finalized his decision to come back to California.

She remembered the day well because it was the last night that she had slept without a gun underneath her pillow. That day, Logan had dropped his bomb about

Francis Boucher, and then left to come back home and meet his daughter. It had been the last day that she could remember not being shit scared of everything. Of everyone.

And Sasha did not like being scared on principal. She was a five-two woman who had hopped from unstable country to unstable country, trying to worm newsworthy stories out of uncompliant—usually male—interviewees for the better part of a decade.

She had faced a lot of scary shit, and her tough exterior—although a purposefully constructed façade—had been carefully designed to exude that. Her black belt in jiu-jitsu helped her peace of mind too.

Or had.

She'd been looking over her shoulder, praying that a stray bullet wouldn't clip her ever since she'd had a run-in with Francis Boucher's goons. The assholes had followed her from the UN's home base after she'd handed in her report for the Human Rights Office of the Commissioner.

Serves you right for sending Boucher a copy, her conscience reminded her.

She still couldn't believe that she'd been so stupid. But it was, after all, her signature move, the story of her life. Just one shitty decision after another because her pride couldn't take being seconded. In anything. And…in Boucher's defense, it had been a *very* detailed report. One that had highlighted everything that he'd been doing in his uranium mine, which, coincidentally, had not entailed only mining.

Her skin prickled as she remembered the things that Boucher's men had taunted her with as they'd chased her down the narrow, dusty streets in Bangui. The sound of their feet beating against the broken tar still chased her in her dreams. They might have been speaking in French, but, unfortunately for her, she was fluent. And being hogtied while they took turns raping her did not make the list of top ten things she wanted to do in her free time.

"Maggie, this is Sasha."

Logan's introduction pulled her from her thoughts. She pasted a megawatt smile on her face to hide the fact that her heart was thumping in her chest, squeezing her air supply so that her breath wanted to come out in small, desperate pants.

Instead, she steeled herself and took a long, silent inhale before looking up to meet Maggie Simmone's eyes. The same big, blue eyes from the photograph smiled kindly back at her. Although they were slightly wide with surprise, she already knew by the calm, accepting look on her face that Maggie Simmone would not turn anyone away if they needed help.

Neither would Logan.

Because her legs started shaking underneath her, she took a step forward and, reaching out a hand, said, "It's so nice to finally meet you, Maggie."

Sasha blinked, surprised when Maggie stepped forward and enfolded her in a hug. "We've really worried about you. The whole family has been waiting for you to arrive."

"You have?" she asked, returning the hug despite her general rules for maintaining reasonable personal space.

Maggie chuckled and took a step back. "Are you hungry?"

"Always."

"Good. We were just making pancakes. Logan, can you go and call the family, tell them to meet at Mom and Dad's at noon?"

When Logan smiled at her and then turned to go and do as he was told, his daughter still perched on his arm, Sasha very nearly started laughing.

In CAR, Logan had been the deadly, silent type. He was the man who usually sat alone in a corner so that he could observe the world around him uninterrupted. But seeing him now, a baby on his hip, a smile on his face, and infatuation in his eyes was...nice, refreshing in a way that her cynical mind hadn't expected.

"Are you sure that you want to involve your family?" she asked, watching as Maggie went about with her pancake making.

Maggie laughed. "Ah, the family don't really understand the concept of personal space." Looking over her shoulder, she added, "You'll see this afternoon."

"But *why*?"

Maggie poured pancake batter into the pan, her back rigid, on guard, and Sasha felt her skin ripple with that same unease. "He's here, isn't he?" When Maggie turned to appraise her, she added, "Charles Rue? He wasn't in CAR when I started making inquiries. People I spoke to thought he'd skipped town."

When Maggie nodded, her shoulders sagged a little, and she offered a watery smile. "He is. Uh, Logan, my brother, and a family friend are going to track him as soon as the extradition order moves forward."

Sasha felt the world slow as her blood pummeled through her ears. Her hands were shaking. She gripped her thighs, digging her nails in until they bit her skin through her jeans.

"Don't worry," Maggie said. "I mean it's one guy against Logan, an LAPD Lieutenant, and an ex-cop turned PI. Oh, and said ex-cop has pulled in the criminal underground to help monitor Charles' movements too."

"What?" Sasha asked, confused.

"It's going to be a lot to take in," Maggie said, not offering more. "Why don't we just have pancakes now, and then when we meet with the family, you can get the full story and catch us up on your side of things?"

Sasha nodded. She was about as confused by the current situation as she'd ever been about anything.

If Rue was in town, why was Maggie so calm? The man was insane. He wasn't just a trained killer, he was…a sociopath. A sociopath who had a major hard-on for trying to one-up Logan Cane.

Sensing that there was no point in bringing it up again before the family meeting, Sasha raked a hand through her hair, sighing. "Ah, can I help with anything?" she asked,.

"Actually, could you take over here while I clear my crap off the table?" Maggie held out a fancy utensil that looked like a spatula.

Sasha eyed it. "Can I clean the crap off the table? Cooking isn't really my forte. At all. Unless you're boiling eggs. I can boil a mean egg."

Maggie laughed. "Sure." Casting a quick look over her shoulder, she said, "Just dump it on the sofa in the lounge for now. I have to clean it up later anyway."

As she cleared away the paperwork from Maggie's table, Sasha's thoughts turned to the Simmone clan. She knew that Logan was competent, but she sure as hell hoped that the other two men that Maggie had mentioned were too. Because if she knew one thing for certain from her interviews with the miners from Boucher's operation, it was that Charles Rue would welcome the challenge.

She'd met him several times before, had known that he was dangerous because Logan had told her to stay away from Rue. Actually, now that she thought about it, that's how she and Logan had met. They'd been with mutual friends at The Watering Hole, a bootleg bar operation informally run by some ex-pats in CAR.

Rue had tried to hit on her. Mostly, she remembered being unimpressed by his rude stare and cockerel-puffed chest, but before Logan had leaned over and told her to keep her distance, she'd been considering the pros and cons of taking Rue home.

Still, until she'd interviewed the miners, she wouldn't have thought it possible that Charles had done the things that they'd told her about.

Sasha had encountered a lot of scary shit in her time as a correspondent. But Boucher and Rue might just take the cake as the worst she'd ever had the displeasure of encountering.

"We're all set for noon," Logan said, coming back through to the kitchen.

"Thanks." Maggie flipped the pancake in the pan, then glanced over her shoulder at Logan and Gracie.

Sasha saw the moment that Maggie's eyes softened, and watched as Logan, sensing Maggie's gaze, shifted and met her eyes. A moment passed between them. It was just a shared look, but Sasha felt her cheeks warm at having witnessed the intimacy between them.

Embarrassed, she hefted an armful of Maggie's scrapbooks and papers off the kitchen table and made for the lounge without saying anything.

Strange, that she could know so much about a man, a *friend*, but never suspect that he was capable of something as simple as an emotional connection with another human.

It was weird.

And, it made her sad. When they'd been in CAR, she and Logan had been two of a kind. They'd been the tough, war-hardened foreigners who people knew not to screw with. She'd felt a kinship with him.

But she'd just realized that they weren't in CAR anymore, and while she'd brought all her baggage back with her and carted it around like a noose around her neck, Logan didn't. He had mastered that separation that allowed him to be a merc in CAR and a dad, a lover, a friend back home.

She envied him that.

Chapter 17

Phil and June Simmone's backyard was like something out of *That 70's Show* or *The Brady Bunch*. Thick, green grass sprawled over the quarter acre, which in Los Angeles may as well have been a ranch. An array of colorful lawn chairs dotted the grass. The lack of order suggested that family gatherings like this one were common enough that June had given up reorganizing her garden furniture once everyone had left.

But still, the chairs, combined with the big, sprawling table at the front of the yard and the barbeque at the side gave the garden a family feel. A feel that was accentuated by the jokes, laughter, and smiles of everyone present.

Sasha was knee-deep in a conversation with Lola, Maggie Simmone's soon-to-be sister-in-law. Someone she generally wouldn't have thought to get along with if she'd seen her walking on the street.

Lola's thin frame, sculpted cheekbones, and sharp chin were all accentuated by doe eyes that expressed exactly what she was feeling at every moment. Sasha could have imagined Lola being the artsy, popular girl in high school. The one who everyone liked but still got to be homecoming queen— as long as she wasn't in the same class as Maggie.

Then again, the Simmone's back yard seemed to be covered with beautiful, grounded people. Jacob, Maggie's brother, and Lola's fiancé, could have stepped off the cover of a sport's mag. His friend, Zac, the one that Maggie had referred to as an 'ex-cop,' could have stripped paint just by walking into the room.

Which was strange because he wasn't good-looking in the same way that the Simmone's were. Zac was...devilish.

He had black, scruffy hair and piercing blue eyes. A crooked nose that had been broken more than once, and a brawler's build—lean and rangy. But it was the way he walked and talked, the way his eyes seemed to promise that you'd have a good time if you trusted him, that made him so goddamn sexy.

Sasha planned on staying far away from him.

Even Phil and June, who must have been pushing seventy, looked like a slice of fresh-baked America, hot out the oven.

And they all *liked* each other. It was like they weren't even scared of the fact that a psychopath was after Logan.

Sasha felt a little unsettled by it.

Having been raised the single daughter of a grease monkey who couldn't talk to her about her period or sex, was probably why she felt awkward in big, social gatherings. Her childhood had been more of the, 'Pass me that wrench,' or 'You fine with pizza?' type of shindig.

And she'd loved every minute of it.

No hovering parents.

No anxious mother waiting for her to come home from a night out.

No salads.

"Where's your brother?" Phil Simmone's big, booming voice carried across the yard to her. She glanced up from her conversation with Lola and Maggie to watch him interact with Jacob.

Her only thought was, *There's* another *one?*

"How many siblings do you have?" she asked Maggie, who was sitting down next to Lola.

"Four." She leaned back in her chair. "Although Lyle and his wife live in New York and Emma is in Europe right now. She's coming home next month."

"Hudson, the baby," Lola picked up where Maggie had left off, "is a doctor so his schedule is wonky. But, he'll make it. He always does for the family stuff."

Hudson. She liked the name, liked how it sounded in her head, the strong *s* making it sound almost like a whisper.

"It's a lot to take in," Lola said, smiling at her. "I'm an only child so this," she swept her arm over the yard, "is still new to me."

"But you wouldn't change anything." Jacob, having heard their conversation, grinned down at her as he approached, his emerald green eyes only for Lola.

"Not a single thing," Lola laughed, meeting his eyes with an equally adoring gaze.

For the second time since knocking on Maggie's door, Sasha felt a long, slow pang of envy grip her stomach and spread. It wasn't malicious.

It *was* startling though.

She had never been the one to lament the fact that she hadn't found someone and settled down in the suburbs. She had always been the party-hard, adventure-prone girl that usually wound up in more trouble than she knew how to handle. Not, she told herself, the girl who longed to have just one man look at her the way that Jake was looking at Lola, or the way that Logan looked at Maggie when he thought she wasn't looking.

"You an only child too?"

Sasha looked back at Lola and nodded. "I am. But it was good."

Sensing that she didn't want to talk about it anymore, Maggie made an obvious play at changing the topic of conversation. "Where is Hudson? Jake, can you call him?"

"I'm right *here*. Jesus! A guy's running five minutes late and everyone starts losing their marbles. You know, Mags, I am an *actual* doctor with *actual* patients. Christ. Do you know what I had to do to get here at noon?"

Because he had come into the backyard from the house, Sasha couldn't see Hudson Simmone from where she was sitting. But there was something about his voice, something about the deep, honey tone of it, that shot straight to her stomach, curled there, and then drew down to her groin.

What the hell.

Turning in her chair, she glanced towards the back door in the direction where the voice had come from.

And then she froze.

Of. Course.

He was gorgeous. All six-foot-six of him was muscled and tanned. Not like Logan or Jacob who clearly spent a significant portion of their week lifting heavy shit. Hudson was tall and lean with sculpted arms that belied good genetics and maybe time in his schedule for three or four bodyweight workouts in his home gym. Or garage.

His dirty blonde hair was long enough to sweep his collar, and fell around either side of his face as if he constantly used a single hand to rake it back off his forehead. When his gaze tracked to where she sat, piercing blue eyes smiled back at her, and she felt a shimmer of interest.

"You must be Sasha," he said, walking towards her, long legs eating the space in only a few strides.

Pushing to her feet, she faced him…or rather, faced his chest. Tilting her head up, she sent him her best smile and held out her hand. "Yes. It's nice to meet you, Hudson."

His huge hand enveloped hers and they shook. There were no tingles or butterflies for her, but, still, it felt nice, safe even, to have contact with a man who wasn't out to kill her.

"Well," Maggie said. "Should we get started then?"

Nodding, Sasha released Hudson's hand and stepped around to her chair, plopping back down so that she could give Maggie her full attention.

Hudson listened half-heartedly to Logan as he took over from Maggie. The other half of his attention, the half that was governed by innate curiosity, kept wandering over to the woman sitting in the lawn chair in front of him.

From behind, when he'd seen her pitch-black hair, cut in a sharp line at her shoulders, she could almost have been a child. She was that small. Then, she'd stood up from her chair to greet him, her tiny waist offset by curvaceous hips and boobs that probably caused traffic accidents when she walked on the street, and he'd struggled to keep his eyes up.

"Sasha is going to tell us where she left off in CAR before we decide anything further," Logan said.

Hudson watched as Sasha Riley pushed to her feet and walked front and center to stand beside Logan, clearly unafraid of being the center of attention. Her smile was bright and calm, her near-black eyes glinting.

She stood with one hip cocked. The gesture would have looked defiant on a child or teenager, but it only accentuated her jean-clad curves and narrow waist. Her arms were crossed over her chest, exposing lean, strong muscles. But the way that the posture lifted her breasts made his gaze want to wander.

He studied her as she recounted her month-long investigation into Francis Boucher and Charles Rue, then detailed her run-in with Boucher's thugs, and her subsequent escape from CAR, south through the Congo. If she was scared at all she didn't show it. Her voice never wavered, her gaze never faltered, although it had fixed on some far-off place over his right shoulder.

When she was done, she turned to Logan and asked, "So, what's the plan?"

"We were planning on waiting for the UN report to come through and for the extradition order to move forward before we began tracking Rue."

Sasha shook her head. "I don't know…"

"Tell us what you're thinking," Maggie added.

Sasha took a moment as if compiling her thoughts. "The US doesn't have extradition treaties with CAR, for starters."

"But Rue is a French national," Zac interjected.

"True, but the crimes we're accusing him of were committed in CAR," Sasha countered. Turning to look at Logan, she added, "Throw in the fact that Rue works for Boucher, who is literally one of the biggest spenders in the second poorest country in the world…"

"So, the government in the Central African Republic won't care that he's killing people?" Jacob asked, his tone incredulous.

"It's not that they don't care necessarily. It's just low on the totem pole of priorities." She shrugged. "Honestly…a lot of the people I interviewed knew that other miners had died before they even signed up…but, the world is different in ways that you can't understand if you've never experienced it."

When Jacob opened his mouth to protest, she raised a hand, stopping him. "I don't mean to undermine your experience, Jake. But you're a California-raised, blue-blooded American. And judging by the fact that you *volunteered* for the LAPD when you could have done anything else, you're an idealist too. CAR is…sometimes as close to the ninth circle of hell as you can get without actually being dead."

"It's a rough place," Logan seconded.

"So," Hudson tensed when all eyes turned on him, "what *can* we do?"

"You want him to be caught and extradited, and he can only be extradited to France…"

Following her line of reasoning, Hudson added, "He's going to have to commit another crime, a big one. On US soil."

"Rue is a psychopath," Logan said. "I wouldn't be surprised if he already has."

"Donny says he's been relatively quiet. No word of him making waves off the grid."

"I don't think the Federal Government would start a manhunt if he was only hurting other bad guys," she replied, looking at Zac. "But he doesn't know that I'm in the US yet."

"Meaning?" Lola piped up.

Hudson glanced to where Lola sat in a garden chair facing Sasha, aware of the fact that her voice was strained, panicked. Because Jake had already told him that she hadn't been sleeping well, he made a mental note to check in on her before he left.

"Once he reports back to Boucher that I'm here and that Logan and I were working together…he'll make a move. That's when we take him."

"So, he has all the cards?" Maggie asked.

"Mnnn," Sasha shook her head, as if unconvinced, "he has a Straight Flush. We have Jack through Ace of spades and are waiting for the dealer to decide our fate."

"I don't like those odds," Lola said, although she was smiling at the analogy.

All Hudson could think was that she played poker, and probably played it well. And as much as he tried to concentrate, he couldn't stop his mind from wondering if she'd beat him in a game of strip.

"So, we stick to the original plan?" Zac offered. "We wait, we look out for Maggie, Gracie, and Sasha, and when he does make a move, *if* he makes a move, we take it as our green light and nab him. Criminal Law one-o-one: Self-defense doesn't count."

"Zac," Maggie laughed, "if you ever get arrested, please call me before you try to sweet-talk your way out."

Logan smiled, but his eyes stayed dark in that way that made Hudson's spine pull tight.

"In the meantime, we file everything that's happened so far…. well, except for Donny's involvement," Jake said.

"We'll have a much stronger case if the LAPD is aware of what's going on when we eventually bring him in. Can you send me a copy of the report you wrote, and give me a statement?" he asked her.

She nodded. "Of course."

"Mags. Logan. You too?"

They nodded.

"In the interim, the girls have to stay together," Logan said. "I'm sorry, Sash," he added, turning to her, "I know you like your independence, but it'll be easier for me to protect you if you're all in one place."

Hudson watched as she shrugged. "No big. This time I'd actually appreciate the help. It's...it's been a long two months."

"Next steps," Logan said. "Zac, you continue running surveillance. Let us know when Rue moves. Jake, file those reports. I'll run point on looking out for the girls. Best case scenario he decides we're not worth the risk and ships out, then we can forget this entire thing ever happened."

"Worst case scenario, the crime that gets him extradited involves one of us," Sasha added, speaking the single thought that nobody else wanted to.

Because it needed to be said, Hudson added, "And we'll deal with that if and when it occurs."

Her gaze tracked to him and, he thought by the stubborn tilt of her chin and the focused set of her eyes, that she might argue. Instead, she nodded once.

Chapter 18

Maggie unlocked the café, before stepping aside and holding the door open so that Sasha, Logan, and Gracie could go through before her.

Both Logan and Sasha carried two five-gallon buckets of paint each. Sasha carried one in each hand, while Logan hefted both with one hand so that he could shoo Gracie in through the door with the other.

Although none of them had wanted the job, it was one that Maggie had to get done in the next week, before her landlord brought his crew in to renovate the bathrooms. Logan had insisted that she couldn't go to the café alone. And seeing as though he couldn't watch all three of them at once, Sasha had offered to tag along and lend her hands to the task.

"Wow!" Sasha's exclamation hit Maggie's ears the moment that she walked through the doors. "This is perfect," she said as she put the paint down and walked towards the back of the room to the bar. "Although I still don't know why you're going with white."

"It's just a placeholder," Maggie replied, placing the huge bag of rollers, trays, painter's tape, and plastic on the floor in the middle of the room next to the paint.

She had specifically chosen eggshell white for the room because she needed a blank slate for each of the different ideas that she had for the three walls. The paint, although boring, was a canvas of sorts, a primer that would give way to her ultimate creation.

She had finally decided on the aesthetic for the café after hundreds of catalog runs and conversations with her landlord. She already knew that the back wall, the half one behind the bar shelves, was going to be covered in mirrored tiles with a gold patina so that the shelves bounced back the reflections of the coffee beans, wines, glasses, and antique décor.

The east-facing wall wasn't going to be a wall at all. It was going to be one floor to ceiling book-shelf that ran the length of the room and included an old-fashioned library ladder. The top shelf was going to be crowded with a row of hanging plants, and, already, she could imagine the long tendrils falling down the front of the rustic, wooden shelves.

The rest of the shelves were going to be where she stocked her inventory of coffee and wines for sale. She'd been toying with the idea of including small-batch, handcrafted preserves, and baked goods from local vendors to her inventory.

The options were limitless.

The last wall, the west-facing one, was going to be wallpapered with a print that she had found online. The wallpaper was black with a mass of Birds of Paradise flowers adding bursts of color. The tropical decor, although loud, would add an accent wall of green to the room to match her plants, while the splashes of red and orange on the flowers would complement the bright serviceware that she was going to pay a small fortune for.

But it'll be worth it.

The paint in eggshell white, although necessary, was going to be largely covered, which was why she'd originally told her landlord that she'd do it herself.

Maggie started opening the paint as Sasha walked through the café, Gracie following close on her heels.

Although not unkind to Gracie, it had become clear to all of them that Sasha was not comfortable around small children after she'd spent the first night dodging and weaving away from Grace. In response, Gracie, obviously fascinated by a new person who didn't lavish her with attention, had taken to hounding Sasha, following her everywhere that she went.

Feeling eyes on her, Maggie turned to face Logan. She ignored the way that her heart stumbled in her chest when his dark, gray gaze met hers. "Watching them interact provides me with endless entertainment," she said, speaking her thoughts.

His eyes tracked to where Sasha was scurrying under the bar hatch towards the kitchen, Gracie right behind her. He smiled and turned back to face her. "Thanks for letting her stay."

"Of course. She's...a friend in need. You know I'd never turn her away, especially considering helping you out was how she landed in trouble in the first place."

He took a step towards her so that they were side-to-side, and Maggie couldn't help but welcome the warm awareness that flooded her senses. She still hadn't figured out how just his proximity made her dizzy after all the years that they'd spent together. But considering that she liked the sensation, she didn't question it.

When he wrapped one big, heavy arm over her shoulders, she nestled in, enjoying the heat that radiated between them. Resting her head on his chest, she breathed in his scent, felt it wrap around her senses and settle in some deep part of her mind that she associated with safety.

The sound of his cellphone ringing had her shifting slightly so that he could pull it from his back pocket, but when she made to move away he tightened his grip on her and squeezed her upper arm.

"Zac?"

The single word, the militant way that Logan answered the phone, drew her back to the present with a vacuum-like deliberateness that made her stomach heave. She could not forget, *would* not forget, that Logan, and the rest of them by default, were in serious danger. And even though things between them were going well, she couldn't forget that their problems were only just beginning.

He listened. "When?"

The way that his body tensed beside her made her own nerves tighten, made her hair follicles pull tight along her spine. When she hazarded a glance up at him, his eyes were dark, nearly black with anger and something else, something that she had always been able to identify in him. Still, seeing the killer in him come alive twisted her stomach with fear.

Not fear *of* him. Fear *for* him.

She had always lived for Logan Cane, had always known that if something happened to him she might not survive her grief. So seeing the way that he embraced the danger in his life twisted her like a knife slicing deep—a knife that he was holding the handle to.

"I'm with all three of them now. Yes." He glanced at her, smiled as if to reassure her. "Will do. Contact Jake. Stay on-call."

He hung up the phone, slid it back into the back pocket of his jeans without looking at her. "What is it?" she asked, knowing that something was wrong.

"Rue just moved. Zac saw him leaving the motel with a single bag. Apparently, he just hopped in the Mercedes and turned west."

"The airport?" she asked. "You think he's leaving?"

"He could be going anywhere…"

"But?"

"By now Sasha's report has to be gaining some traction with the UN. I can imagine Boucher's getting nervous."

Maggie felt a shimmer of genuine happiness, one that started in her stomach and spread through her entire body. "How will we know?"

"Zac's tracking the car using Donny's resources. We just have to sit tight and stay safe. Time will tell."

Sighing, she rolled her neck before letting it fall back on his arm. He turned her then, used the arm already looped around her to shift her body so that they stood face to face.

"I'm not going to let anyone hurt you."

"He's not coming after me," she argued. "He might, *might*, try and get close to us, but only so that he can get under your skin."

"Well, I can protect myself if and when that happens."

She looked up into sincere eyes. "Unless he shoots you from a hundred yards away," she said quietly, aware of the fact that Sasha and Gracie were wandering about nearby.

"He's not the type. Especially considering it's me."

He rubbed her arms up and down, sending a shiver of need up her spine. "He'll want to draw me out. Challenge me."

"He's an egomaniac."

"And a psychopath."

She grinned. "And a psychopath."

He pulled her into his chest then, linked both of his arms around her waist even as she loped hers around his. Maggie rested her cheek on his solid chest, heard the heavy thump of his heart under her ear. "I'm really glad that you came home," she whispered, aware of the fact that all of her wants, wishes, needs, and desires seemed to be met the moment that their skin touched.

His arms tightened around her, and he pulled her a little closer so that there was no space between them. "Me too."

He was quiet for a moment, then he added, "What do I have to do to get you to wear the ring again?"

Maggie felt her heart come to a screeching halt as the moment shattered around her. She must have tensed because he took a step back so that he could look down and meet her eyes.

"I...I just don't have the bandwidth to think about it right now, Logan. *Please*...don't be offended. You...you have so much going on, and once it's over you'll be able to think straight again, you'll be able to decide what you really want."

"You still don't think I'm going to stay." It was not a question.

Maggie felt her heart split in two at the defeat in his voice. "I need time to get used to the idea," she countered instead, unwilling to admit that she was petrified of letting herself believe that he was going to be around long term. The last time that she'd believed him, she'd ended up in his condo alone, with a ring on her finger, and a fiancé in the wind.

After a moment, he exhaled. "It's okay. I...I didn't expect you to just forgive me and take me back." He tilted her chin up with one hand, forcing her eyes back to his. "But I am going to stay."

He leaned down to brush his lips on her temple.

Desperately needing to bridge the gap that seemed to have widened between them, she raised her hand to the nape of his neck and pulled his head down so that she could take his lips instead.

The kiss was gentle, a melding of lips, tongues, and breath that was meant to pull them both back from the rabbit hole they'd fallen down. Instead, it hollowed her out.

As his hands moved to her ass, and his lips broke contact with her to trail down her throat, all she could think about was how much she needed him, and that if he did leave it would crush her even though she had promised herself that she'd be fine.

She wasn't a fool, she knew that history usually repeated itself. But there was still a small part of her that knew that this time it was different. *They* were different. And maybe that would make a difference. Maybe that would be enough.

"Jesus, Cane. Get a room. There's a minor in the building."

Sasha's voice broke the moment, and Maggie took a step away from Logan as her cheeks flooded with warmth.

Even though they were both grinning, she felt the physical distance between them as surely as if she'd lost a limb.

Needing to give her hands something to do, she reached forward and spilled the contents of the bag onto the old, herringbone floor.

Gracie, hearing the noise, tottered over and plopped to her bum so that she could rifle through the paint supplies. Maggie let her be.

"Okay," she said, coming up with three rollers in her hands. "I guess we'll each just pick a wall and get to it?"

"So, just tape the wainscoting and window seams, lay down the plastic, and get going?" Sasha asked, repeating the instructions that Maggie had given her earlier.

Maggie nodded. "Yup. We don't need a primer because there's a coat of flat paint on the walls already."

Sasha wandered over to where she stood and, once she'd taken the roller from Maggie, picked up a paint tray, a roll of tape, and a ream of plastic. When she stood back up, she had a skeptical look on her face.

"What is it?" Maggie asked.

"I gave you the disclaimer about not having an artistic bone in my body, right?"

Chuckling, Maggie leaned over and started passing Logan his quota of the supplies. "Just don't swallow the paint or the turpentine and you'll be good."

"Okay. Remind me which wall the wallpaper's going on?"

When Maggie pointed, Sasha nodded and marched across the room to the west wall. Gracie, seeing it as another opportunity to impress herself on their house guest, pushed to her feet and made her way across the room.

"Gracie," Maggie called after her, afraid that she'd get in Sasha's way.

"Don't worry about it," Sasha replied, her black eyes glinting with humor as she watched Gracie's approach. "Just don't let her swallow the paint or turpentine, right?"

Maggie smiled, and although she wasn't one-hundred-percent comfortable with leaving Gracie alone to terrorize Sasha, she turned her back on them.

Logan, obviously seeing her deliberate attempt to mask her mom-nerves, chuckled. "They'll be fine."

"Yeah." Picking up her roller, she moved with him to the east wall. "I told Hudson that we were doing this today," she whispered.

"Let me guess. He's coming to help?"

Maggie chuckled. "So, I'm not the only one who noticed?"

"They seemed to hit it off." Logan snorted. "Poor guy doesn't know what he's getting into."

Maggie cast a glance over her shoulder, but seeing that Sasha was engrossed with teaching Gracie how to unroll the tape, she carried on with, "You don't think she's interested?"

Hearing the concern in her voice, he looked up from the sheet of plastic that he'd been unraveling. "I think she might be. I just don't think she's into anything serious per se." He shrugged. "Sasha lives three hundred and twenty days of the year in a foreign country, Mags."

Maggie sighed. Of course, Hudson would choose to go after the one girl that wasn't interested in a relationship. If her baby brother was good at one thing—aside from being a doctor—it was pursuing women who didn't want to stick it out through the long haul. "For someone who wants a relationship, the poor guy doesn't have a clue."

"Hudson?" Logan frowned. "I don't know, Mags. He seems to do okay in that department."

She handed him the tape, making sure to keep her voice low as she stepped over the plastic that he had laid down. "Come on. Every girlfriend of his in the last ten years has broken up with him for the *exact* same reason," she whispered.

"What?"

"When he asked them to take it to the next level."

"What?" he said again, his brow furrowed with confusion.

Maggie nodded. She could tell by the way that he stared into space that he was trying to remember what he could about Hudson's girlfriends. "You're male so you think that because he's young and successful he must only want to get laid."

"He doesn't?"

"That's part of it. Obviously. He is a young, successful male."

Logan chuckled. "But?"

"He's a total romantic."

He fell silent as he leaned down to tape the edge of the window frame, but when he stood again, he said, "I seem to remember him flying his last girlfriend to Paris for her birthday."

"She was a fashion student at the FIA," Maggie confirmed with a nod. "He flew her to fashion week. Literally bribed Emma to get them unlimited access."

"What happened to her?"

Maggie had forgotten that Logan had shipped out around the same time that Hudson and Rose had broken up. She only remembered now because the memory of her and Hudson spending a three-day weekend binge-watching Netflix and eating ice-cream together in Logan's unfurnished apartment snuck its way into her mind.

"She broke it off a few days after they got back. Said he was moving too fast."

"Ouch."

"Yeah. He was heartbroken."

"How long did they date again?" he asked.

Maggie laughed. "Five months."

"He flew her to fashion week? In Paris? After they'd been together for five months?"

She nodded, feeling a small hint of shame at the fact that she was finding amusement in her baby brother's suffering. She knew that Hudson couldn't help it. Knew that he was sweet and sensitive despite his six-foot-six height and surfer-bro manner of communicating.

"Jesus."

"Uh-huh."

"Weird that I never saw that before," he said as he rolled the first touch of white paint over the faded blue wall.

Maggie watched as he moved the roller over the wall, felt blood heat beneath her skin as her eyes tracked the way that his forearms flexed with every change in direction. When her gaze wandered to the line where his right bicep rose out of the sleeve of his shirt, she felt a long, slow pull of lust that started in her belly and spread to her thighs.

"Maggie," he said without looking at her, his voice hoarse, "if you don't stop biting your lip like that, I'm going to humiliate our guest by hauling you to the bathroom and having my way with you."

She hadn't even realized that she'd been doing it, so she released her bottom lip from between her teeth. The image of him throwing her over his shoulder and storming through to the bathroom held way more appeal than it should. She picked up her roller and drowned it in the paint tray.

By the time that Hudson arrived nearly an hour later, Maggie and Logan had plastered the first layer of paint on the east wall. Sasha, who had split her time between painting and managing Gracie, had only painted a quarter of the west wall. She was only five-two, so her line of paint ended nearly five feet below where the wall met the tall ceiling.

"Jesus! Why isn't the door open?" Hudson asked as he came inside. "Can't you smell that?"

Maggie and Logan looked at each other and broke into twin grins. They'd been so caught up in the task that they hadn't noticed the cloying cloud of paint fumes in the room.

Maggie moved over to greet Hudson, took in the old, baggy Stanford University shirt that he wore for the paint job. "Thanks for volunteering," she said.

He pulled her in for a quick hug before his eyes tracked over to where Sasha was focusing on painting the other bottom quarter of the west wall.

"Why don't you grab the ladder and help Sasha out," she said. "Logan and I don't need it until the first coat dries."

He grinned down at her and she rolled her eyes. "I'm going to check this place out first," he said, moving towards the back exactly as Sasha had done when they'd first arrived.

He took a good five minutes to walk the space, casually chatted as he walked through to the back. "The kitchen needs a lot of work," he shouted from the back of the room.

When he wandered back out, she replied, "I know."

"Max Murphy doing it for you?" he asked, referring to Zac's older brother.

"No," she replied. "The landlord is handling the kitchen and bathroom renovations so they're using their contractors."

Logan's phone rang again, and he pulled it out, answered with, "Zac?"

Hudson nodded and moved past her to grab the ladder. "Is Gracie with Mom and Dad?" he asked, lifting the heavy step ladder with one hand.

"What?" Maggie frowned and turned to look back at Sasha, just as Logan turned to do the same, the phone at his ear.

Gracie wasn't there.

"What?" Logan said to Zac. Without dropping the phone, he stalked ran through to the back of the café. Maggie felt her stomach slide to the floor as panic closed her throat. She couldn't move.

"Fuck!" Even though she hadn't made it to the back, she knew by his tone that Gracie wasn't there.

Turning back to the room, she tried to calm her racing heart. *She has to be here.*

Her eyes ran over Hudson, standing forlornly with the ladder, his big, blue eyes wide with surprise, then over to Sasha. Before she even looked at the door, she knew that it had been left open by the wide-eyed look of fear on Sasha's face.

Maggie turned slowly. "Oh, my God." The door stood open, propped with an old brick that Hudson must have found outside. "Logan!" she called as she made for the door.

"Maggie…" She turned back to look at Hudson, noticed the look of shock on his face again. His pupils were big and black, nearly swallowing his pale irises.

"Oh, hell no!" Sasha flew at him, gave him one hard shove that seemed to pull him back to the present. "Snap out of it! We need to help!"

Maggie listened through the blood pounding in her head. *She's probably just outside the door. Waiting for me to come and find her.*

So why couldn't she move? It was as if her feet were cemented to the ground, holding her in place even as her mind screamed at her to hurry, to go find Gracie.

Suddenly Logan was behind her, propelling her the rest of the way. He didn't stop moving until they were out of the door and standing on the sidewalk. "Zac said Rue was in the neighborhood."

She watched silently as he looked left and right. When Sasha and Hudson came out of the café, he said, "You go right. We'll go left. It's only been a few minutes so come back once you get to the end of the block. She can't have gone further than that if she's alone."

Her hands started to tremble, and her breath came in small, frantic gasps. "Maggie!" Logan's voice came through to her. "Stop. We need to move. Now!"

Nodding, she lifted her head and started after him, followed just behind him as he ran.

It took them ninety seconds to get to the end of the block. Maggie felt the tears falling down her cheeks as she looked around frantically. A few people milled about the neighborhood, enjoying the sunny Saturday.

"You see a little girl come this way?" Logan shouted to a man sitting on the stairs of an old apartment complex.

He shook his head no.

Logan pulled the phone back up to his ear. After ten seconds, Maggie heard him say, "Zac! Gracie's gone."

Hearing the words, hearing the calm, even tone in which Logan said them took the blood from her limbs in one quick rush.

"Okay. Call Jake. Call Donny. Meet me at Maggie's place as soon as possible." Logan listened to what Zac said over the phone, and Maggie watched through a haze as his eyes darkened, turning nearly black. She knew by the way that he was looking away from her that whatever Zac had told him had not been good.

"Alright. And Zac," his voice was heavy with something that made Maggie's spine pull tight, "bring me another gun, preferably a SIG or Glock."

He hung up the phone and, grabbing her hand, started back towards the café, his long legs and fast pace forcing her to run so that she could keep up with him.

Maggie put one foot in front of the other, trying to keep up. When they came back to the door, Sasha and Hudson were already back waiting for them. Without Gracie.

"Nothing?" he asked.

Sasha's eyes were brimming, and Maggie looked down when she stretched out her hand in front of her. A kpinga, the replica to the one that she'd found in her car, was in Sasha's hand.

Chapter 19

Logan was going to kill Charles Rue. Of that he was certain. By the time that Zac and Jake had pulled up to the café, Maggie had fallen into quiet tears. Although she was crying, her blue eyes were calm despite her bloodless face and shaking hands.

Hudson and Sasha stood on either side of her, their presence a welcome distraction to Logan. He needed to focus and quiet his mind. But seeing the grief in Maggie's eyes was making it hard to function beyond the need to take her in his arms.

So he blocked her out, blocked them all out, and focused on the task at hand. He focused on the roaring rage that was tunneling through his veins at the thought of Gracie, alone, with Rue.

He still wasn't sure how the man had managed to grab her in the space of five minutes, he didn't care either. Rue had signed his death warrant when he'd touched her.

They needed to move quickly. The longer that Gracie was with Charles, the less likely it became that he'd leave her completely unscathed.

Because he didn't want Maggie to hear what he had to say, he nodded his head, indicating to Jake's cruiser, which was parked a little down the road.

Zac and Jake followed.

When they came to a stop, he crossed his arms over his chest. "We have an hour, maybe two."

"You think he'll hurt her?" Jake asked.

Logan relaxed his clenched fists. He didn't say anything, and Zac, sensing that he was in unchartered territory, took over.

He pulled the Glock that Logan had requested out of the waistband of his jeans, and handed it to him. Logan saw the slight hesitation in Zac's actions and the wariness in Jake's eyes, but he didn't care that his friends were worried about what he'd do. *He* didn't care what he'd do, as long as he got Gracie back to Maggie.

"He's heading south. Donny says that Rue hasn't made contact with any of his guys since he bought the car, but that we should call if we need backup."

"Let's go," Logan replied, opening the door to Jacob's cruiser. "We can plan on the way."

"Someone going to tell Maggie?" Zac asked, looking at him.

Logan rolled his neck because he knew that it was his responsibility. But he also didn't know how he could face her. How could he look her in the eye after he'd promised to keep them safe only moments before? He had failed her. He had failed them both.

He slammed the door with a sharp, "Fuck," and hurried to where Maggie, Sasha, and Hudson stood on the sidewalk watching them.

He didn't have any time to lose, so he started talking before he was even in front of them, "Sasha. Hudson. I need you to give me a minute. Then take Maggie home and stay with her until I come back."

They both nodded and went back inside the café to give them a moment.

When he turned his eyes on Maggie, he felt his chest rip in two. Her blue eyes were red and puffy from crying, and she'd wrapped both of her arms around her midsection as if she were trying to keep herself from falling apart.

For a moment, he didn't know what to say, and he just stood there looking down at her as everything that he wanted to tell her filled the space between them.

After nearly ten seconds, she reached out a hand and touched his face, forcing his gaze back to her. "Bring our baby home."

Her voice broke at the end, and she dropped her hand. Before she could turn away, he pulled her into his arms. He felt some of his grief push through to the surface when she gripped the back of his shirt as if he were her lifeline.

"I'm going to bring her back." He took a step back so that he could look at her. When she nodded, he crushed his mouth to hers in a fierce kiss that tore through his chest. Then just as quickly, he let her go and turned away.

He'd only been with Maggie for a minute, but by the time that he got back to the cruiser, Zac and Jake were in the front. The car was idling, ready to go. The moment that he closed the door, Jake pulled away from the curb and turned on his siren.

"We'll take the siren down when we get closer to his location. But for now, it'll help us make up the distance."

Logan didn't argue as they sped through a red light with traffic stopped on either side to let them through.

"LAPD SWAT is on standby," Jake said. "We sent them the tracking info, and they're following close behind. We've sent out an amber alert with the car's information."

"Donny and co. are in commns. too," Zac added. "They can pin him in one location if he moves into any of Donny's territory."

Logan felt the weight in his chest increase, but he knew this game better than anyone. "Tell them to stand down until I give the green light," he said.

"Do you think that's the best idea?"

He looked forward from his position in the back seat, stared at Jake for a full ten seconds. "He has Gracie."

Zac and Jake exchanged concerned glances from their position in the front, and Logan felt a dull, throb of anger. He didn't say anything else. He knew that he was not in the right frame of mind to be having this particular conversation.

He didn't even know how he could begin to explain to them. How did he describe that Gracie had become more important to him in the last month than anyone, even Maggie? How did he tell them that when she smiled at him and called him, 'Da,' his entire heart slammed against his chest? How did he describe what it felt like when they were both drifting off to sleep, and he could feel her tiny heart ticking through her chest in time with his?

He couldn't. So, he didn't try.

He had never loved anyone more than Maggie Simmone until the first time that she'd plopped Gracie in his arms. She'd been rifling through the freezer looking for ice to put on the bruise that Donny had given him, but in that exact moment, his life had changed.

"He's stopped," Zac said, pulling Logan's attention away from his thoughts.

"Where?"

"Port of Los Angeles Harbor."

"What?" Jake glanced at him. "Why the port?"

"It doesn't matter," Logan said, stopping his mind from thinking of all the ways that Gracie could go missing without a trace from the port. "Let's just find them."

Not needing any more prompting, Jake accelerated through a series of red lights. His cruiser reached a hundred miles an hour on the small side streets, as the siren wailed mournfully.

Logan kept his eyes trained on the red light on the dashboard. He focused on the glaring flashes to try and distract himself from the helplessness of being trapped in a car on the way to rescue his daughter. The bright red color of the light blurred in his mind, carried his thoughts to blood, and the fact that after today, he'd have one other person's on his hands.

The thought did not make him sad.

Not this time.

Chapter 20

The Port of Los Angeles Harbor was publicly accessible from South Seaside Drive. Although he had never had reason to visit the water's edge district, Logan felt his skin pull tight with unease as he studied the setting.

Jake had turned his lights and siren off, and moved the unmarked cruiser forward slowly towards the point where Donny Flynn's tracker had stopped.

The harbor was surrounded by a temporary chain-link fence that was covered in green netting as if it were closed for construction. Although standard security, the fencing made the industrial district look and feel even more ominous.

Behind the netting, Logan could see eight round cylinders rising from the ground. Each one was probably the size of a three-story apartment complex, and he wondered what they were used for. If he hadn't known that they were at the edge of the water in Los Angeles, he would have placed the silos in the middle of the country at an industrial brewery.

Two cranes poked the cloudless sky above the silos, their horizontal arms slouched and unmoving. Still. The hook blocks on the ends of the cranes' arms that were used for lifting the shipping containers made the machines look as if they had little faces that were turned down in sadness.

They were only a few hundred yards away, so Logan checked the Glock's magazine one last time. He had sixteen rounds. It was enough considering that he only intended on using one.

When the car came to a rolling stop, he looked out the window so that he could take in the concrete-paved lot and shipping warehouse. A pile of molding lumber and a chain-link gate that had been left wide open were the only things separating them from the old warehouse. The black Mercedes sat outside, its engine off.

"Remember that he might not be expecting us to have found him so fast," Zac began. "He doesn't know that Donny has trackers in all of his cars."

"And don't kill him if you can avoid it," Jake said. "The last thing that I need is to explain that I watched as you took Zac's Glock on a human hunting mission."

Zac cleared his voice. "Actually, that particular Glock has been filed…"

Logan almost smiled when Jake groaned and let his head fall back on the seat of the car. "You're buying illegal weapons now?" he asked, looking at Zac with a horrified expression on his face.

Zac shrugged. "Only for this *one* occasion. And I bought the gun legally—I know a guy—*then* had it filed. Like I'm going to give Logan a weapon registered in my name right now."

On any other occasion, the information would have settled his mind, would have made him feel calmer about the fact that he was hunting a human being. Today, he didn't care. He knew that he was going to kill Rue anyway, so whether he did it with the weapon registered to him, or with one that'd had the serial number filed off didn't matter. He'd deal with the consequences later.

"I need one of you to cover my six, and one of you to stay in the cruiser and bring the backup if we need it," he said.

"SWAT is five minutes out," Jake said. "I'll meet them here and bring them in after ten." When Logan opened his mouth to protest, Jake held up a hand, cutting him off. "I'm breaking all the rules by letting you two go in alone at all. Ten minutes starting," he looked at his watch, "thirty seconds ago is all you have."

Logan was out the door two seconds later.

He didn't need to look back to know that Zac had also climbed out and was following him, close behind. He knew Zac's skill-set and trusted that he would be effective backup.

Crouching low to the ground, Logan ran through the gate towards the parked black Mercedes. When he came up to the car, he hunkered down and waited until Zac came up to his side.

Speaking quietly, he said, "I'm going in the front. You go around back and make sure that there's no exit. If there is, secure it so that he can't make a run for it. If there isn't a way out, filter back to the front and set up outside. Either way, if I miss him, you get to play housekeeping."

Zac nodded, his blue eyes narrowed with focus. "I've got it covered. Go get our girl."

Without another word, Logan slipped around the front of the car and made his way towards the warehouse door. His Glock was in both hands in front of him, the barrel pointing to the ground.

When he came abreast of the door, he pushed the corner with his boot. It creaked open, giving him just enough room to slip inside the black bowels of the shipping room without letting too much outside light in.

The smell of mold and mildew hit his nose first, filling his brain with the sense of claustrophobia as he wondered exactly what was decaying in the room.

Pausing, he took a moment to let his eyes adjust. The room was nearly pitch black, but even through the darkness, he could make out the looming forms of dozens of shipping containers. They sat side-by-side, like institutionalized aunties who were afraid of the dark place that they had been locked up in.

Quietly, he crouched low as he made his way through one of the wider aisles. He ignored the feeling of the containers as they trapped him in, their metal sides caging him. He knew that the set-up would impair his mobility if

229

Rue caught him off guard. He also knew that he had limited time and next to no other options. So he surged forward, his weapon now raised in front of him.

He could hear his heart beating in his chest, feel the adrenaline pumping through his veins. He welcomed both, welcomed the rush of awareness that he felt as his instincts took over. His mind quieted completely.

A noise towards the back of the warehouse caught his attention, and he paused for a moment to listen.

Silence.

He took a single step forward, stopped. Listened.

He estimated that he had less than five minutes before SWAT burst in. So, he put one foot in front of the other, and silently padded towards the back of the warehouse again, his confident steps hurried but silent.

As he came around one of the last shipping containers, he noticed a small ball of light coming from the farthest corner of the room. Crouching as low to the ground as he could, he focused on the sound of Gracie's whimpers, on the sound of Rue's scuffled steps.

He knew instinctively that they were just around the next container. He stopped moving and listened to pinpoint Rue's location. If Rue spoke, Logan could take him out before he even knew that he was there, then move on to helping whoever else was inside.

He had already deduced by the echoing silence and the lack of other vehicles outside, that Rue was alone. That he'd made the trip without any of his usual goons. The thought stilled Logan's heart, and he felt relief in knowing that Boucher's connections did not extend to California.

He peeked his head around the corner of the last container that stood between him and Gracie, so that he could observe the scene.

Gracie was sitting on the dirty floor, her hands and mouth duct-taped. Her face was red and puffy from crying, and streaks of dirt clung to her right cheek as if she'd lost her balance and fallen on the packed dirt ground. He could see that she was struggling to breathe through the tape that was blocking her screams. Her eyes were wide with fright, and, although her little hands were taped together at the wrist, her fists were bunched.

Rue stood a little off to the side, looking down at her, his face a dark mask of anger. His hair had grown out and spiked in every direction, making him look like an evil scientist from an old movie—one on a shitload of steroids. His green eyes were shadowed as if he hadn't been sleeping. They flickered around his surroundings frantically, searching the shadows.

Logan could see only one weapon on Rue's person, a Browning 380 with a sleek, silver barrel.

Raising his gun, he leveled it on Rue's chest, tightened his finger ever-so-slightly over the trigger. He took a deep breath, caught it in his chest, then began a long, slow exhale.

As if in slow motion, he watched out of the corner of his eye as Gracie's head turned to where he was crouched on the floor. Her little face transformed rapidly when she saw him. She raised her bound arms towards his hiding spot, but not before Rue snatched her off the ground. The sharp movement caught her off guard, sending her into a second round of muffled wails.

Logan came out from behind the container, his eyes and gun trained on Rue.

Rue back-peddled, Gracie in his arms. "Well, I wasn't expecting you so soon, Cane." A manic grin crossed Rue's features.

Gracie whimpered, earning a vicious shake from Rue that sent her small body rocking back and forth like a rag doll.

"Don't hurt her," Logan said, calmly, his eyes unwavering.

"Or, what?"

"I'm already planning on leaving you for the fishes, Rue. Let my daughter go, and I'll think twice about pelleting you slowly from your sack to your forehead. I'll make it quick instead."

Rue laughed, his black eyes twinkling. "You aren't holding the cards here, Cane," he said, his voice filled with genuine happiness.

When Rue trained the cold barrel of his gun against Gracie's head, Logan felt his blood freeze, felt his heart slow completely.

As if she could sense his reaction, Gracie quietened down, her muffled wails choking out. Logan focused on her face for a brief second, then took another step towards them.

Rue pressed the cold metal firmly against Gracie's temple, forcing a soft mewl out of her.

"The LAPD is outside, Rue. Where are you going to go? Huh? Add the murder of a one-year-old child to kidnapping and assault? Doesn't seem like a good idea to me."

Rue glanced behind Logan as if he were trying to see the door from where he stood. "The LAPD would never let you come in here for me," he said, his Cheshire smile growing wider.

"Not usually. But Maggie's brother is the lieutenant in charge. He'd much rather send me in than one of his own."

He saw a flicker of doubt cross Rue's face, and made a split hair's decision to pursue it. "What is it that you want? I know that Boucher didn't send you over here to kidnap my child."

"Boss didn't give specifics." Rue shrugged. "He said to make a point, leave a scar." Leaning down he rubbed his cheek against Gracie's face, his course stubble causing her face to crinkle in alarm. "I figure she's about as close to irreparable damage that I can do."

"Boucher isn't going to survive the UN's investigation," Logan countered, channeling his rage. "He's going to pay for his crimes wherever in the world he runs to."

"Boucher is running?" Rue asked, his hand relaxing on the gun.

Logan took another step forward. Interesting that Rue no longer knew what Boucher was up to. The knowledge could only mean that Francis had decided to cut his losses and sever contact with Rue.

"Even if he hasn't, he's thrown you to the wind."

"You don't know anything," Rue spat.

"Come on, Charles," he laughed, despite the furious tapping of his heart against his chest. "We're in the same line of work. I *know* that you're disposable because I am too." Shrugging, he added, "It's part of the appeal to guys like Boucher."

"Even if that's true, Cane. I've waited a long time for this."

"What is *this* exactly?"

"The opportunity to show Boucher that his golden boy is a pussy-whipped yank with no balls."

Logan was confused for a moment. "I don't know what you're talking about. I was a contract. Planning on leaving after two years anyway."

"Boucher was prepping you to take over as his second," Rue said, his dark eyes glinting dangerously.

He laughed, a deep cackle that echoed through the dark warehouse, pulling Logan's nerves tight. "Do you know," he carried on, ignoring the fact that Logan had taken two steps closer already, "that Boucher only pulled me into the mines after ten *years*? Then you show up, and within *months* he's restructuring security to make space for you."

"I don't know what you're talking about."

He could sense that Rue was close to snapping, knew that whatever part of his mind had remained intact while they'd been in CAR had been fractured now. It had succumbed to the same sickness that had kept him working for Boucher for so long.

"It was a test, you asshole! And you failed!"

Raising the gun back up to Gracie's head, he grinned.

Logan felt the world tilt. He had seen that look on Rue's face before, knew that what came next would not be according to his plan. "Do not hurt my child, Charles."

"Too late."

A single shot rang out.

Logan dove forward at the same instant. Without pausing, he grabbed Gracie, flinging her to the side in the dirt so that he could pin Rue's body beneath his.

He felt the warm blood soak through his shirt, felt the sticky weight of it against his skin.

There was no resistance, no fight.

It was only in looking down at Rue that he realized why. He was dead. A single bullet wound bloomed on the left side of Rue's chest. Even from his position half on top of him, Logan knew by the flood of blood, that the sniper round had gone clean through the heart.

Rue hadn't felt a thing. He hadn't even seen it coming. *Unfortunately.*

He gave himself three long seconds to calm down, to level his breathing. Then, pushing himself off the body, he turned to go to Gracie. She lay just off to the right where he'd thrown her in his panic. Her little body was covered in dirt and a spatter of blood stretched down her entire left side.

She was silent, her big, gray eyes wide, her face ashen.

Logan's hands trembled but he reached for her anyway. Picking her up, he cradled her against his chest for a moment. Despite his efforts to calm himself, his heart was racing, pounding against his skin with heavy thumps and starts. The fear he'd successfully banked before rose in his throat, suffocating him.

He could feel her in his arms, and yet, he wasn't sure it was real. He held her for what seemed like a lifetime, but could only have been seconds, too afraid to loosen his hold.

She had messed herself. He could feel the weight of her fear in her diaper, he could smell it. He imagined her alone with Rue, so afraid and confused. And it sickened him.

He had failed her at the only thing he was supposed to be good at. And, worse, he knew that although Charles Rue was dead, Boucher was still very much alive.

As the LAPD swarmed the scene, their guns raised, their boots thudding on the packed dirt floor, Logan worked on removing the tape. Other than the few scrapes from when he'd thrown her, Gracie seemed physically unharmed. Mentally...he had no idea how one even began to assess a one-year-old.

As soon as the last strip came off, he bent his head and kissed Gracie on her right cheek.

She whimpered and wrapped her arms around his neck, burying her face in his shirt.

She had started trembling in his arms, so he pried her away from his neck so that he could look at her. Her pupils were dilated, and Logan knew that the shock could be just as dangerous as a physical wound.

"Gracie," he said, as he rubbed a hand over her head. When her eyes didn't focus on him, he rubbed her pale cheek with one of his calloused palms, just rough enough so that her gaze flickered. "Hey, baby. Look at Daddy. Look over here."

When she finally turned her eyes on him, he gave her a smacking kiss in the hope that the sound would bring her back.

She didn't respond, just wrapped her little arms around his neck again in a vice-like grip, but Logan didn't try and break free this time. He needed the contact as much as she did. Cradling her bottom on one arm, he fished his phone out from his pocket. Out of the corner of his eye, he could see Jake issuing orders to the swarm of police crowding the scene. He could see Zac, standing a little off to the side spectating.

Turning away, he made his way for the door as he dialed Maggie.

The phone rang once before she answered. "Logan?"

He couldn't speak for a moment, found himself blinking through the tears that were choking his throat.

"Logan...*Please. Please...*"

"She's fine," he managed.

"Oh, thank God!"

He didn't have to be standing next to her to know that she was crying too. He could hear it in the strangled sobs that were coming through the phone line.

"I'm bringing her home now." Because he couldn't say more without breaking down completely, he hung up the phone.

Chapter 21

The moment that Logan stepped out of Jake's cruiser with Gracie in his arms, Maggie ran out of the front door. She made it as far as the driveway before bursting into tears again, but she didn't let the fact that she was running with blurred vision slow her down.

She'd been a wreck from the moment that she had realized that Gracie was gone. She had been borderline catatonic until Logan's call had come through to her nearly an hour before. She'd just sat on the sofa with Spunk, praying to whichever god would listen that her baby girl would be okay as her family had swarmed around her.

And none of that mattered now because she could see Gracie clinging to Logan's neck like a lifeline. Her face was buried in his shoulder, and she could see that they were both alive and okay.

When she came to stand in front of him, a small gasp escaped her lips, and she smacked a hand to her mouth to bank down the sob that rose in her throat. They were both covered in blood, so much of it that she could smell the rusty scent as it wafted off them.

She felt her head swim as she took in the bloom of red over Logan's chest. It covered his entire torso except where Gracie's body hid it. Feeling a wave of nausea rise in her stomach, she reached out a hand and touched Gracie's back, then raised her other one to Logan's face.

Their daughter shuddered under her palm. She didn't move her head from Logan's neck, and Maggie had to refrain from prying her off so that she could look at her. "Are you..." she swallowed her sob even as tears flowed down her face.

"We're both okay," he said quietly. "She's just experiencing a little residual shock. The medics checked her over onsite."

When she walked into his chest and wrapped her arms around both of them, Logan wrapped his free arm around her tightly. "You're going to get blood all over yourself," he whispered into her hair.

"As long as it's not yours, I don't care."

Hearing her voice, Gracie lifted her head out of the crook of Logan's neck and turned to glance at her. The moment that their eyes met, Gracie burst into fresh wails and reached out her arms.

Maggie took her from Logan then, felt her own body respond to the familiar weight of her baby in her arms. Her legs felt as if they weren't going to hold, so she leaned into Logan's chest, sighed when he caged them both in against him, supporting their weight easily.

They stood there like that for minutes, holding each other in the driveway, needing the physical contact just to be sure that everything was okay.

Maggie felt the heavy sickness that had been sitting in her stomach begin to subside, and, glancing back up at Logan, she said, "Why don't we go inside? Everyone came."

He nodded, turning towards the house.

The moment that she opened the door, they were swarmed by the family. Even Sarah and Matt, Lola's best friends, and Sarah's cousin, Donny, had shown up in case they needed to help.

Now, Maggie let a begrudging chuckle free as Gracie was pried from her arms and passed first to Grandma, then to each member of the family after that. While everyone fussed over her, made jokes, and generally tried to act normal, Maggie leaned back into Logan's chest.

His arms wrapped around her, and even though she could feel the sticky blood on him through her clothes,

Maggie didn't care. She rested a moment before turning in his arms so that she could look into his gray eyes.

He looked sad.

Reaching a hand up to his face, she brought his gaze back down to her. "What is it?"

He shook his head once, and she knew it was a solid refusal to acknowledge the tears that were swimming in his eyes. Clearing his throat, he managed, "I thought…"

She knew what he was going to say, and had only survived the past three hours by convincing herself that such things didn't happen. She reached up and locked her arms around his neck. "Me too. But she's okay."

"I have never been more scared," he admitted, his eyes glazing over.

He pulled away from her slightly, gripped her upper arms in his hands so that he could take a step back. Maggie frowned at the deliberate distance that he had put between them. "What aren't you telling me," she said, aware that the group of people in her house had moved through to the lounge.

"I can't ever go through that again."

Her heart shuddered to a stop in her chest, and she fisted her hands at her sides. "You're leaving us. *Now?* After…all this?"

Despite all of her earlier promises to herself, she felt as if the world had just split in two, and that she was being thrust into the abyss without a lifeline.

Shaking his head, he took a step forward. Maggie moved out of his reach. "I'm not leaving," he ground out fiercely.

"So, why are you going?" she returned, her tone snapping. "You forget that I've survived several rounds in this rodeo."

"I can't live knowing that he's out there!" His voice had risen to a shout, but he bit out the next words quietly. "That he could hurt her. To get back at *me*."

"Boucher?"

When he nodded, she felt her world cave at the corners a little. Of course, he would be worrying about the next psychopath before they'd even washed the blood off them from the first.

"I have to go, Mags. If something happened to Gracie...or you..."

His voice broke, and she watched as he raised his index finger and thumb to his eyes as if he could physically staunch the tears.

She knew that he was struggling, that he was in uncharted territory. For all his faults, Logan Cane was still the strongest man that she'd ever known. But, now, he was lost. The fear of Gracie being taken had hollowed him out. It had shown a side of himself that she wasn't sure he'd ever been aware of until that moment in the café when they'd realized their daughter was gone. He was...mortal. Not a soldier, not a weapon. He was a dad, and she knew he'd just realized how much more he had to lose.

She wasn't sure how she felt about what he wanted to do either. Hunting a man...even an evil man...was a gray area...wasn't it?

But then she thought of Gracie, just one year old. She thought of all the miners, thought of all the boys and girls in CAR whose parents had died at Boucher's hands. And the gray area solidified in her mind, turning black. "Go."

He lowered his hand to look at her, and she saw the surprise in his eyes. "You'll...you'll wait for me to get back?"

"As if the last twenty-five years haven't been proof enough?" she asked. She crossed her arms over her chest as if she could hold herself together.

"Will you still marry me after a year?" he asked, his gray eyes bright with the grin that she had loved for as long as she could remember.

"Nope."

His face fell.

"New deal terms," she said.

"I'm listening."

"The year re-starts every time that you leave."

"Meaning?"

"On the day that marks when you've been home for three-hundred-and-sixty-five days *in a row*, I'll marry you."

His smile registered in his eyes, lighting them almost silver. "Ah, Maggie." He rubbed his chest over where his heart was. "You're killing me."

"Sorry, Logan. That's just the new rule."

He squinted his eyes at her as if he was contemplating her deal. After a moment, he smiled. "Why delay the inevitable?"

"Because we have a very long history of inevitable delays, and this time I need the extra year."

"For what?"

"Ah, planning a really, really big, *expensive* wedding."

He laughed, and the sound pulled her stomach into a tight ball. "Okay, so we delay a little longer. My terms aren't so simple."

She raised a single eyebrow. "Oh yeah?"

Holding up one finger, he began, "You have to wear the ring. I can't have some investment banker or Hollywood actor moving in on my girl while I'm gone."

She nodded, although her heart tripped a little in her chest. She'd been waiting a long time to wear that damn ring. "Seems fair."

He held up his second finger. "We have to have at least two more kids, with the option of a fourth."

"Yeah. No. I'm *forty-two*," she laughed. "*As if!* I doubt that's even possible. And probably dangerous. My eggs are practically fossils." Still, she countered with, "One more *after* we're married."

"Jesus, you drive a hard bargain, lady." Smiling, he raised a hand to touch her face, leaned forward to plant a kiss on her forehead. "Last condition."

She tensed.

"You have to help me find a job, and be patient with me when I end up hating it," he said. "God, I've never even written a resume before."

She wanted to laugh at the absurdity of it, but she didn't because she could tell by the faraway look in his eyes that he was worried.

"Luckily for you, my friend," Zac's voice broke their negotiations, "I don't require one."

Maggie watched as Logan's head whipped up to look at Zac, who was standing in the doorway, looking at them with raised eyebrows. "You were serious about that?"

"Dead serious. Although seeing you covered in somebody else's blood is making me question my sanity."

Logan didn't reply at first, and Zac added, "You'd be doing me a favor. I'm so inundated that I'm turning clients down. I tried to poach Jake, but he's just too by the rules." Zac snorted. "Says he wants to be Chief of Police. Can you believe that idiot?"

"What's the pay like?" Maggie asked. "He wants another kid…"

"Eh," Zac waved his wand in a see-saw motion in front of him, "usually solid. Sometimes spotty. People have a weird tendency to commit fewer crimes over the holidays, so I like to take a month-long vacation around Christmas."

"Luckily I'll be away for the next few months then," Logan said. "If the CAR government doesn't work with Sasha's UN report to arrest Boucher…"

"When are you coming back?" Zac asked, ignoring Logan's stilted explanation. "I need someone in the new year."

"I'll be back as soon as humanly possible. Definitely before the new year."

"I like a man who can tie up loose ends," Zac said with a final shrug.

When Zac held out his hand, Logan didn't hesitate. He reached forward and shook it, and Maggie felt a deep calm take ahold of her.

"You two need to get cleaned up," he added, scrunching his nose as he took a solid step back. "You really smell. And June has started making her pot pie, and I *do not* want any delays when it is on the table on account of you being all bloody and gross."

With one final wink, he stepped back through towards the lounge, leaving Maggie and Logan alone once again.

"He is so *weird*," she laughed.

When she turned to face Logan, he was looking at her, his head tilted to the side, a soft smile on his face. Reaching up a single hand, she pushed his long hair back from his face. "What?"

"You've never really been with anyone else all this time?"

"*That's* what you're thinking about right now?" she asked, laughing. *Men.* "But, to answer your question, *no* I have not."

"I want you to know…" he trailed off, embarrassed by whatever he was trying to tell her. "Me either."

"What?"

"Me either."

"You haven't slept with anyone else since we-"

"Before. Since your sixteenth birthday party, when I looked up and saw you in your bikini, all pale, creamy skin, and big, blue eyes."

Maggie didn't say anything. In fact, she found it hard to breathe around the lump in her throat at all.

"You looked up and saw me checking you out, and instead of blushing or looking away, you smiled this completely self-aware smile that just crushed me. I felt my heart drop to my feet…among other things."

"Are you teasing me?" she asked, astounded. It wasn't that she didn't believe him, it was just that the whole situation was slightly unbelievable. Logan Cane could have had anyone that he wanted.

He shook his head, and she knew that he was telling her the truth. "I have only ever wanted you since I was seventeen years old. Nobody else."

Maggie's heart beat a jackhammer pulse in her chest, and she stared up at him, lost for words.

"I'm sorry it took me so long to figure everything out, Mags. You...you've always scared the living hell out of me."

"I love you," she replied. "It's always only ever been you."

"We'll start for real in a few months."

"How about we start with a shower first?" she suggested.

When his gray eyes snapped to her, their wolfish gleam lit a fire in her belly, a fire that spread through her blood, setting everything ablaze.

"Deal."

When he held out his hand for a shake, she took it, right before he crushed his mouth to hers.

Epilogue

As the Christmas season got into full swing in LA, Maggie settled into a comfortable routine working on getting the café up to speed. She had spent the time since Logan had left immersed in her business, often working from the time that she woke up to the time that she fell into her bed, exhausted. She allowed herself occasional breaks to walk Spunk, set up Christmas decorations, or play with Gracie—when her daughter wasn't with Phil and June.

It had been thirty-two days since Logan had flown out of LAX, back to the Central African Republic. Thirty-two days since he had slipped the ring back on her finger, and promised her that he'd see her soon. Thirty-two days since she'd felt his hands on her.

He hadn't called her. Not even once. But Maggie knew that he was back in CAR on unofficial business and that he was off-grid. So, she didn't lament the fact that they hadn't spoken even though she missed hearing his voice.

More than anything, she just wanted to know that he was okay and that he would be coming home to them soon.

Although, thanks to her lack of ability to focus on anything else, the café was done. The bathrooms and kitchen were ready, the wallpaper, bookcase, furniture, and even the plants were in all place. All she had left to do was unpack her serviceware, glassware, and the décor that she'd bought. And sign off on the employee contracts for the six full-time staff that she had officially hired—three for the day shift and three for the night shift, plus another four part-time employees to help out on weekends.

Everything was ready. And every time that she walked into the space, she felt a new sense of purpose, a sense of pride.

She'd done it.

She'd taken her idea and the knowledge that she wanted control of her life, of her time, and she had run with it. Now, nearly fifteen months after she'd quit her career in law to have Gracie, she finally had a place of her own.

Maggie's Place.

The name had come to her in the third week after Logan had left. She'd been lying awake in her bed replaying the horror of discovering that Gracie had disappeared from the café. That she'd been taken from right under their noses.

In the first week after the incident, the memories had echoed in her head and filled her stomach with an unease that had kept her from sleep. Those nights, she'd taken to walking through to Gracie's room to check on her. Sometimes, she'd stand in the doorway and watch her sleep. Other times, she'd need to walk in and lay her hand on her daughter's chest, just to feel the contact, feel the gentle rise and fall of her chest under her hand.

It was only in the second week when the anxiety had eased and she'd been able to fall asleep, that the nightmares started. Nightmares where she was running up and down on the sidewalk behind Logan. In the dream, she knew that she was looking for something, something that was important, but she didn't know what.

By the third week, the nightmares had subsided to sleep memories on replay. It was somewhere in that week that she had woken up with her heart pounding in her throat, and the memory of Logan staring back at her in the forefront of her mind. His eyes filled with horror as he'd spoken to Zac on the phone. He'd said, "Meet me at Maggie's place as soon as possible."

Somehow, the name had been born from the worst experience in her existence. An experience that she knew beyond a doubt would be the worst experience of her entire existence even when she took her last breath.

But, it worked.

It was hers. Her place.

So, the sign had been ordered and anchored above the door. Already neighbors were stopping by when she was in and asking her when she was going to open and telling her how excited that they were to have a café and bar in the neighborhood.

Seeing the awe-struck expressions on their faces when she'd welcomed them inside had been the best thing she'd gotten out of her new business so far.

Now all you need to do is open.

It was not the first time that she'd thought about nailing down a date for opening night, but she pushed it aside, choosing to focus on her wine supplier's list in front of her instead.

It wasn't that she wasn't chomping at the bit to get going. Because she was. It was that she wanted Logan to be home when she finally opened. She wanted him there, by her side. It was more than just needing him there, it was…a symbol of their new start, of their new life together.

And so, after thirty-two days without him, she was still waiting to finish those last few tasks that would put the final touches to Maggie's Place.

When her front door opened, and June's greeting drifted through to her, she replied, "In the kitchen!"

The patter of small feet on the tiled floor made her smile. Gracie's squeal of excitement echoed down the hallway, followed by her mom's exaggerated shuffle as she pretended to chase her.

When the two burst into the kitchen, June close on Gracie's heels, Maggie laughed and scooped Gracie into the air. "I caught you!" she said, laughing as she took a pretend bite out of Gracie's neck.

Gracie giggled. "Mama! No!"

"No!" she parroted.

"This little lady is picking up a new word every day," June affirmed.

Maggie glanced up at her mom. "I know. I can't keep up. Just now, I'm not going to be able to pick you up, huh?"

"No!" Gracie said again.

Moving her to her hip, Maggie asked, "How was she today?"

"An angel."

"Good." Maggie smiled at Gracie. "Although Gama is probably not a reliable source."

"Her favorite word is still 'Da'. She says it every hour still."

"Yeah, I know."

"Heard anything?" June asked.

Maggie shook her head no. She didn't want to talk to her mom about it. She didn't want her parents to take her own worry home with them. "He'll be okay," she said, more to convince herself than her mother.

"I know, baby." June raised a hand to her face. "But will you?"

And that was the problem. Her family, too used to Logan up and leaving, thought that he wasn't coming back. *But he is.*

She couldn't explain to them how she knew it to be true.

Maggie Simmone had always had a sense for things. But with Logan...Fate, kismet, destiny. He was hers. She could *feel* when he was close.

It was that pull now that made her turn to her mother and say, "He's coming back for good this time, Mom. Soon. I...I just...have that feeling."

Never one to argue when it concerned the happiness of her children, June Simmone shrugged, and Maggie found herself wanting to laugh at the gesture. "You know I've never been wrong about this."

"I know. Hell, you and that boy have been goners since you gave each other goo-goo eyes at your sixteenth birthday party."

"You knew about that?"

"Knew about it? I told your father right then that you two were going to get married and have a big family."

Maggie laughed, imagining her dad being less than happy about the situation at the time. Logan hadn't exactly been displaying any signs of being a productive member of society at seventeen. "What did Dad say?"

"Oh, you know your father. Never one for words. Just turned to me, and said, 'I'm surprisingly fine with that. Nice kid'."

Maggie laughed at June's gruff imitation of Phil, sending Gracie into a fit of giggles too. "Well, that about sums up our story."

"You heard from Hudson?" June asked.

"Yeah, he called yesterday. They're traveling from Egypt to Morocco tomorrow. I think he said they're there for a week before they fly to Kenya, then Cape Town, then home. He's officially out of vacation time end of January so they have to be back by then."

"Who'd have thought."

Maggie shook her head. She'd have pegged Hudson and Sasha to hook up, maybe break each other's hearts eventually. But if someone had told her that they'd have a shotgun court wedding before a month-long honeymoon traipsing through Africa, she would have lost a lot of money betting to the contrary.

Still, she was happy for them. Happy that her little brother had somehow convinced the feisty Sasha Riley that she couldn't live without him.

"Anyway," June sighed, "I better get going. Your father wants to take me to bingo. I swear Maggie, it's like he's trying to put us in an early grave."

Maggie snorted, used to June's discontentment with Phil's choice of activities. "Oh, and don't forget that Lola wants to go shopping for the nursery this weekend."

"Have I ever forgotten about anything about my grandchildren?"

"I guess not. See you tomorrow, Mom. I love you."

"Love you too, girls." June gave them each a kiss before moving down the hallway so that she could let herself out.

Maggie listened to the door open and close, then sat back down with Gracie on her lap. She had missed her, so she cuddled Gracie close, inhaling her baby scent.

"Want to see what Mama did today?" she asked, pulling the wine lists from the stack of papers on her desk.

She'd selected the wines for the cellar, decided on her first quarter's by-the-glass menu, and called her suppliers to organize the deliveries.

"Da! Da!"

The sound brought a swift pang of longing to Maggie's stomach, and she kissed Gracie on the head again. "Yeah, Daddy is coming home soon, baby."

"Da!" Gracie shouted, thrusting her upper body over the arm that was caging her in.

"Gracie!" Maggie floundered, and reached for her with her spare hand, just as Gracie was lifted from her belly dive.

Maggie looked up into gray eyes that she'd known almost her entire life, at Logan. Her heart thumped wildly in her chest. Her eyes blurred instantly with unshed tears.

"Hi, Mags," he said, his voice breaking on her name.

"Logan," she whispered, right before she flew into his arms.

"Da!" Gracie giggled as he kissed, first, Maggie, then her.

When his lips found Maggie's a second time, she let herself melt into his embrace, uncaring that big, fat tears were rolling down her face. "You're home."

"For good," he said, against her lips. "I missed you both so much."

"We missed you too." Her hands were shaking, so she rested them on his chest, perfectly content to feel the hard planes of him underneath his shirt.

Needing to know what had happened, she whispered, "Boucher?"

Logan shook his head. "I was waiting for a green light, but I never got it."

"He's…"

"He went missing a few days after I arrived. I lay low, thinking he'd heard a rumor that I was back and was waiting me out."

"He never surfaced?"

"No. He did. His body was found buried in a mine shaft ten days ago."

"Someone else got to him?"

He nodded, his eyes shuttering slightly. "From what I heard, it was pretty bad. The mine had been intentionally collapsed."

"How…"

"Most likely a lot of people, working together." He paused as if thinking about it. "I think everyone has a breaking point. For me it was Gracie."

"For the miners…"

He shrugged. "Maybe watching their entire community at Boucher's whim for years and not having any means to do anything about it. How many Gracie's did they watch suffer?"

Needing to quell the thought, she shushed him.

His free arm snaked around her midsection, pulling her close. Maggie sighed and rested her head next to her hands. Her heart beat staccato in her chest, and she breathed a deep breath to try and calm herself.

The lungful of his pine scent swooped through her senses, leaving her dizzy and hyper-aware at the same time.

"My girls," he whispered, pulling them both close, "how did I ever live without you?"

"Never again." Because she meant it, Maggie added an inch of space between them so that she could look up into his eyes.

His hair was pulled back and tied in a small, loose bun at the back of his neck. His face was unshaven, adding a layer of course, sandy scruff. Her breath caught in her throat.

He dipped his head so that they were looking directly into each other's eyes. "Never again," he affirmed before dropping his lips to hers.

To My Readers

To all of my amazing readers,

Thank you so much for picking up a copy of *Too Close to Home*, and if you made it all the way to this note, then thank you for powering through to the end.

For those of you who enjoyed reading *Too Close to Home*, please share your thoughts with the world by writing a review on Amazon, or drop me a line at hello@tess-shepherd.com. Reviews are important to all authors, but especially for indies who are trying to do it all themselves.

If you'd like to catch up with Logan, Maggie, and Gracie, stay tuned for *The Kismet Equation*, coming early 2022. Sarah Boyle and Matthew Carmon have a *lot* to say to each other. You can read a sneak peek on the next page…

Lots of love,

Tess

The Kismet
Equation

Prologue

There was only one thing in the entire world that could have made Sarah Boyle more uncomfortable at that moment. And it was happening.

Matthew Carmon was walking towards her. Straight towards her. She could tell by his confident stride and the rigid set of his shoulders that he was heading in her direction. And she knew by the grim set of his mouth that he was as happy about it as she was.

It was bad enough that she'd broken down in front of Jake and Lola. It was worse having to walk through the stark white hallways of the hospital, the frantic squeak of her tennis shoes drawing people's attention to her choked sobs. But it was hell on earth to have her tears witnessed by Matt.

He was her nemesis.

She couldn't do anything about the hair she'd hurriedly pulled into a messy bun on her way to the hospital, or about her tear-stained red, splotchy skin and swollen eyes—both of which were a redhead's punishment for crying in the first place—but she'd be damned if she let him see another tear fall. So, she swiped at her eyes with the sleeve of her sweatshirt and quickly sniffled before he was in hearing distance.

She averted her gaze when his footsteps padded nearer, pretending to study a discarded magazine on the small table next to her chair. It was a dated copy of Vogue, which seemed a little out of place in the sparse waiting room of LA General Hospital.

The cover model on the magazine was leaning forward, showing just a touch of cleavage, the laugh in her eyes suggesting it was deliberate. Sarah supposed it was meant to

1

be seductive, but to her, it seemed as if the woman—adorned in a red, sparkling gown and bedazzled with glinting emeralds—was laughing at her. Mocking her.

Sarah wasn't dressed appropriately. She wore black sweatpants and a sweatshirt five sizes too big for her, sneakers, and no makeup.

The sweatpants and sweatshirts had been left behind by an ex-boyfriend of hers and, although she should have thrown them away, she hadn't because, well, they were *so* comfortable. And it didn't seem fair to let the clothes take the blame for her ex being an asshole.

Regardless, she hadn't exactly been thinking of fashion when Zac had picked her up to rush over to the hospital, and she definitely hadn't thought she'd be facing Matthew Carmon.

She flipped the magazine, hiding the model's mocking smile.

Matt came to a stop in front of her.

He didn't say anything. Not one word. But she knew he was watching her, waiting. She could feel the singular sensation of his gaze, weighted on her skin.

She didn't acknowledge him in the hope that he would just go away.

He sighed. Loudly. "Sarah." Her name, said in his deep voice, echoed in the empty waiting room.

Worried that her words would still come out choked, she didn't reply. But because her tears had mostly dried, she pried her gaze away from the back of the magazine and tilted her face towards him.

He stood directly in front of her, his hands tucked into the pockets of his faded, blue jeans, his white-blond hair a little messy, as if he'd also gotten out of bed to come to the hospital. His blue eyes were hooded, tired in a way that she'd never associated with him. He was usually so…crisp.

Matthew Carmon was never unkempt. He walked around as if he'd just been dressed and groomed by a

Hollywood wardrobe team for a Hurley ad. But tonight he looked a little…rumpled.

Noticing her silent examination, he raised a single eyebrow. "It's not my best look. But…I had to come to make sure…"

His mention of Lola washed over her, bringing the last thirty hours to the forefront of her mind again and, with the memories, a fresh swell of tears. Her eyes burned with them, so she ground her jaw and remained silent as Matt blurred in front of her.

"Sarah…"

After a moment, he took the seat next to her, leaned forward so that he could link his hands, his elbows on his thighs.

They sat like that for ten minutes.

Neither one of them moved as life went on in the hospital. Sarah stared down the long, white hallway as nurses and doctors came and went, their movements routine, their faces calm.

A young man with deep olive skin was the only other person in the waiting room; he sat alone in a single plastic-covered chair, his dark eyes vacant. She couldn't help but wonder what tragedy had brought him to LA General. Alone.

The thought was a sobering one. Tapping her fingers on her leg, she took a deep breath and turned to face Matt. She couldn't talk about Lola. Not yet. Probably not ever. "Nice w-weather we're h-having today."

Next to her, Matt turned his head to stare at her. He looked as if he wasn't quite sure if she was losing the plot but was too afraid to ask. Eventually, he nodded. Just once. "Great weather."

Well, feck.

Just when she thought he wouldn't try again, he added, "Maybe it'll rain. We could use more rain."

"That we could."

And this, she remembered, was the problem with them. They had nothing in common. Their stilted conversation about the weather was the exact reason that the blind date Lola had set them up on had tanked in one glorious shouting match—because unless they were arguing, they didn't know how to communicate with one another.

"It's been a really dry year." He looked straight ahead, avoiding eye contact.

"We do live in a desert," she replied drily, impatient with the small talk.

She thought she saw his mouth twitch. But it resumed its neutral expression so quickly she wasn't entirely sure if she'd imagined it.

Feeling strangely off-kilter, she cracked her knuckles. "What are you doing here, Matt?"

"I told you. I came to see that Lola and Jake were alright…I can't…wrap my head around it. I mean, what are the chances?" His last words were almost whispered.

"Point zero zero zero three nine percent. In North America."

"What?"

"I Googled it. According to the United Nations Office of Drugs and Crime, your chance of being randomly killed by a serial murderer is point zero zero zero three nine percent." Because it had plagued her since she'd looked the statistic up, she asked, "Does that seem high to you? It seems high to me."

"And it has to be higher for us, living in LA."

"But lower for you because, well, you're male." She'd meant to be sassy, to pull them both out of the path they were going down, but when she turned to look at him, she saw that he was nodding in agreement, his eyes sad.

"I guess you're right."

Through the fatigue and grief, Sarah felt rage, hot and ripe, rise in her chest and bubble out her mouth in a bitter stream. "If he hadn't died, I would have finished him off for what he did."

He looked at her, studying her face as she said the words.

"I-I would have." She glared back at him, begging him to contradict her.

Strangely, he just executed a curt nod and replied, "I believe you."

His words didn't settle her. Quite the opposite. They flared a long-hidden spark of panic in her chest, one that flamed to life and spread outwards. *Why would he say that? Does he know who I am?*

He couldn't.

He's an accountant.

Who's really good with computers. And went on a date with you. She stared at him, trying to gauge if there'd been any subtext behind his words. She knew that it was highly unlikely that he'd done more than Google her before their blind date...but still. If anyone could have traced her past, she knew that it'd be Matt.

He seemed to sense the shift in her because he stared back, his blue eyes unflinching. "What?"

Deflect and defer, the little voice in her head reminded her. "I can't get a read on you."

"What's to know?" he asked. "Born and bred in Manhattan Beach. Undergrad and Masters...right here in LA. Moved to Westlake almost a decade ago when I landed the job. Met you and Lola. You know the rest."

Seeing an opportunity to contradict him, she countered with, "Mnnn, not exactly. Because up until the disastrous blind date last week, I only knew your name and that you lived next door to Lola."

"Well," he shrugged, "now you know the rest."

"Unfortunately," she mumbled, just loud enough for him to hear.

He groaned—honest to God, groaned—and ran his hands through his hair quickly. "Christ's sake, Sarah."

"What?"

"You're insufferable."

"No. You're insufferable." *Oh, good one.*

He seemed to agree with her internal monologue because his mouth did that twitchy thing again. "That's all you've got?"

"No. I'm just…getting warmed up, that's all."

"Right. Well, seeing as though it clearly takes you a while, do you mind if we get moving while you think about it. There's nothing we can do here, and I promised Zac I'd get you home."

"I caught a ride with Zac," she replied, her voice cold. "I'll wait for him."

"He left."

"*What?*"

"He said something about needing to give a statement or…I don't know. But I've been burdened with the task of getting you home safe and sound. Please," he pushed to his feet, "just come."

"I'll catch an Uber."

"Now you're just being stubborn. I live five minutes from you."

He didn't raise his voice at all even though she was deliberately dancing on his last nerve, which she found both impressive and slightly irritating. "I'm a grown woman. I can get home just fine."

"Five seconds."

"Excuse me?"

He shrugged nonchalantly. "Five seconds to start walking."

"Or what?" Pushing to her feet, she came to stand in front of him. Unfortunately, she had to crane her neck back to look up at him, which doused the effect a little. But she didn't care.

"Sarah…" His voice took a patronizing tone. "Do this math. I have a foot of height on you and outweigh you by a hundred pounds."

"I'm still waiting for the math…" She tapped her foot on the hospital floor, the frantic beat in time to her thundering pulse. *The gall of the man!*

"I will haul you over my shoulder and carry you out of here like a temperamental child if you don't move in three, two…" He bent over slightly as if preparing to grab her.

"Fine!" Throwing her hands in the air, she spun around. "For feck's sake!" In the far corner of the waiting room, the man with the olive skin looked at her, his eyes wide. "Sorry," Sarah whisper-shouted, waving her hands in Matt's direction as if his presence was all the excuse she needed.

Snatching her purse off the seat, she looped it over her shoulder and stormed past. She made it twenty steps down the hallway before she realized that he hadn't followed. Spinning on her heel, she turned to glare at him.

He just smiled and indicated the opposite direction with a quick shake of his head. "This way."

Perfect.

Deliberately calming herself, Sarah stalked past him, keeping her eyes trained forward even when she felt him behind her.

Worst. Day. Ever.

Strangely, Matt couldn't have agreed more. He'd spent the last thirty hours worrying about Lola, worrying that she wouldn't pull out of the drug-induced coma the doctors had put her in. He hadn't slept in nearly two days. He hadn't showered in at least twenty-four hours. And to top it all off, the Tasmanian Devil herself had spent every minute since just rearing to test his already sour mood.

And what was she wearing? Whatever it was swallowed her tiny, curvy figure whole, leaving just her head poking

7

out, her mane of red hair piled in a messy bunch on top. The sweatpants were so baggy that she'd had to hold the waistband up as she stormed out of the hospital. "You planning on going to an Eminem concert after this?"

She turned her head slowly, her green eyes glinting. "No. But for your information, I do a mean Lose Yourself karaoke after few shots."

Matt tried not to laugh as she tugged at the sweatshirt, her hands moving frantically as she yanked it up and over her head before scrunching it up on her lap.

Turning a little in the seat, he opened his mouth to tease her, intrigued that her Irish accent chose to show when she was mad…then snapped it shut.

She'd taken her sweatshirt off.

She wore a lace contraption that hugged her curves before disappearing into her sweatpants like a one-piece bathing suit. It was the color of pre-dawn—black with a hint of blue—and perfectly contrasted her shock of burnt red hair. It was something made for nighttime rendezvous not for emergency visits to the hospital.

The boning pushed her small breasts up so that, even in the dark car, he could make out the smattering of freckles riding the tops of her cleavage. Inexplicably, his body tightened. *Oh, no. Not her.* "What are you wearing?"

"Ah, my pajamas."

"That," he waved his hand in her general direction while he kept the other on the steering wheel of the car, "does not constitute pajamas."

"I sleep in them. Therefore, *they are pajamas.*"

"Them? You have more than one of those?"

"Oh, Matt," she shook her head as if sad, but the wicked smile painted on her lips as she turned to face him fully ruined her attempt, "I have dozens."

"Put your sweatshirt back on."

"Nope." Crossing her arms under her chest, she turned to look out the passenger window, ignoring him.

"Sarah…"

"Yes?"

"I mean it."

"Oh, I know."

Ignoring his compulsion to look again, he stared at the road ahead. "What game are you playing?"

"Ah, it's called 'Piss Matthew Carmon off as Much as Possible'."

"Why?" Slapping his hand on the steering wheel, he shot her a dark look. "Why are you like this?"

"Because you're infuriating! And insufferable! And a-a Sagittarius."

"How do you even know that? And what does my astrological sign have to do with anything?"

"I'm a Leo. I should have known before I said yes to that date that we weren't compatible. Maybe then we could have been friends."

"We could never be friends."

He heard her short intake of breath but didn't apologize. She deserved it. She had been impossible. From the moment he'd taken the job and moved down the street from her, she'd been there, filling his head and plaguing his peace of mind.

"You just hate me because you're still in love with Lola and you've only just realized you'll never have her."

The words were quiet. But they were clear. Scathing.

Matt acknowledged them with a small nod. He wouldn't deny that he'd become inexplicably attached to Lola. She was sweet and kind, soft and caring where Sarah was more likely to start a fire to get you moving in the right direction. "I never loved her in the way you're implying," he said finally, breaking the awkward silence. "We never had a chance to get that close."

"It's none of my business."

"No. It's not."

They fell into another tension-filled silence as they made their way through the narrower streets of Westlake.

Driving through the neighborhood in the dark, moonless night, Matt could imagine how easy it had been for James Barrowman to lure his victims off the roads and to their deaths. The thought made him grind his jaw. What he wouldn't give for thirty minutes alone with the asshole.

Too bad he's dead.

"I hate this neighborhood now." Sarah had been looking out her window, but as she spoke, she turned to face him.

She was crying again, her eyes two pools of emerald set in a pale face. "Every time I drive through it, I think of those girls, dying alone in the dark with nothing but that-that monster's hands on their throats. I see Lola...When they carried her out on the stretcher...I thought..."

"It's okay." Because he didn't want to think about it himself, he added, "He's gone now."

"It's not me," she countered, her voice steely. "It's the damage already done. Those women aren't coming back. Jordan Holt will never be tucked into bed by his ma again. He's only ten. And every time I drive through here now, that's what I think about."

"You planning on moving?"

Matt tried his best to ignore the way her breasts rose as they filled with a deep sigh.

"No. Not for a while yet. I want to make sure that Lola's okay. That she and Jake work out."

"You don't think they will?"

She shrugged. "I want them to. But..."

"Can you really love someone after only a few weeks of knowing them?"

"Well, yes. I fall in love all the time." She giggled and Matt felt his bunched shoulders relax. "But is it true love? Well, that's another question entirely. On the off chance that it's just a fling for Jake, I want to make sure I'm here for Lola. She's…she's always been there for me."

"She's a good friend."

"Do you know she set us up because I had just broken up with someone?" she asked.

Matt shook his head, but he could feel the smile tugging. "I thought it was because she realized that I had a little crush on her and she wanted to douse it."

"Well, that too."

Chuckling, he pulled his car into Sarah's driveway. He rolled down his window at the intercom. "What's the code?"

"Ah. Yeah, no way in hell, Carmon." Before he could argue, she unbuckled her seatbelt and climbed across his lap so that she could lean out his window and punch the code in.

"Sarah, you're not a fucking housecat," he said as her weight shifted dangerously close to his junk.

"Calm down. I just need a little length."

She stretched as she reached out the window, and Matt's entire body tensed as her perfume, something with roses in it, inundated him. Feeling her hand on his thigh, he glanced down at it, caught an eyeful of cleavage. His body responded instantly, hardened instantly. *Fuck.*

Think of James Barrowman. A serial killer just tried to murder one of your closest friends. It didn't work. *Think of…Goddamnit! Anything!*

The sound of the arched gates swinging open had Sarah crawling back to her seat, but judging by her sudden silence and the red blush flooding her cheeks, she hadn't missed his body's reaction.

As silence flooded the car, stifling both of them, he drove up the long, winding driveway, came to a sudden stop in front of the mansion.

The house was huge; Matt pegged it at around five thousand square feet. It was a tasteful rendition of an Italian villa, with a slanted shingle roof. Pretty, wrought-iron balconies hugged the upstairs French doors that looked over her perfectly landscaped lawn. Ginormous terracotta pots stood sentry in front of the huge wooden doors. He couldn't see far enough to make out what the pots held, but if he knew anything about Sarah, he knew that the plants would be colorful.

The sound of her clearing her voice forced his gaze back to her. "Thank you," she said, "for driving me home."

"Sure."

She didn't make a move to get out, didn't open the door and run away as fast as she could—which he'd been expecting. Instead, she sat still, staring forward at the walnut doors of her home, her bottom lip caught between her teeth.

"Are you okay?"

"I…" Turning in her seat, she looked at him.

"What?"

"I don't know if I can go in just yet. It's…a big house to be alone in. Especially tonight."

Nodding cautiously, he added, "I'll stay as long as you need."

"Why?"

"Sarah?"

"Yes?"

"Don't look a gift horse in the mouth." Exhausted, Matt pressed down on the electric recline, ignoring her laughing green eyes as the chair crawled to a horizontal position.

He stared at the ceiling of his Maserati, barely refrained from smiling when the faint electronic whir of her chair reclining filled the confined space. He ignored her as she curled up on her side in the passenger seat, her eyes taking him in.

"Why don't you just come in with me? You can stay the night. I have spare bedrooms you know," she whispered.

"I don't think that's a good idea."

"Oh." She was silent for a beat, then she sighed. "Hey, Matt?"

"Yes?"

"Thank you."

"It's not a problem." He wanted to say more, to explain, but, because the right words didn't come to him, he didn't. Instead, he asked, "Can you really rap Lose Yourself?"

"Every goddamn line."

There was a smile in her voice, and when he turned his head to look at her, she was studying him, her green eyes hooded with fatigue. Her hair was coming out of the knot she'd tied it in and wisps of burnt red fell about her freckled face.

Right then, he thought she was beautiful.

Steer clear, Carmon. He knew who she was, who she really was. And she was dangerous.

Wasn't that why he'd decided to keep his distance from her all those years ago? He'd moved into the understated neighborhood, taken one look at his cute neighbor and her pretty best friend, and decided to fish a little to find out more about them.

The problem being, while his search on Lola Michaels turned up a neighborhood artist from an upper-middle-class background, Sarah Boyle's past had led him down the rabbit hole to Rogan Barry's daughter, AKA, Sarah Aileen Barry. Her father was the modern equivalent of Bernard McLaughlin: wealthy, charismatic, and—if the rumors were true—exceptionally dangerous.

He'd avoided her from that moment on. Well, until the disastrous blind date that Lola had set them up on a few days earlier—the date where they'd officially gotten to know each other...and fought like a pair of rabid cats.

Feeling suddenly itchy at the thought, he broke the silence with, "I forgot I haven't let my dog out."

He inclined his chair.

13

It wasn't necessarily a lie—he hadn't let Nugget out. It wasn't necessarily the truth either—Nugget could have gone another ten hours just dozing on the couch.

"Oh…You should go."

He hated the tinge of fear that had crept into her voice. Still, she reset her chair without saying anything else, the whirr of the incline pulling the tension in the car to an unbearable level. With one last wide-eyed look at him, she opened her door and climbed out of the car.

Turning, she leaned forward, one hand on the door, and Matt deliberately looked away when her breasts shifted with the gesture.

"Thanks, Matt."

"Don't mention it."

"Bye." She whispered the word, then shut the door.

He watched her as she walked back to her front door, her shoulders slightly rounded, waited until she was back inside before circling the car around the front fountain.

He stopped again before heading down her long, winding driveway. He thought about who she was, tried to remind himself that getting to know her would be the beginning of the end for him.

But the image of her fearful eyes and hunched shoulders haunted him. She might be Rogan Barry's daughter, but he knew that she had been genuinely scared for one reason: she would never have shown him her fear if she'd been able to stifle it.

She hated him.

She'd literally said, "I think I might hate you," before storming out of their blind date, leaving an amused Jake and a wide-eyed Lola staring at him as if he had the answer as to why they didn't get along.

Fuck. He knew what would happen if he left too; he'd end up lying in his bed, wide awake, getting more and more irritated with her for stealing his sleep. Circling the fountain again, he parked in front of the wide, double doors, climbed out of the Maserati, and walked to the front door.

With one last sigh, he raised his hand and punched the doorbell before he had time to change his mind.

He heard her soft footsteps approach, then pause just behind the door. "Matt?"

"It's me. I...I'm going to stay. Nugget will be fine."

The door swung open.

Made in the USA
Middletown, DE
27 August 2021